YIELD the Night

Steel & Stone: Book 3

ANNETTE MARIE

STEEL & STONE

Chase the Dark
Bind the Soul
Yield the Night
Reap the Shadows

CHAPTER
-1-

PIPER pressed her nose to the car window as the Consulate came into view. Her first sight of it in two months.

The car rumbled down the gravel drive, passing the large expanse of lawn that surrounded the massive manor. It looked exactly as she remembered, the glowing windows beckoning amidst the late evening shadows. She touched the cold glass with one finger, her eyes on the front door as her excitement built. She was home. Finally home.

The car stopped in front of the main entrance. She pushed the door open and dragged her suitcase off the seat beside her. She didn't bother saying anything to the driver. He was a hired security professional, and recent experience with his type had taught her not to bother with pleasantries; they never replied. Cheerful bunch.

Predictably, the moment she shut the door the car rolled into motion. Good riddance. She'd been shadowed by enough security guards over the last eight weeks to last a lifetime.

She rushed up the steps, suitcase bouncing on its wheels behind her. Flinging the door open, she stepped into the wide foyer. Her boots clicked loudly on the marble floor. She stopped in the center of the space, eyeing the glossy reception desk, the grand stairway, and the multitude of doors and halls leading off it. The silence pressed down on her.

She stood for a moment, waiting for something to happen. Slowly, her anticipation died away. Her shoulders slumped. So maybe it wasn't fair to expect a grand welcoming when she was home a day early, but still. How many hints had she dropped to Uncle Calder that she wasn't planning on spending her birthday alone in a dorm room? Short of mailing him step-by-step instructions, she'd given him every opportunity to arrange a little birthday celebration.

Shaking her head, she and her suitcase headed down the left-hand hall. At the far end, a carved wooden door blocked her path, hiding the spacious office within. She tried the handle—locked. Her father only locked his office when he left the Consulate.

With a sigh, she went around the bend, down another hall, and into the main-floor kitchen. The lights were off, leaving the dining table and granite island in shadows. Memories drifted like the shadows and she almost expected to feel hands tickle across her sides and a purring voice to whisper, "Hello beautiful," in her ear. She shook off the nostalgia and focused on the present.

The entire floor was silent. Consulates were never empty. Where was everyone?

"Hello?" she called. "Anyone hoooome?"

Scowling—such an anticlimactic homecoming—she turned to leave.

"Oh, Piper. It's you."

Starting slightly, she turned back as a woman came up the stairs from the lower level. Her wild red curls bounced as she sauntered into the kitchen, grinning. "The prodigal returns! It's been quiet here without you."

Piper snorted at the prodigal comment. "Hey, Kindra. Where is everyone?"

"Not here," she replied casually. "You're back early. Calder has been gushing about your homecoming for days."

Piper shoved her suitcase in the corner and perched on a barstool in front of the island. Trust Uncle Calder to go on about family stuff to the Consulate's guests, though apparently she hadn't been obvious enough with her hints about arriving in time for her birthday.

"I convinced the school to send me home tonight instead of tomorrow morning when everyone else leaves. They were only too happy to get rid of me ahead of schedule."

Piper may have set a new record for detentions while at Westwood Academy. She couldn't help it if the stuck-up brats at that school had practically *begged* her to bring them back down to reality. Really, she hadn't been able to help herself.

Kindra slid into the seat beside her, movements sleek and almost predatory. Lots of daemons moved like that, like wolves on the prowl. Kindra was cool though. Only a few years older than Piper and perpetually easygoing, she was always good company. She hired out her services as a delivery woman, transporting valuable items between Earth and her home in the Underworld. She often spent her time between jobs at the Consulate.

"A boarding school, huh?" the daemon said. "How was it?"

"Ugh. It was boring. And snobby. And the human kids were just—" She shook her head. "When they found out I was from a Consulate, it was endless stupid questions. Do daemons suck your blood? Do they all have pentagrams tattooed on their backs? Do they eat babies? Gah."

Kindra laughed, tossing her curls over one shoulder. Her long, soft grey sweater and leggings made Piper yearn for something to wear besides her jeans and long-sleeve top. She hadn't brought enough clothes to the school and was sick of wearing the same things over and over.

"So," Piper asked, looking pointedly around the dark kitchen, "where is everyone?"

Kindra shrugged. "Marcelo is downstairs with Raanan and Fia."

Piper grimaced. Marcelo was her least favorite of the Consuls who worked at the Griffiths Consulate. He refused to get over the time she'd broken his nose.

"There's only the three of you here?" The Consulate usually had closer to a dozen daemons in residence on any given day. "Why so few?"

Kindra's eyebrows shot up. "Why would anyone *want* to be here?"

Piper blinked. "Huh?"

After a moment of confusion, Kindra's expression cleared. "I guess you didn't hear about it at the school."

"Hear about what?"

"The attacks."

"The *what*?"

The daemon slid out of her chair to flick the nearby light switch. An orange glow bloomed, shining on the grey counters. Kindra pulled a crinkled newspaper from a stack on the table and dropped it in front of Piper on the kitchen island.

Piper didn't have to ask for an explanation. The black letters of the headline screamed at her: SIXTH CONSULATE DESTROYED. Eyes wide, she yanked the paper closer and read at top speed. Six Consulates across the east coast had been demolished overnight by unknown attackers. There were no survivors so far, with five to ten daemons killed at each location, along with two to four Consuls.

"Holy shit," she breathed.

"One each day since last Saturday," Kindra said. "Most daemons have found other places to sleep."

"No kidding," Piper muttered, skimming through the details of the investigation. A combination of explosives and magic had been used to reduce two-story manors to rubble in the space of an hour or less. In the second attack, it appeared a daemon had survived the explosion only to be shot in the head once he'd crawled out of the wreckage.

"I—I can't even—" She shook her head and looked up. "Why would someone destroy Consulates?"

Kindra shrugged. "That is what the Consuls want to know. The Head Consul and Calder are at an emergency meeting in the city right now."

No wonder her father and uncle weren't here. She supposed she would have to forgive them for missing her birthday.

She looked at the photo, a blurry shot of rubble and smoke. She'd seen what a demolished Consulate looked like; she'd been inside one at the time it exploded. She read the line again about the survivor who'd been shot dead. Shivering, she set the newspaper down.

"I'm surprised I didn't hear about this at school."

"I don't think humans care much," Kindra remarked. "The Head Consul will sort it out. They're talking about increasing security."

Piper scowled. The Head Consul would fix things. Her father could fix anything, as long as it wasn't something *she* wanted his help with.

"Piper," Kindra said, her voice suddenly intense. Her green eyes turned into laser beams. "I need to know something."

"What?" she asked warily.

The daemon leaned closer, not blinking. "It's very important."

"Okay."

"I need to know . . . what's going on between you and the Underworld daemon Ash?"

Piper's mouth fell open. She sucked in a breath to answer and choked on saliva.

"N-nothing!" she hacked. "Why do you need to know *that*?"

"Nothing?" Kindra scoffed. "Did you not go missing for a week then turn up at the Consulate with him? Everyone is talking about how the Head Consul tried to murder him with a death spell back in May."

"*What*? That did not happen. There were no death spells."

"No?" Disappointment dragged at her face. "But it sounded so juicy. No one knows anything about Ash beyond his kill count."

"His kill . . ." Piper frowned. *She* didn't know his kill count. "Ash is not a murderer. Okay, well, yeah, he's killed people, but he's not a bad guy."

Kindra's moping dissolved into excitement. "Oh, so you know him well then? How well?" She wiggled her eyebrows suggestively.

Heat rose in Piper's cheeks. She'd forgotten Kindra was the biggest gossip this side of the Underworld.

"Not *that* well," she said firmly. A couple kisses didn't count. Even if those kisses had involved a lot of passion and maybe some wandering hands—but still. "We're just—we're friends, okay?"

Kindra blinked. "Lovers with the draconian assassin I would believe. But *friends*? No one is friends with Ash."

Piper was really starting to dislike this conversation. "Believe what you want."

Doubt heavy in her expression, Kindra shrugged. "Well, I'm glad you're back. I haven't seen a fistfight in *weeks*. When's your next shift? I can keep you company at reception and you can tell me more stupid things human children believe about us."

Piper clenched her hands as her mood worsened. "I don't know."

"Let me know then when you get your schedule," Kindra said cheerfully.

Piper stood abruptly, not wanting to admit there were neither schedules nor shifts in her future. "Well, seeing as I won't be getting a surprise birthday party, I'm going to throw my own."

Kindra's mouth popped open. "It's your birthday?"

"Yup."

"How old?"

"Eighteen."

"Oooh, eighteen!" Kindra's grin faded as she looked around the silent Consulate. "Your family isn't here . . ."

"I noticed that."

"But they should be here for your eighteenth birthday."

Piper shrugged. "That meeting is more important."

Kindra shot to her feet, gesturing grandly. "We should have a party for you right now!"

"Isn't that what I just said?"

Kindra ignored the question, her eyes alight. "What kind of party do you want?"

"The kind where we bake cookies, sit around in sweatpants, and trade stories about all the ass we've kicked lately."

The daemon, who under the right circumstances was a lethally efficient killer, clapped her hands in delight. "Perfect! Can we make cookies with chocolate chips?"

Piper laughed. All things aside, it was good to be home.

CHAPTER

- 2 -

VERY few things could trump a chocolate chip cookie still warm from the oven. Piper's eyes rolled back as the chocolate melted on her tongue. So good.

Kindra took a big bite and sighed contentedly. They were sprawled on the sofa in the sitting area just off the kitchen, the daemon in her sweater and leggings, Piper in fitted yoga pants, a red tank top, and a black hoodie. She'd tied her hair in a high, messy ponytail, vaguely wishing her current auburn locks were her preferred dye job of black with red streaks.

She also wore a leather band wrapped twice around her wrist, a memento from Ash. She traced a finger over the buckle with a sigh.

"You have no idea how nice it is to relax," she said. "The security at Westwood was over the top. Bodyguards everywhere. I swear the only privacy I ever got was in the shower, and even then I'm not so sure."

"Fun," Kindra commented. She eyed her sixth cookie, perhaps measuring how it might affect her willow-thin figure—or not. "Was anything about the boarding school pleasant?"

"Not really." She didn't want to admit that between her total disinterest in non-daemon-related academia and the classes she'd missed while in detention, she'd barely scraped by with passing grades.

"Any cute boys?"

Piper snorted. "I suppose, but they were all afraid of me."

"Afraid? Why?"

"Probably because I got in a fight on my third day and beat up a couple of them."

"Oh, well, those kinds of things happen at school."

"It's not usually girls beating up boys though," Piper remarked dryly. "And then there were the security guards . . ."

Kindra looked worried. "What about them?"

"Well, one of them grabbed me from behind while I was fighting the boys, and I kind of . . . threw him onto the floor." It hadn't been a difficult shoulder throw, but it must have looked pretty impressive to the rest of the cafeteria.

"You threw a security guard?"

"He surprised me. It was a reflex." The fight had happened a little more than a week after escaping Samael, so she'd still been pretty jumpy.

"What happened then?"

"Then another security guard came running in, and it really looked like he was going to tackle me, so . . ."

Eyes wide, Kindra shook her head slightly. "You beat up the security guards too, didn't you?"

"Well, '*beat up*' would be a bit of a stretch. But the principal told me I would be expelled if I used physical force on anyone again, so that was it for fights. But the other kids just wouldn't let it go."

"So human boys don't like tough girls at all?"

"I guess not. They seemed to like the giggly girls a lot more." She shrugged. "I really don't fit in with humans."

"You belong here anyway."

Piper smiled, emotions swelling. She was far more used to hearing how she *didn't* belong at the Consulate. As a haemon without magic, she was—according to her critics—ill-equipped to be a Consul.

Of course, Kindra had no idea why Piper had been sent to the high-security boarding school. Samael had already had her kidnapped once, and she was pretty sure his new plan involved eliminating her before someone else decided to make her their personal Sahar-wielder.

"So clearly you aren't suited to human boys," Kindra said, holding up another cookie. Her examination complete, she nibbled on an edge. "Tell me about Ash. How did you become . . . friends?"

Piper raised her eyebrows, too content to get offended over the doubtful pause before "friends."

"It's a long story," she said. And not one she wanted to share with casual acquaintances.

"What's he like beneath all those black clothes and cold stares? I've never spoken to him."

"Umm." She picked a cookie off the plate between them and frowned at it. "Fearless," she finally said. "Reckless. Loyal."

"*Paaaaa*ssionate?" Kindra drawled.

Piper blushed, refusing to answer.

Kindra sighed. "Fine. Be mean. Tell me what happened two months ago when you went missing. Did you two run off together?"

Piper shook her head. She didn't want to get into that story either. The last eight weeks had done little to heal Piper's emotional wounds from the preceding week in Samael's tender care.

Seeing that an answer wasn't forthcoming, Kindra shifted on the sofa, leaning a little closer. "Tell me then. How do you feel about him?"

"Huh?"

"How do you feel about Ash?"

"We're friends, like I said," she replied quickly.

Kindra gave her a look. "But do you want more than that, hmm?"

Piper glanced down, pressing her lips together. Why was she even having this conversation, especially with a daemon? She wasn't great with feelings at the best of times. Other girls always seemed to know exactly how they felt when it came to everything and everyone, but she'd never had much time to worry about feelings. She'd been too busy training or kicking ass.

And Ash, well. Things were complicated. She couldn't deny she was attracted to him. She couldn't deny she was drawn to him in other ways besides physical desire. But he was still a mystery, still a stranger in so many ways. But whenever she tried to convince herself that, really, she didn't know him at all, her mind would conjure up a perfect memory of his dark eyes, gleaming with fire and determination, staring through her skin and scorching her soul with their intensity.

"It doesn't matter," she finally answered, her voice flat. "He's never coming back here. He's gone for good."

He, Seiya—his sister—and Lyre had gone deep underground, hiding from Samael's relentless spies, and she'd done a pretty good job over the last two months of convincing herself she would never see any of them again. But the thought still made her ache inside.

Kindra opened her mouth to respond but thumping footsteps made them both turn toward the back of the kitchen. Marcelo appeared at the top of the stairs and stopped at the sight of them. His eyebrows shot up and his dark gaze snapped over Piper. His buzz cut, sturdy build, and heavy boots made him look more like a soldier than a Consul. The ugly bump on his nose from a badly healed break ruined his look a bit.

"Piper? What are you doing here?" His tone was much closer to disgruntled surprise than welcoming.

"I live here."

He snorted. "Not anymore."

"Uh, actually, I do. I was at school, not banished."

He folded his arms, biceps bulging. "The only people allowed in Consulates are Consuls, Apprentice Consuls, and daemons. Ergo, you shouldn't be here."

"Are you drunk, Marcelo?" Kindra snapped. "You said it yourself. Apprentice Consuls belong here just as much as you do."

"They do. But since there are no Apprentice Consuls in this Consulate right now, the point is moot."

Kindra looked sharply at Piper, who flexed her jaw, wishing she could break Marcelo's ugly nose a second time.

"Piper's apprenticeship was cancelled two months ago," he informed Kindra, barely suppressing his smug delight. "I don't know what the official reason is, but 'gross incompetence' is probably pretty close."

"Piper is a good Apprentice!" Kindra said angrily.

He snorted again. "I spent more time cleaning up her messes than doing my job. But the last two months have been great. It's been so quiet it's almost been boring, but that's how it's supposed to be."

Waving a dismissive hand at Piper, he smiled coolly. "We all knew you wouldn't make it. We were surprised you lasted this long. Even *I* think your father has been pretty damn cruel, stringing you along for so many years. You'll have a better time of things once you settle into a human community."

"I'm not going to a human community," she ground out.

"You sure as hell aren't staying here."

She bared her teeth at him. "You've been enjoying the peace and quiet, haven't you? You like it better that way because then maybe no one will notice that you couldn't beat a daemon in a fight if your life depended on it."

He sneered. "Talk all you want, but you won't be here long. Your father is already planning how to get rid of you again."

With a nasty chuckle, he strode over to the fridge, grabbed a can of soda, and disappeared back down the stairs. Piper glared after him, hands clenched into fists.

"Piper . . ." Kindra said softly. "I'm sorry."

She stood, motions jerky with anger. "I'll be back in a few minutes."

Striding out of the kitchen, she headed for the grand staircase at the front of the manor. Marcelo's words rang in her head. *Already planning how to get rid of you again.* It wouldn't surprise her. Quinn wanted her as far away from the Consulate—any Consulate—as he could possibly get her.

She half-jogged up the stairs and stopped at the top, breathing hard. To her left were four Consul suites; to her right, an open-concept living, dining, and kitchen space where live-in and on-shift Consuls could relax. Two months ago, she'd been standing in almost this exact spot, her suitcase beside her, about to head down to the foyer to watch for the car from the school, when Quinn had told her that her apprenticeship had been cancelled. He'd told her literally ten minutes before she was to leave.

Her current situation was too *unstable*, he'd said. She wasn't in a position to dedicate the proper effort to her training. She needed time off to get her life back in order.

Though he'd referenced recent events, she suspected his real feelings on the matter were a little different. He'd treated her strangely ever since he'd learned she could wield the Sahar. She could draw only one conclusion: he thought *she* was unstable. He was afraid she'd become fragile or even unhinged after everything that had happened to her. And his idea of the best approach to his daughter's potential psychosis and her ability to wield massively destructive levels of magic was to get her as far away from daemons as physically possible.

Fury surged through her. She'd charged through an army of daemons to reach him and Miysis, then she'd used the Sahar to open up an escape route for them. And her reward? The cancelation of her apprenticeship. If anything, she'd proved herself to be strong and capable, but instead, Quinn thought she was damaged and brittle.

Jaw clenched, she stalked into her bedroom and shut the door, barely managing not to slam it. Damn Marcelo for digging at old wounds. Dropping into her desk chair, she rubbed her face and massaged her aching temples.

Propping her elbows on the desk, she stared listlessly around her room. She'd been so delighted to return home that she hadn't given a lot of thought to what came next. Unless she convinced her father to reinstate her apprenticeship, she couldn't live at the Consulate anymore. Marcelo was right. A random haemon hanging around would create all kinds of complications; deprived of her authority as an apprentice, she would be a target for any daemon in a bad mood. Besides that, without training or shifts to complete, she'd have nothing to do.

Without an apprenticeship, she would have to leave. But where would she go? This was the only life she'd ever known.

YIELD THE NIGHT | 13

She stared in the general direction of her desk for several minutes, thoughts spinning through her head, before she realized what she was seeing. The corner of a red piece of paper peeked out from beneath a battered textbook on advanced first aid—a textbook she would no longer need to study without her apprenticeship.

Brow furrowed, she pulled the paper out. She didn't own any red stationery that she could recall and she was certain the sheet hadn't been there when she'd left for Westwood. Unfolding it, she discovered it had been torn from a larger page. What appeared to be a cheap menu was printed on one side. She flipped it over to find unfamiliar handwriting scrawled on the opposite side.

MIDNIGHT ON SATURDAY
AT THE WELL.
— L.

She stared at the message, then looked at the desk. A note hidden in her room. Only two people with names that started with an L would want to meet her in secret. Since Lilith wasn't the "secret handwritten messages" type—as far as she knew—that meant the note had to be from Lyre.

Excitement erupted inside her like fire in her veins. Lyre had been here. In her room. When? Her excitement turned into anxiety. How long ago? What if he'd hid the note weeks ago, thinking she would be home to find it? No, he'd known she was going to a boarding school. It was common knowledge that today was the last day of the winter semester for schools across the region.

So he must have hidden the note just this week. Maybe he'd even been in the Consulate that very day. He must mean tomorrow night. There was an old well on the Consulate property, dry for decades; she knew the spot.

Her hands twitched, wanting to clench the note tight. So close. She'd been so close to seeing him—and Ash—again. Just when she'd finally accepted that they were gone forever, this! But why? Her exhilaration waned a second time. Why did Lyre want a secret meeting? Why was he back from the Underworld? Were Ash and

Seiya with him? She'd assumed they were together, but what if something had gone wrong? What if Lyre wanted to meet her because he had bad news?

The last bit of her happy bubble popped as another thought occurred to her.

What if the note wasn't from Lyre at all?

She didn't know what Lyre's handwriting looked like. What if it was a trick? Some plot of Samael's or Lilith's to lure her out into the forest by herself in the middle of the night?

Her hand clenched, crushing the note. There was no way to know for sure without going to the meeting point tomorrow night and hoping for the best. Biting her lip, she smoothed out the paper. She didn't know why, but her gut said it really was from Lyre. She would have to take the risk.

"Piper!"

Hearing the alarm in Kindra's voice, Piper sprang to her feet. She stuffed the note in her pocket and ran for her bedroom door.

"What's wrong?" she yelled as she threw the door open.

"I smell smoke," Kindra yelled from somewhere downstairs. "Something is on fire!"

A zing of fear ran through her and an image rose in her mind: the grainy newspaper photograph of the destroyed Consulate. Panic surged and she bolted toward the stairs.

She got ten steps down the hall before an ear-shattering explosion rocked the Consulate.

She hit the floor. The building heaved. Light bulbs shattered, plunging her into darkness. Another detonation went off in the west wing. Wood and metal screamed as support beams gave way.

With snapping sounds like gunfire, one end of the living area fell into the foyer. The floor plunged downward, turning into a ramp. She scrabbled desperately for a handhold as furniture and debris slid off the edge and crashed down into the entryway. Friction lost out and suddenly she was sliding fast. She screamed as she went over the edge. She landed hard and fell into a painful roll, crashing into an upside-down sofa. Debris rained down on her.

A third detonation tore through the front of the manor.

The earth bucked and trembled. The dining room table, a casualty from the upstairs kitchen, lay on its side a few feet away. She dove toward it. Tucking herself against the heavy wooden top, she covered her head with her arms as the front wall of the building buckled inward. Wood and bricks smashed down on the foyer, but the table shielded her from the worst of it.

Breathing hard, limbs shaking, she shoved a chunk of drywall off and staggered to her feet. Cool night air whipped across her face but she barely spared a glance at the front lawn, which was now one with the demolished foyer. Half the manor was still standing.

"Kindra!" she screamed.

Stumbling over rubble—thank goodness she was wearing her leather boots—she ran into the hall, still calling for the daemon. Kindra had just been shouting to her; the daemon couldn't be that far. The hall was pitch black, and as soon as she entered, she smelled it— smoke. Something was burning.

She almost ran into a barricade at the end of the hall that separated her from the main-floor kitchen. Part of the upper floor had buried the hallway.

"Kindra!" she yelled desperately.

Kicking at the debris, she found a loose spot. She yanked a few two-by-fours out of the way and squeezed through the tiny gap. Halfway to the other side, the debris shifted and the hole tightened, squeezing her middle. With a terrified gasp, she squirmed out, scraping her hips on the splintered wood. As soon as she pulled her feet free, the gap caved in and she heard another wave of rubble fall from the upper level.

Scrambling away, Piper turned toward the kitchen and saw where the smoke was coming from. The kitchen was on fire. Flames danced over every surface, greedily devouring the wooden cupboards.

She spun away from the kitchen and toward the living room, eyes scouring the remains of the sitting area where, just a few minutes ago, she'd been sitting, eating cookies. A deafening crash rent the air as another part of the house caved in on itself. Breathing fast, she focused on the living room again. A wall had collapsed over half the room, burying the sofa, but—

Her heart leaped into her throat. Red curls peeked out from beneath the broken wall.

Piper dashed to the wreckage and grabbed a heavy piece of drywall with studs still attached and bent nails sticking out from the back. Straining, she dragged it off and flipped it aside. Kindra was sprawled amidst the remains of a bookshelf.

"K-Kindra!" she coughed. It was becoming hard to breathe. Smoke burned her eyes.

She grabbed the daemon's arm and pulled it around her shoulder. Gritting her teeth, she stood, heaving Kindra up. The dead weight was almost too much for her. Kindra shuddered.

"Piper?" she groaned.

"Kindra, hang on, okay? This way."

Kindra got her feet under her and staggered beside Piper, leaning heavily on her. The heat from the fire beat at her as she led them toward the kitchen. The fastest way out of the manor was through the back door, except it was on fire too. She half-dragged Kindra to the edge of the inferno. With one arm shielding her face, she kicked the door hard. The flames jumped from the impact but the door remained intact. Teeth bared, she kicked again. The door flew open and Piper hauled Kindra out as the scorching heat singed her face.

Fresh air swept into her lungs as she led Kindra away from the building and onto the lawn. Cold drops of water peppered her face; it was starting to rain. A dozen yards out, her legs buckled and she fell on the grass. Kindra dropped to her knees, one hand pressed to her head. Blood streaked the side of her face.

"What happened?" she whispered, eyes still dazed.

Piper shook her head, looking back at the building. The corner with the kitchen was the only part of the manor still standing, but the flames were quickly consuming it. Somewhere in the destruction, all her worldly belongings had been crushed and were burning. And somewhere inside, Marcelo and two daemons were either trapped or dead.

"It's the seventh attack," Kindra said hoarsely, also staring at the wreckage. "One every night this week . . ."

Piper didn't answer, unable to speak. Her heart pounded and her head spun. She kind of thought she might throw up. Or pass out. Or both. She should do something. There was something she should be doing, right? Search for Marcelo? Call for help? Maybe she and Kindra could dig them out. She rubbed her hand over her face, smearing soot and raindrops across her skin.

A thought popped into her head, snapping her out of her daze.

"Kindra," she hissed. "We have to get out of here."

"What? No, we need to—"

"Now!"

"But—"

Piper grabbed her arm and hauled her to her feet. She ran for the dark line of trees at the edge of the lawn. They ducked into the foliage and Piper crouched behind a thorny bush.

"Don't you remember what the article said?" she whispered, pulling Kindra into the shadows with her. Rain pattered on the leaves overhead. "That daemon who survived the explosion was killed afterward, shot in the head."

No sooner did she finish speaking than shadowed figures appeared, slowly circling the Consulate. Kindra went still and silent, her jaw tight as she watched the strangers. Piper's hands clenched. The six men came around to survey the demolished half of the building, their backs to Piper and Kindra as they examined the rubble, searching for survivors to finish off. Even in the uncertain light, Piper could tell they were armed; they carried themselves with that stiff-shouldered stance of men with heavy guns. She gritted her teeth. They were the ones who'd been blowing up Consulates for a week. The ones who'd blown up her home.

Kindra shifted her weight. Piper glanced over—and gasped.

"Kindra, no—"

The daemon rose to her feet, shedding her glamour in the same movement. Her wild red hair drifted outward, suddenly immune to gravity. Her ears were now pointed, cheeks hollow beneath dramatically sharp cheekbones. Her eyes were huge and black as coal. Her body, more willowy and lightweight than ever, coiled in readiness. Narrow red things—scales? feathers?—rose in lines on her arms like a cat's hair standing on end.

Before Piper could even finish her protest, Kindra sprang out of the trees. With impossible speed, she flashed across the expanse of lawn. Piper swore under her breath and ran out after her, keeping low.

Kindra was on the first man before he could turn. Piper didn't see what Kindra did but the man screamed as he fell. The others spun toward the daemon. She dashed away, almost too fast for the eye to follow, then reappeared, making a grab for a second one. The third got his gun up and fired but Kindra abandoned her target and flashed away, a dark blur. His gun flipped up, hitting him in the face, struck by an invisible blow from the daemon. He staggered, brandishing his rifle and wildly looking around for Kindra.

Between the darkness, the haze of rain, and the lethal daemon, none of them noticed Piper coming.

She rushed in and swung her leg up in a hard kick, her booted foot hitting the nearest man's hand before he could pull the trigger, crushing his fingers against the metal. He yelped and twisted toward her, but she grabbed his gun and wrenched it hard, probably breaking more of his fingers as she tore it from his grip. As soon as she'd disarmed him, she slammed the stock into his face, knocking him clear off his feet.

To her left, another man yelled in panic as Kindra caught him. He collapsed and the daemon sped away as the remaining three let loose deafening sprays of bullets at the empty space where she'd just been. Tossing the rifle aside, Piper dove toward them, dropped low, and swept her leg into the nearest one's ankles. He fell, landing hard on his back. Piper jumped on him and smashed her elbow into his temple. Two left.

Kindra appeared again, this time behind the second last man, and grabbed his head, clearly intending to break his neck.

The last man whirled to face his comrade—and opened fire.

Piper screamed. Kindra fell backward, the man she'd been about to kill collapsing on top of her, riddled with his companion's bullets. Neither moved.

The last man spun around and leveled his gun at Piper's chest. She braced for the blazing agony of bullets.

But he didn't fire.

"I don't believe it," he said flatly. He glanced swiftly over his shoulder. "Sergeant!"

Piper looked in the same direction. Three more men were running toward them, clutching their weapons and breathing hard. They slowed as they drew near and raised their guns toward Piper as their eyes scoured the bloody scene.

"What the hell happened?" one of them barked.

The man who'd shot Kindra didn't immediately answer. He was still staring at Piper, his face hidden behind a black ski mask, the barrel of his gun barely a foot from her chest. Cold rain peppered them, the flickering flames of the Consulate fire reflecting off the wet metal of the gun. Her gaze darted from the dark heap that was Kindra beneath a dead man, and back to the man who'd killed her. Tears stung her eyes. Rage closed her throat. Her right hand clenched and unclenched. If she only had the Sahar, she would show these bastards what a real explosion looked like.

"What *happened*?" the leader demanded again.

The guy in front of her snapped out of his reverie.

"Do you know who this is?" he asked, the words edged with an emotion she couldn't name—something between fury and fear.

"No idea."

"That's Piper Griffiths."

"*What?*" The leader peered at Piper. "Are you sure?"

"Of course I am," the man retorted.

"What's she doing here? She wasn't supposed to be here."

"Holy shit," another muttered. "Good thing she didn't die."

Piper looked between them, confusion battling fright.

The one who'd recognized her lifted his rifle and rested it on his shoulder. With his free hand, he grabbed the bottom of his ski mask and pulled it up to reveal a cold, angry sneer.

Her heart skipped in her chest.

"Fancy seeing you again," he said. "Last time we met you left me to die in a burning Consulate. Shame I couldn't return the favor."

She stared, barely able to comprehend what she was seeing—*who* she was seeing. The first time she'd met him, his smile had been friendly and open, his sandy hair a little longer and his face smooth with carefree youth. Shortly after that, she'd strangled him unconscious so she could rescue her uncle.

His name was Travis. And he was a Gaian.

CHAPTER
-3-

PIPER stared at the bare wall across from her and wondered why the hell these things kept happening to her. Abducted again, less than twelve hours after arriving home. It wasn't fair.

Beneath her disgust at her awful luck, fury and fear simmered. Fury at the Gaians for destroying her home. For killing Marcelo and the two daemons in the basement. Above all, fury at Travis for killing Kindra.

Fear twisted her stomach because she didn't know what was going to happen next. But she wasn't terrified. She wasn't trembling. It was hard to fear the Gaians, who had already revealed they had no plans to kill her. Her last abductor had been a thousand times more terrible. The Gaians might be capable of murder but Samael had turned torture and killing into an art.

After capturing her, Travis and the others had taken her to their vehicle. She'd been bound and blindfolded for the three-hour—by her best guess—drive. Still blindfolded, she'd been led into a building and dropped off inside her new accommodations: a closet. A big closet, but still a closet. Likely in a basement since they'd gone down some stairs and the air was dank in her nose. She wasn't tied up anymore, which was nice. But she couldn't break the lock on the door or otherwise get out, which wasn't so nice.

She sat with her back against the far wall, watching the door. Light leaked in from the gaps around it. She sighed. She must be jaded; being kidnapped just didn't faze her anymore. Or maybe she was still in shock from surviving the attack on the Consulate.

Letting her head fall back against the wall, she twisted the leather band around her wrist, thinking about Ash and Lyre. Her hand drifted toward her pocket where Lyre's note was tucked away. What would he do when she didn't show up and he discovered the destroyed Consulate? What then? The questions circled in her head, and a few hours of worrying passed before footsteps sounded in the hallway. A key slid into the lock. The handle turned.

Piper squinted as the door opened, flooding the room with light.

"Piper!"

A silhouetted form swooped down on her.

"Sweetheart, are you okay? Are you hurt?"

Arms clamped around her, squeezing the breath out of her.

"Mom?" she wheezed.

"Of course, Piper." Mona leaned back and, her vision adjusting to the light, Piper saw tears in her mom's hazel eyes. "I'm so glad you're all right. I almost fainted when they told me you were inside the Consulate." She stood up and tugged on Piper's hand. "Your clothes are filthy, sweetie. Let's get you into something more comfortable."

Piper followed her mom out of the closet, glancing in bemusement at the concrete walls and floor of the hall. Free from her cell already. That had been easy. A man and a woman, both clad in black like Travis, stood in the hallway, their stares suspicious.

"Come along, Piper," Mona said cheerfully. "Ignore them. You aren't a prisoner."

Piper's eyebrows shot up. Not a prisoner, really? She followed her mother down the hall, their escorts keeping pace behind her. Emotions roiled, threatening to crack her cool facade. It had been over three months since she'd seen her mother, and before that, she'd thought her mother was dead. She still hadn't come to grips with this new mother: a Gaian leader.

Piper had no idea what sort of building they were in but she was surprised when Mona led her to an elevator. She pushed the call button and the doors opened. The four of them got in and Piper saw all of the buttons—twenty-five, to be exact. She hadn't expected the building to be this large. Mona pressed the button for Floor 12 and the doors closed. Piper suppressed a cringe as the elevator rattled and creaked upward, shuddering to a stop after a painful two minutes.

The doors opened and they stepped inside a drab hallway. It soon opened into a wide space filled with rows of dusty cubicles; headsets lay on desks as though the workers would be back at any moment. The computer equipment had long since been poached but who needed a hundred cheap headsets?

"Where are we?" she asked.

Mona smiled over her shoulder. "We've had possession of this building for some time. This is home. We'll get you a real room soon, but this will have to do for now."

They passed the sea of cubicles and entered a hall lined with office doors. Mona opened the one at the end. Piper warily walked in, eyeing the dust-coated executive's desk in the corner. A new cot had been set up along the wall, with a cardboard box sitting on top of the folded blankets. Glancing back at her mother, she stepped up to the window and pulled down the horizontal blinds to peek out. The city beyond was cloaked in near darkness, skyscrapers silhouetted against the faint light of the approaching dawn.

The door closed and Piper turned. The two nameless guards had left. Mona sat on the cot and patted the spot beside her. Piper reluctantly sat with a strong sense of déjà vu—sitting on the sofa beside her mother while they had their first conversation in nine years.

"I know your belongings were destroyed," Mona said, her forehead crinkling. "I collected some clothes for you, just something for the time being. Hopefully some of it will fit."

Piper gave a stiff nod, not prepared to offer any thanks yet.

"Sweetheart . . ." Mona folded her hands in her lap and sighed. "You probably have some questions."

"Yup," she replied with cutting nonchalance. "Let's start with why the Gaians blew up my Consulate. I almost died. Another Consul and three daemons did die. Did I mention the third daemon was shot to death by one of your guys? Oh, and did I mention that guy shot another Gaian while he was at it?"

Mona sighed again. "It's all for the greater good, Piper. You weren't supposed to return from Westwood Academy until late this morning."

"I was early." Piper shook her head. "I can't believe you destroyed the Consulate. What if Father and Uncle Calder had been there? Maybe *you* don't care but they're my family."

Mona's eyes widened. "I would never hurt you like that. We knew they weren't there. That's why we picked tonight. I wouldn't let your father and uncle be killed, sweetheart. I wouldn't do that to you."

She decided it wasn't the best time to analyze her mother's moral spectrum, where "don't upset your estranged daughter" ranked higher than "preserve human life." Taking a deep breath, she struggled to keep her emotions on a tight leash. When she had spoken to her father about the things Mona had said during their previous encounter, Quinn had informed her that Mona was insane. Piper didn't know whether that was true but there was a good chance her mother was a few cards short of a full deck.

"So what's the grand plan?" she asked, her voice cool. "What's the justification for all the murder?"

"Fewer daemons have died this week than humans killed by daemons last month," Mona replied sharply. She paused. "We need to talk."

"We are talking."

Mona gave her a long look. "About your future."

"You want me to stay with you."

Mona nodded. "I want you to join me. Join the Gaians."

"Look, Mom—"

She held up a hand. "Piper, just listen. I know you don't agree with some of the things we've done. Maybe you don't agree with our goals. But you'll come to understand them. We can be a family. Not just you and me, but all of us. You belong with us. You belong here."

Piper shook her head, her chest tightening. Belonging was a dream she thought she'd given up on a long time ago, but Mona's words had more effect than she would have anticipated. As a magic-less haemon in a world of magic, she'd never been good enough for her father, the other Consuls, or daemons.

But belonging with the Gaians? They hadn't seemed like one big happy family when Travis was shooting his partner.

Mona stood up. "I'm sure you're tired; you've been up all night. We can talk again later in the day when I give you a tour." She beamed. "I'm so glad you're here. And so glad you're safe. Oh—and happy birthday, sweetheart!" She leaned down and hugged Piper.

Piper nodded, mumbling, "Good night."

Mona closed the door behind her, and a moment later, the lock clicked into place. Not a prisoner indeed.

Heaving a sigh, she moved the box onto the floor, unable to work up enough energy to look inside it. She lay on the cot, exhaustion crashing over her. Twenty-four hours ago, she'd been sleeping in her dorm room, dreaming about being home. Twelve hours ago, she'd been walking into the Consulate for the first time in two months.

Now, the Consulate was gone and Piper was a prisoner—of her own mother. Whatever Mona might say, Piper knew she wouldn't be allowed to leave. The locked door was enough of an indicator. She would never be given her freedom, not now that she knew where they were hiding a major base of operations.

Even if someone figured out who was behind the attacks, no one would know where to look for her. An image rose in her mind of Lyre standing in front of the smoldering remains of the Consulate, wondering where she was.

She closed her eyes and a bitter smile tugged at her lips. A prisoner she might be but one thought comforted her: no matter how bad the Gaians were, they couldn't be as bad as Samael.

      e   e   e

Mona was irritatingly perky when she woke Piper that evening. Her mother just didn't seem to get that Piper wasn't a fan of her new prisoner status—whether or not Mona wanted to admit that her daughter was a captive. Piper tried not to scowl too obviously as she followed her mother through the building. A new pair of guards once again trailed in their wake.

"This floor is the communal area for our residents." Mona waved a hand at the massive open space on the fourteenth floor.

A few dozen people were scattered about the four areas: kitchen, living room, workout/games, and some kind of practice area. Three children around ten years old were sitting on a sofa, giggling over something Piper couldn't see. A few nearby adults glanced curiously at Piper. As her mom led her to the practice area, she tugged self-consciously at the end of her ponytail. A shower would have been nice but she hadn't been given that option yet. At least she had clean clothes instead of looking like she'd been dragged through a fire pit.

The pickings in her box of clothes had been slim. Her shorts had begun life as jeans and the person who'd wielded the scissors hadn't done a very neat job. The only other option had been men's sweatpants, so she'd chosen to deal with the tickly white threads hanging off the shorts. Her red top had been protected from the dirt and smoke by her hoodie so she'd kept it on, layering on a loose-knit sweater with black and grey stripes, an oversized hood, and a plunging V-neck.

"This is the practice area for magical self-defense," Mona explained, gesturing. "Our more experienced members teach the newer ones."

They stopped to watch. The teacher had her students, varying in age from teenagers to forty-somethings, lined up in a row facing stacks of cardboard boxes. At her call, they made wild throwing motions. Three-quarters of the boxes went flying into the wall behind them. The teacher applauded.

Mona smiled. "As you can see, a beginner class. Did you know the majority of haemons born to human parents are never taught how to use their magic? Many, especially the younger ones who live here, left their families to find others like themselves. Some of them didn't even know what they were until we found them."

Piper blinked. She'd had no idea.

"This class has only been practicing for a couple of weeks. Their control is improving quickly." Mona started walking again, heading for the kitchen where a few people were clustered around the table with plates of food. Two massive pots were steaming on the stove and other dishes sat on the counter, waiting for the hungry hordes to descend.

"We take in a lot of teenagers," Mona continued, pointing her chin at a pair of girls in their mid-teens discussing something over their dinners. "They often run away from home, unable to fit in with humans. Or, if they don't know their true parentage, they're unable to understand what's happening to them and go looking for others in the same situation."

Piper nodded slowly. It made sense. Daemons almost exclusively disguised themselves with glamour while on Earth; many women probably had no idea their one-night-stands had actually been with a daemon. How would she know to warn her child about the inevitable onset of magic at puberty? Having grown-up with daily exposure to haemons and daemons, Piper had never given much thought to what it was like for haemons born into a human family in an all-human community. For rural towns especially, daemons were an exotic rarity one never expected to see and weren't entirely sure existed.

"We have a network in place for abandoned infants." Mona glanced at Piper. "When we find them, we place them with couples here. Since we don't allow haemons to reproduce together, we have many eager adoptive parents."

"People abandon their babies?" Piper mumbled. Another thing she'd never thought about. Gaians not allowing their members to have children together made sense; for haemons who could reproduce—not many, as the majority was as sterile as mules—they risked a fifty percent chance of having a female child who would die before reaching puberty. Piper was the only female alive with two haemon parents.

"Yes, more frequently than you'd imagine," Mona answered. "Many humans don't want haemon children and conceived unintentionally, without knowing their partner was a daemon, or as a result of force. Mothers will often leave their newborns at medical centers. We take them all and ensure the children grow up loved in a community that welcomes them."

She looked at Piper, gauging her reaction. "Then there are the female daemons who accidentally become pregnant. We suspect the majority of their newborns are never found, but the ones we hear about, we take in as well."

Piper nodded again, unsure what to say. She wasn't ready to admit that the Gaians did some good things, not after what they'd done last night, but she honestly couldn't find any faults in their efforts to protect haemon children and create homes for haemons who'd been rejected by human communities.

They stopped beside the long, banquet-style table. Mona gestured around the room.

"Those who live here don't have any other home. The majority of our members live normal lives in human communities, but for those without homes, we make space as best we can. It's not perfect but we've tried to make it as comfortable as possible. We have several facilities like this across the country." She patted the table. "Why don't you sit and have some dinner? I have some things to take care of. Just hang out here for a bit and I'll come get you soon."

"Okay," Piper agreed. It wasn't really a choice. Mona gave her a quick hug and hurried off.

Her two shadow guards sat a little ways away and picked up newspapers from the piles scattered across the table. She shot them a narrow-eyed look, not buying their casual act for a minute. One of the two flicked a glance at her, meeting her stare with dark eyes. He was well built, with pale hair somewhere between blond and ashy brown. He held himself like a man who knew how to fight.

They stared at each other for a heartbeat longer before he turned back to his newspaper. Her escape plans would have to take him into consideration; she wasn't sure she wanted to go head to head with him. He gave her a bad feeling.

She looked toward the kitchen, chewing her lip. The long strip of counter and appliances accommodated a lot of cupboards and drawers where plates and utensils might be hiding.

"Hey."

She turned. A girl stood beside her, shoulders hunched, two plates in her hands.

"Um . . . do you want some food?"

Piper tried not to look too surprised. "Uh—yeah, sure."

She accepted a plate and followed the girl to the counter. They served themselves in silence, dishing out noodles, tomato sauce, and salad, before taking a seat at the table. The girl glanced shyly at Piper, nervously fidgeting with a lock of blond hair, half-heartedly brushed at some point much earlier in the day. The casual look matched the sweats and t-shirt she wore. She hesitantly passed Piper a fork.

"I saw you getting the tour," she said so quietly Piper had to lean closer to hear her. "I figured you were new and wouldn't . . ."

"You guessed right," Piper said, putting on her cheerful face. "Thanks. I had no idea where to find the dishes."

The girl smiled, her round face relaxing. "I'm Kylee."

"I'm Piper." She twirled some noodles around her fork then looked over and discovered Kylee staring at her.

"You're Ms. Santo's daughter?" the girl asked.

Piper managed not to cringe. "Yeah, that's me."

"That's cool. Ms. Santo has mentioned you a couple of times. She must be really happy that you're here now. When did you arrive?"

"Early this morning."

"Oh, so you just got here. I've been here for a month. I'm a newbie too."

"Why did you come here?"

"My mom and stepdad kicked me out after I was expelled from school for blowing up a desk."

Piper snorted down a laugh and shoveled a forkful of pasta into her mouth. "Why did you blow up a desk?"

"I didn't mean to. My parents forbade me from ever using magic and I couldn't control it. But my teacher was . . . calling me names and I got so upset and it just . . . happened."

Piper knew what being humiliated in front of peers felt like. "Are you happier here?"

Kylee's face lit up. "Oh yeah! Everyone here likes me. I start magic lessons with the next group in a week. I can't wait."

"I bet that'll be fun. So I'm guessing your biological dad . . .?"

Kylee frowned at her bowl. "He must have been a daemon, though my mom didn't know it when she met him. She didn't like talking about him."

"I'm sorry. You probably don't like daemons much, huh?"

"Definitely not. I've never met my dad. No one here knows their daemon parent. They make children but then abandon them. I don't think that's right. And they all do it. It's pretty heartless."

Piper couldn't argue there. She focused on her meal, her thoughts twisted with ideas and realities she'd never bothered to consider before. As she and Kylee ate, the room began to fill up. People glanced at her curiously, the newcomer, as they served themselves dinner or sat in the living area to catch up with friends. The lesson at the other end of the room concluded and the tired but happy students came to get drinks, talking excitedly about their progress.

"Hey look," Kylee said suddenly, her eyes lighting up. "The scouts are back."

Piper looked over at the entrance to the communal area. Four guys in black were striding across the room toward the kitchen.

"Scouts?"

"Yeah! Usually they're just looking for runaways and stuff, but they've been working on a big project lately. I hope I'm good enough with magic to become a scout. I'd love to help rescue other haemons."

Big project, huh? Were any of the regular members aware of the Consulate attacks? These scouting guys had probably been out choosing Consulates for their demolition schedule. Piper almost returned to her plate for her last bite when one of the men caught her eye. Fury flooded through her, burning in her veins. Travis.

"Piper." He stopped beside her, sandy hair flattened from the ski mask he'd been wearing the night before while destroying her home, murdering her friend, and abducting her. The other three stopped behind him. "How do you like your new home?"

Kylee shrank away from the cold hostility in his voice. Piper turned halfway toward him, propping one elbow casually on the table as she fought back her swirling anger. The spray of blood as Kindra fell kept replaying in her head.

"Hey there, Travis. Finished with all the murder and mayhem for the day?"

Kylee's eyes went wide.

Travis smirked. "It's not murder when it's daemons, Piper. I told you that last time."

"Yeah, I remember, along with how quick you were to pull the trigger on your own comrade. Was that not murder either?"

He paled slightly but managed a cold snort in reply. The friendly chatterer from three months ago was long gone. Was she responsible for the change in him? She had a hard time believing her attack could have caused such a drastic transformation in him, from a naive and trusting young man to a callous killer.

"I brought something for you," he said, pulling a folded newspaper from under his arm. "Picked it up this morning and figured you'd enjoy it."

He shook it out and read loudly from the front page. "Griffiths Consulate Destroyed, Head Consul's Daughter Presumed Dead."

Her mouth fell open. She snatched it from his unresisting hands and flipped it around. The headline blared from across the top. She skimmed the first few paragraphs. There was almost no info, just a reiteration of the previous attacks and the ongoing search for bodies. Westwood Academy had confirmed dropping her off last night and all evidence suggested she'd been inside when the explosions had gone off. There was no mention of Kindra's body; the Gaians must have dumped it somewhere.

The rest of the article was speculation about what the Consul Board of Directors would do next. The Head Consul hadn't been available for comment. Piper dropped the paper on the table.

Travis leaned down. "I thought you'd like to know that the whole world thinks you're dead, which includes anyone you were hoping would come to your rescue."

She fought to keep her reaction off her face. Oh shit. Double shit. She hadn't thought of that. How would her father and uncle know she was missing if they thought she was dead and buried under the Consulate's rubble? Would Lyre think she was dead too? Who would look for her?

"Piper," Kylee whispered, "what does he mean by 'rescue'? Don't you want to be here?"

"Piper needs some reeducation," Travis said, his glare locked on Piper's. "She's a glam-girl and doesn't have a clue what daemons are really like."

Piper's hands clenched at the insult, a derogatory term for women with daemon fetishes. "*You* don't have a clue. You're just a little boy so terrified of monsters you shot your own friend to keep the scary daemon away from you."

He smirked and leaned in, getting right in her face. "And I'd do it again," he hissed. "That murderous bitch got what she deserved—"

She grabbed the back of his head and slammed his face into the table.

He lurched back, spewing curses, blood running from his nose. She sprang to her feet, her surge of anger waning as quickly as her temper had snapped, but the image of Kindra falling still kept playing in her mind—the sound of the gunshot, the thud as she hit the ground.

Travis wound up for a punch that would break her jaw. She slid aside, grabbed his other arm, and spun him around using his own momentum, making him stagger in the wrong direction. He reoriented and took another swing. She ducked under it, the breeze ruffling her hair, and saw his friend rushing her. Damn it.

She danced away from the new guy's punch. The others closed in. She sighed, struggling to control her anger. However many months of martial arts training these guys had, it was just enough to make them overconfident. Block the incoming punch, strike to the gut, kick to the knee, and one went down. Rinse, repeat. When Travis came at her again, it took all her self-control not to break any bones as she put him on the ground.

"Piper!"

She looked up from the middle of a circle of moaning guys clutching their bruises. Her mother stood at the entrance to the space, mouth hanging open. Piper belatedly noticed the entire room was watching. Her two shadow Gaians hadn't moved from their seats; the creepy one was smirking.

"He wanted a fight," she said loudly, pointing at Travis. She looked around at Kylee, who was possibly about to faint. "You saw, right?"

Kylee gaped at her, not making a sound.

Mona's mouth thinned. "Come with me. Travis, report to your supervisor."

She shook her head and turned, striding away. Whispers erupted throughout the room, shocked voices quietly exclaiming. Piper glanced at Kylee and shrugged. The girl managed a weak smile. As Piper turned to leave, the two teens sitting nearby gave her grins and thumbs-up. She wondered who else didn't much like Travis.

Hurrying out of the room, Piper caught up with her mother in front of the elevator. She braced herself for a lecture but Mona merely frowned at her.

"This community doesn't tolerate senseless infighting. I expect you to show more respect."

"I am *not* a member of this—"

The elevator dinged and the doors opened.

"Don't make any decisions yet," Mona said. She suddenly smiled. "The Council is waiting for you."

CHAPTER

-4-

THE ELEVATOR rattled as it ascended. Piper silently watched the floors tick by.

Why didn't Mona get it? Piper didn't want to be part of her special *community*. Introducing her to a bunch of people and making her feel sorry for the poor abandoned haemon kids wouldn't change that. She could list a lot of good reasons why she hated the Gaians, starting with her mother leaving the family when Piper was a kid and ending with the whole "hello, you kidnapped me" thing going on at this very moment.

When the light for the twenty-fourth floor lit up, the elevator groaned to a halt and the doors creaked open. Oh, this had to be the executive level of the building. Two glass doors opened into a reception area with a curved desk of glossy mahogany. Mona led her straight through and down a wide hall. The door at the end opened before they reached it and an older man in a suit waved them in. A long conference table took up most of the room, with six people already seated around it, three men and three women.

Her mother sat and the door-opening guy took his seat as well. That left the chair at the head of the table for Piper. She sat, eyeing the others warily. These were the leaders of the Gaians, the men and women responsible for the destruction of her home.

"Welcome, Piper," the nearest man said. His deep-set eyes were serious above a broad nose and full mouth. The dark skin of his bald head gleamed under the fluorescent lights. He was around thirty, maybe a little older. "I am Chairman Walter."

Piper gave him a cold look. "So should I thank *you* for attacking my Consulate last night and kidnapping me?"

"It's not like that, Piper—" Mona began anxiously.

Walter held up a hand. "She has every right to be upset. From her perspective, we have not been allies of any kind."

That was an understatement. Piper folded her arms and waited, anxiety slowly churning in her stomach.

"Piper, we want to change your perspective. In spite of recent events, we are your allies. We are the allies of every human and haemon. We want to make the world a better, safer place. With daemons here, spreading fear and corrupting our attempts to rebuild, our progress as a society has stalled."

He gestured toward the window at the back of the room. A downtown vista, though of what city she wasn't sure, stretched out as far as she could see. From above, the impression was overwhelmingly drab and rundown.

"Not since the Dark Ages has humanity gone so long with so little progress. Seventy years. What kind of progress could we make if we removed the outside threats from our world?"

Piper pulled a disbelieving face. "You're blaming *daemons* for our lack of progress since the war? Based on what?"

"Cities. When have you ever heard of great innovations coming from tiny, isolated towns? We need people to live in the cities again but as long as daemons are here, they won't."

"There are lots of people in cities."

"No. Statistically there are very few. Over seventy percent of the population resides in rural communities and towns with no more than 5,000 inhabitants."

Piper grimaced and swallowed her arguments. Might as well let him finish his spiel.

"People are afraid of daemons. Too many are unwilling to work or live in cities where daemons reside. Remember, Piper, outside well-trained Consuls, people can't recognize daemons. To a human, anyone could be a daemon waiting for a chance to prey on them."

"Daemons aren't vampires," she said shortly. "They don't—"

"They prey on humans more than you'd like to admit, but that is beside the point. Humans believe daemons are a threat to them—and they aren't wrong—so they stay away. If we remove daemons from the cities, people will return. We can rebuild the infrastructure, improve the power grid, kick-start the economy. Innovation and progress will begin again. As people return to the cities and society begins to function, higher education will once more become possible. We can reverse this slide back into the middle ages where the common people are nothing but ignorant farmers."

That sounded all grand and everything, but she didn't believe daemons were the root of the problem. She couldn't say what the root was, but without hard facts, all she saw was a scapegoat.

"That is our goal. We are not extremists out to destroy the daemon race. We simply want them to return to their worlds while we put ours back together. When things are stable again, we can work out fair and controlled ways for daemons to visit again."

"Let's say you did get them all to leave, how would you control their visits? How would you even know they were here?" It wasn't like policing a land border; daemons could drop in through ley lines anywhere on the planet.

"Some of our brightest minds have developed new technologies to help identify ley line disturbances." Walter smiled benevolently. "But I'm sure you're wondering what this has to do with you. Because we don't intend to bar daemons from Earth entirely—nor would that be feasible—we need to create a system to control the daemons who do come here. Such a system does not currently exist."

She frowned. "The Consulates—"

"The Consulate system doesn't work, Piper," Walter interrupted. "You know this."

She flinched. She used to believe wholly in the Consulates. Daemons needed them for safe accommodations on Earth, and they needed the Consuls as fair ambassadors between them and the human government. But she'd since come to realize that the system only worked for weaker daemons. Powerful daemons didn't need Consulates or the protection they offered. And the daemons that did need protection were often guilty of something illicit, even if it was unrelated to human laws.

"The Consulate system was born thousands of years ago to shelter daemons coming to Earth," Walter said. "It was never intended to control or police them. Seventy years ago, when daemons came out to the public, the Consulates were thrust into a position of authority without the power to fulfill their responsibilities. The world continues to change but the Consulates have not—or will not—evolve to keep pace."

Piper pressed her lips together. Her only goal for most of her life had been to become a Consul, and she had been far more concerned with that than whatever problems existed within the organization. She hadn't been walking around with her eyes closed; she knew there were some issues, but she'd never thought of them as something serious enough to undermine the system's effectiveness. She'd never considered the possibility that it was irredeemably flawed.

"Consulates and prefects need to be abolished," Walter continued, "and replaced by a new system with the authority and ability to police daemons effectively."

Piper shook her head. "If there was an easy way to police daemons, the Consulates would already be doing it."

"Would they? The Consulates exist for the convenience of daemons, not the protection of humans. The new system would protect humans and haemons alike, and hold daemons accountable for their actions."

"And how are you planning to do that?"

"Knowledge, technology, and magic."

She raised her eyebrows questioningly.

"Knowledge of daemons—how and where they travel, the limits of their abilities, their weaknesses. Technology to empower us—the ability to track them, restrict their movements, and subdue them when necessary. And, of course, magic of our own to counter even the most powerful daemons."

Piper barely held back a derisive snort. *No* haemon could compare to a reaper or a draconian. Did Walter have any idea what he was talking about?

"Piper," he said, folding his hands on the table and leaning toward her. "Your experience, knowledge and training afford you the opportunity to be instrumental in the creation and leadership of this new system."

His words took a moment for her to process. She looked from face to face, waiting for someone to crack a smile or yell, "Gotcha!" Silence met her stare as they waited for her to absorb Walter's words. She gave her head a sharp shake.

"Me?"

"Your familiarity with daemons and their natures, and your unique ability to meet them on equal ground—a talent many Consuls struggle with—are exceptional. You're a natural leader, a natural fighter, and you possess an unquestioning sense of justice. You are uniquely qualified to influence the development of the system."

She looked from him to her mother and back again. "I *just* turned eighteen and you want me to help build your new super-Consul force?"

"You would not be working alone. This isn't something that would happen overnight. This will be an ongoing effort of years, not months."

She shook her head. "Well, you forgot one thing. Your three 'keys to success' included magic, and in case you forgot, I don't have any."

Walter's teeth flashed in a smile. "Actually, you have more magic than anyone in this room."

She gave him an icy look. "I have magic that's sealed. That equals zero magic, not extra magic."

"You don't have *accessible* magic at the moment, but we have a solution."

Her breath caught before she scowled. "My mother's idea of unlocking half my magic and hoping it doesn't kill me isn't a solution."

"Actually," the woman beside Mona said, "we want to unlock all your magic."

"So you definitely want to kill me."

"Not at all," the woman replied coolly, clearly unimpressed by Piper's attitude.

"We have devoted an entire team to researching your unique situation," Mona said earnestly. "We discovered three other female survivors of haemon parents: Calanthe Nikas, Natania Roth, and Raina Golovkin. They lived at least a hundred years ago but we were able to dig up some records on all of them. Calanthe in particular was the subject of an entire research paper by a Consul."

Mona leaned toward Piper. "Calanthe had *all* her magic. She was more powerful than any haemon and rivaled daemons with her abilities. You could be that strong too."

Piper froze in her seat, not daring to let hope take hold. To be as powerful as a daemon . . .

"But how did she survive?" she asked.

The other woman replied before Mona could. "Calanthe did not have magic as a child. Hers may have been sealed off like yours, or perhaps she developed it later than usual. Either way, our theory is that the dual magic is dangerous only to children because they do not have the control needed to manage it."

Piper looked between them. "But you're just guessing."

"Raina, Natania, and Calanthe all survived," Mona pointed out. "You're past the danger point. You're old enough—"

"Hold on," Piper cut in, desperation making her voice go high. "You're just leaping to conclusions based on some sketchy old documents. You have no idea what—"

"Don't you think it's worth finding out?" Mona asked, her stare intense. "Do you want to spend the rest of your life powerless, or do you want to take a chance and find out if you can be the most powerful one of us all?"

"A chance that could kill me."

"You risk your life on a daily basis. You take chances all the time that could get you killed. How is this any different?"

"I take calculated risks to defend myself when my life is *already* in danger. I'm not deliberately taking life-threatening risks for nothing more than—than ambition."

Mona made a sharp gesture with one hand. "Your life is in danger every day as an Apprentice Consul. Claiming your magic would be proactive self-defense, giving you the power to go head to head with daemons instead of being at a constant disadvantage."

"We understand it's a risk," Walter said. "But consider your options. Your goal is to become a Consul, but I think you already doubt the effectiveness of the system. The title of Consul would not always protect you and you're defenseless against all but the weakest daemons. That's assuming you can become a Consul without magic."

"If you don't become a Consul," Mona said, "what will you do? What future do you have? Will you move out of the city and join a rural community? Marry a farmer and raise his children?"

"With us," Walter said, "you have a future where you can shape change. With your magic, you can help us create an effective system to control daemons. This is your chance to make a difference, to change the world for the better."

Piper's head swiveled between Mona and Walter. She shrunk in her chair. Having a larger purpose in life was one of the big attractors of the Consul job, but she'd already lost her apprenticeship. Was this her chance to start over? Instead of being the weakest member of a flawed system, she could spearhead something new, something effective. Something with real power.

But removing the seal on her magic? Yes, she'd daydreamed about it since the day she found out she had magic locked inside her. How could she not? Being a magic-less haemon had made her a second-class citizen in the Consul world. But the chances were high, very high, that removing the seal would kill her. She hadn't forgotten the debilitating headaches from her childhood, the pain so terrible she would vomit or have a seizure. Maybe those other women had found a way to live with their magic, but Piper had no idea what trick they'd used or if she had the ability to duplicate it.

Walter folded his hands on the table. "With your magic unsealed, you would have the respect of daemons, not grudging tolerance for the baseless authority they allow Consuls."

She pressed a hand to her face. "I need to think about this."

"Yes, of course," Walter said. "There is a meeting the day after tomorrow. We would like your answer before then."

Her mouth went dry. She swallowed. "I need to think about it," she repeated.

Mona rose to her feet. "Come, Piper. Let's go back to your room. I'm sure you need some time alone with your thoughts."

Piper rose to her feet, her mind numb. So much to think about, so many long-held convictions cracking under the weight of new information. She had two days to decide the course of her future, assuming she could trust a word Walter had said.

CHAPTER

-5-

SPRAWLED on a sofa in the communal living area, Piper tried hard to tune out the chatter of a dozen voices. Haemons ranging in age from twelve to thirty sat nearby, talking about this and that. A lot of speculation about the big meeting the following day. They all seemed determined to make her feel welcome and kept asking her questions. She didn't want to be rude, but she really wasn't interested in conversation. She had too much on her mind.

Kylee sat beside her, reading a battered paperback. The girl had been a little awkward with Piper after her fight with Travis, but Piper had managed to brush it off as nothing more than bad history between them. Her worries appeased, Kylee was quietly delighted to just sit beside the cool new girl.

Piper rubbed two fingers across her forehead. She'd tossed and turned all night, reliving her conversation with the Council over and over until the words kept spinning in her head. She definitely wasn't onboard with the Gaians' methods, but she wasn't entirely opposed to their goals.

She wanted to be part of something bigger and the Council offered that. She couldn't believe she was giving their proposition serious thought, but their plans weren't totally crazy. In fact, they had some serious logic on their side. If Piper was willing to admit the Consulate system was seriously flawed, then she couldn't deny that a new system had the potential to do so much better. And to have the opportunity to help build it . . .

Her eyes travelled across the smiling and laughing faces around her. When had there ever been this much carefree laughter in a Consulate? The reason her mother had left was starting to make sense to Piper.

The Consulate wasn't a carefree place to live in. It wasn't a happy place. It was challenging, demanding constant vigilance and frequent exposure to danger. Piper had thrived in its atmosphere but it was the only way of life she'd ever known. It had probably been very different for Mona. With her husband absorbed in his work and her home filled with dangerous strangers, maybe she had just burnt out. When she'd found the Gaians and they'd welcomed her into a group that stood against everything she hated—the constant presence of daemons and the threat they represented—she hadn't been able to say no.

The Gaians didn't have the same strict, disciplinarian atmosphere of the Consulates. Aside from a contained number of individuals possessing a cruel disregard for others' lives, Piper's overall impression was one of almost laughable incompetence. They had bungled everything they'd attempted. The ones who'd attacked the Consulate had failed to get the Sahar Stone, and then they had kidnapped the wrong man in a desperate attempt not to leave empty-handed. The group that had tried to capture Piper when she'd gone back to the Consulate a few days later had barely slowed her down. And when Miysis's guards, prefects, and then a choronzon had attacked their hideout at the abandoned Consulate, they'd been woefully outclassed.

Either way, the average Gaian wasn't a soldier in a war against daemon-kind. They were simple outcasts looking for a place to belong, and that was something she could support wholeheartedly.

She was no closer to making a decision now than in the meeting yesterday. There was no way she could decide by tomorrow. She needed more information. She needed to know more about their plans, how she would be involved, and what other plots they had up their sleeves. Would she be expected to participate in the destruction of the remaining Consulates? Could she really help them bring down the organization she'd dedicated her life to? That was assuming it was possible to shift their methods away from the careless violence they'd so far exhibited. She wasn't even sure she wanted to do that. A large part of her just wanted to get the hell out and never see another Gaian again.

She closed her eyes, a headache building in her forehead. Whether she was even remotely interested in joining them was very much a secondary question to the one that had taken root in her brain and grown into a voracious monster overnight.

Magic.

Her magic.

Dared she risk her life to regain her magic? Not just any magic, but magic more powerful than any other haemon's. Magic to rival daemons. It could kill her, or it could make all her dreams possible. If only she had more information. If she knew for certain that controlling her magic was a matter of willpower, she would go for it. But what if there was no way to control the outcome? What if it was predetermined? That her magic would kill her, no matter what. No way to fight. No way to survive.

She hated being helpless. Could she make herself helpless to her own magic?

She'd experienced powerful magic before; the Sahar had given her more magic than she could control. She'd seen what it could do. Mainly, it killed. Easily. And in large numbers. It terrified her.

Unlike the Sahar, her magic wouldn't be tainted with hatred, and she would be using it to defend, not attack. Assuming it didn't kill her. The questions and options spun, pulling all her thoughts into a whirlwind that made her head ache. She pressed a hand to her forehead as the feeling of being trapped closed in around her.

She needed air. She needed to breathe.

She needed to escape.

Eyes opening, she casually scanned the room. It was time to find out how tight the security around here was. She could make decisions later. Right now, she wanted her freedom above all else.

She stretched and yawned. "Hey Kylee, where's your room? I don't think I've seen that level yet."

Kylee looked up, smiling. "It's on the eighth floor. Want a tour?"

"Sure."

They rose off the sofa and climbed over the legs of the other lounging haemons. She and Kylee strolled across the room and into the hallway. Out of the corner of her eye, she watched two older haemons nonchalantly follow—her ever-present shadows. One was that creepy, pale-haired guy again.

At the end of the hall, Kylee prodded the call button for the elevator. The two guards drifted closer, supposedly in deep conversation. Piper didn't know why they bothered pretending. The doors dinged and rattled open. She and Kylee got on. The two guards started forward quickly.

As they reached the doors, Piper said, "Oh, I forgot something," and stepped into the elevator's threshold as though she were getting off. The guards backed up so she could exit. She stepped out.

The doors rattled into motion. At the last second, Piper hopped backward into the elevator and waved as the doors shut. One merely looked startled, but chagrin flashed across the face of the creepy one.

Kylee blinked at her. "What was that all about?"

"Oh, just . . . you know, admirers, I guess. They've been following me around."

With a smile, Kylee poked at the already lit Floor 8 button. "People seem to like you a lot."

Piper shrugged, her mind racing through Step 2 of her plan. Or to be more precise, racing to figure out what Step 2 was supposed to be.

"A couple of the boys were talking about you earlier. I think they want to ask you out after seeing your . . . fight."

Piper twitched. Oh joy. That would be fun. She needed out of here.

The doors creaked open. Piper let Kylee get off then stopped in the doorway. "Actually, I did forget something."

"Oh." Brow furrowed, Kylee turned to get back on.

"No, no," Piper said as the doors began to close. "Just wait there." She smiled, guilt squeezing her as Kylee's confused frown disappeared.

Since a better plan hadn't occurred to her, she hit the M button. Hopefully her guards would waste time checking the eighth floor before coming after her. As the elevator trundled downward, she pulled her hood up and tucked her hair inside it. Shoving her hands into her pockets, she affected a slouch and waited for the doors to open.

As soon as a large enough gap appeared, she slipped through and into a lobby with chipped marble floors and a dry fountain with a broken sculpture in the middle. The entryway opened up to the second floor, with balconies on either side looking over the fountain. It was a straight stretch to the triple set of glass doors—most of the glass missing—and the fading afternoon sun beyond.

She strode straight for the doors, eyes scanning alertly while she kept her body language relaxed. Nothing to see here. Just a haemon teen out for some fresh air.

"Hey there."

It wasn't an aggressive call. Glancing over, she didn't break stride. Two people came into view on the other side of a wide pillar. They were sitting behind a desk, looking bored and sleepy.

"Don't forget to sign out," the woman called out in a friendly tone. "Don't want to get barred on your way back in."

Piper didn't slow, just extracted one hand and gave a casual wave.

"Hey, you need to sign out."

She sped up. Footsteps sounded behind her—the two Gaians circling the desk to follow her. She broke into a run, shooting for the doors. Dodging crumbled marble, she jumped a smashed statue and aimed for one of the broken doors—

An unseen blow caught her in the chest, knocking her backward. She stumbled and tripped, falling to one knee. Where had that come from? Damn hood had cut off her peripheral vision.

A man stood in front of her, dressed in dark, military-like clothing. Shoving her hood off to prevent a repeat blindsiding, she spun and kicked hard. Her boot hit his ankle. He staggered. She sprang up and struck his diaphragm. He backpedalled, faint surprised registering on his face.

Two more guys came running as the first two caught up with her. Damn it. She'd been expecting more goons like Travis guarding the entrance, but these guys were older and probably a lot more skilled.

Dropping to the floor again, she swept out her leg, taking out the legs of one man. The other jumped over her kick but stumbled on the landing. She jumped to her feet and spun around to see a hand flashing toward her. She threw herself backward, going into a backflip as she kicked out with one foot, forcing her attacker back. On landing, she dropped into a crouch to avoid the fist of the woman.

Spinning around, she ran at the two between her and the doors. At the last second, she turned on one and jumped, slamming both feet into his chest. Her weight and momentum knocked him over backward. She landed on his chest and bolted for freedom. The Gaians scrambled after her as she shot out of the broken doors and onto the sidewalk. A sharp wind gusted across her face, wonderfully fresh. She skidded around the corner and tore down the sidewalk.

The air a few feet in front of her rippled. A flash of black.

Something hit her in the face, snapping her head back and throwing her off her feet. She hit the ground, her head slamming against the sidewalk. Sparks flashed across her vision, almost obscuring the black swirl as it shimmered and solidified into a man— the creepy, pale-haired guard she'd left in front of the elevator on the fourteenth floor barely five minutes ago.

With dark eyes colder than ice, he leaned down and grabbed her chin with rough fingers. Tingles rushed across her skin—magic. As the other Gaians ran over, his spell swept through her, sucking her mind into darkness.

o   o   o

Piper sat cross-legged on her cot, glaring out the window at the dark buildings silhouetted against the fading sunlight. Locked up again. What a delightful pattern this was becoming.

Her muscles ached and her head throbbed, but that was the least of her concerns. She closed her eyes and gently massaged her temples as she went over her failed escape. That flash of darkness. That blow out of nowhere. The sudden appearance of the creepy guard.

She knew what that flash of darkness had been; she'd seen it before. Teleportation was a skill possessed only by reapers.

Even knowing that, she could hardly believe it, though it explained how the guy had gotten outside the building so fast. But how could she have failed to recognize him as a daemon? He'd been following her since yesterday. She'd been trained to recognize daemons in glamour. Could he be a haemon with reaper blood who'd somehow unlocked a caste ability? Or was he a daemon very skilled in hiding his true nature? She didn't know whether either alternative was possible, but her gut said he was a reaper.

If he was, what the hell was he doing masquerading as a Gaian?

Her hands clenched into fists. Did Samael know Piper's mother was a Gaian? Had he planted a spy on the off chance she would renew contact with Mona? And what would this supposed spy do now that she'd been trapped here? He definitely didn't want her to escape, nor did he seem to want her dead—yet. Had the guard already told Samael she was here?

Whatever his plan might be, she couldn't stay where she was and wait for the Hades assassins to close in. She needed to escape now more than ever.

Exhaling, she prodded the painful lump on the back of her head. No Plan B came to mind. Her father and uncle thought she was dead. Chances were Lyre thought the same after discovering the half-demolished Consulate last night, which meant Ash would believe it too. Her only potential ally was her mother, but she couldn't tell Mona about the reaper, not unless she intended to explain why a reaper was after her. There was no way she was telling her mother, and thereby the Council, that she could use the Sahar.

Almost as though the thought had summoned her, Mona opened Piper's door and stepped inside. Her mouth was a thin, angry line. Walter came in behind her, all shiny bald head and ebony skin. He didn't look any happier.

Piper turned to face them, quickly hiding her anxiety.

"I asked you not to wander around," Mona began, clearly revving up to go into full Righteous Parental Lecture mode.

"And that is such a legitimate request," Piper cut in with biting sarcasm, "when you're holding me here against my will."

"You're not a prisoner, you—"

"If I'm not a prisoner then why did your goons attack me when I tried to leave? Why did that guy knock me out? And why am I locked up *again*?"

Mona swelled like a bullfrog.

"You're not a fool, Piper," Walter said before Mona could explode. She deflated with an irritated glare at her counterpart. "I know you understand perfectly well that by being here, you are privy to highly confidential information. Of course we need to protect that information."

"So why do you keep pretending I'm not a prisoner?"

"We don't intend to keep you imprisoned. What use would that be? What possible purpose could it serve? We brought you here because we want you to join us. We want your help. If you choose not to, then we will arrange to return you to your father with the necessary precautions."

Her eyes narrowed. "Such as what?"

"I assume you don't know what city you're in?"

"No."

"So, you see, we can't have you walking out the door. But we certainly don't intend to keep you here if you decide you'd prefer to leave."

She scowled. "It's hard for me to decide anything when I'm stuck here."

"Unfortunately, that's the reality of the situation. We're going to have to insist you remain in your room until tomorrow afternoon. We'll see then what you've decided and proceed from there, either preparing permanent accommodations for you or arranging to send you home."

"I don't have a home. You blew it up."

Mona folded her arms and glowered.

"We need to get back to work," Walter said. "We'll send someone in with your dinner."

She nodded curtly. They left, locking the door behind them. Huffing, she flopped back on her cot. Walter's insistence that they would send her back to her father if she turned them down made sense; Mona certainly wouldn't let them permanently silence her daughter. Keeping her prisoner would eat up their resources and they had to realize that Piper would be a troublesome inmate. Sending her home with no more information than "an office building in a city and a black guy named Walter" wouldn't get anyone very far in locating them. Come to think of it, Walter probably wasn't even his real name, and he hadn't introduced any other member of the Council either.

Throwing an arm over her face to block out the light, she closed her eyes. A reaper was way more than she could handle alone; as long as he was preventing her escape, she was stuck here. But what would he do if the Gaians themselves tried to take her back to her father? Would he strike then? She would have to be very careful.

Tomorrow she had to decide what she would do. Join the Gaians and unseal her magic? The answer should have been obvious. No to both. A resounding no. But she couldn't quite let either idea go. They tantalized her with *maybe's* and *if only's* that made her heart squeeze with longing. Purpose. Power. She wanted both.

Rolling onto her side, she wished there was someone, anyone, she could talk to. Someone to tell her she was crazy for considering the offer. Someone to tell her this was her chance to get what she'd always wanted. Or someone to tell her everything would be okay no matter what she decided.

CHAPTER

- 6 -

PIPER was waiting when Mona came to get her the following afternoon. She stood as the door opened, tugging the ratty hems of her shorts down.

Mona gave her a long look. "Are you ready?"

She nodded. Mona scanned her expression, trying to decipher her mood. Piper folded her arms and raised her eyebrows. Her mother motioned for her to follow.

The hall was empty, as was the elevator. Mona hit the button for the top floor. They waited in silence as they ascended, if the creaking of the elevator counted as silence. She let out a huge breath when it dinged and the doors opened. She strode out and shook the tension out of her hands. Mona led her past a set of open double doors. Piper glanced in and saw an immense meeting room with a wall of windows. At the far end, three steps led up to a dais where a podium and a single wooden chair sat. The room was large enough to hold a dinner function for a few hundred people.

"Is that where the meeting is happening?" Piper asked, catching up to her mother.

"Yes, people will be arriving soon."

How many people were they expecting? The Council sure was leaving it to the last minute to find out what Piper would decide. The sun had already begun to set.

The hall ran the length of the building before ending at a small antechamber. Walter and the rest of the Council waited around a table inside, but one member was missing. The cranky woman wasn't there. Piper glanced around at the bare space. A second door probably led into the meeting room beside the dais.

The Council members were in their finest suits and jackets. The men wore ties, the women necklaces. Piper felt ludicrously underdressed.

"Piper, welcome," Walter said, gesturing for her to sit. "Since time is short, I'll skip the prelude. Have you made a decision?"

She folded her hands in her lap and surveyed each person. Finally, her gaze came to rest on her mother.

"I've given it a lot of thought. I really like what the Gaians do to help haemons and build a community for them. I think that's great."

She glanced at Walter before turning back to Mona and continuing. "As for the Consulates, I admit they have their flaws. But I don't think they should be destroyed, and I won't help you tear them down, especially not when you plan to use outright violence to do it. I won't help you kill innocent people."

Mona stared at her lap, her brow furrowed, refusing to meet Piper's eyes. She exhaled and turned to Walter instead. He nodded solemnly.

"I see. I'm very sorry to hear that."

"Well . . . thanks for the offer anyway." But not for the kidnapping. She could have done without that part.

Walter waved at one of the other Council members. "Could you see if the drivers are ready for Piper?"

She leaned back in her chair, relaxing for the first time. She really had been worried that they would say she had to stay for another week or month or year until she agreed to join them. In fact, they'd taken it so calmly she wasn't sure how to react. Mona continued to stare dejectedly at her lap, chewing on her lower lip. Piper buried a stab of guilt. Now she just had to worry about the reaper ambushing her on the way out.

Twenty seconds later, the door opened again, but it was just the cranky woman finally joining them. As she passed behind Piper's chair toward her seat, her footsteps paused. Piper started to turn—and the woman slapped a damp cloth over her nose and mouth.

Piper gasped involuntarily as she jerked away from the woman's hand. Sweet-smelling air coated her tongue like slime. She lurched out of her seat, tearing herself out of the woman's grasp. The room spun and rocked like waves under her feet. Hands grabbed her and shoved her down into her chair. Someone pinned her arms against her sides. She kicked off the table, trying to topple her chair, but the hands held her down as the world spun around and around.

Walter gripped her jaw. Before she knew what he was doing, he'd forced her head up and jammed a syringe into her mouth. Liquid gushed across her tongue, bitter and syrupy, and then someone put the cloth back over her face. Walter held her jaw closed with bruising force, preventing her from spitting. She fought to free herself even as the room whirled and her vision blurred.

Her lungs burned. Against her will, she inhaled a desperate breath through her nose. Another wave of terrible dizziness. The room faded to black.

Her vision slowly returned, but she had no idea how much time had passed. Her head was filled with swirling clouds of vapor, her thoughts lost in a fog. She slumped in her chair with no will to move.

Mona patted her arm. "Don't worry, Piper. It's a harmless drug, just to keep you calm."

Alarm whispered through the haze in her head. Her chair moved as someone pulled it away from the table. She wobbled in her seat. The room rolled and twirled in every direction. When it steadied, Walter was standing in front of her. He peered into her eyes. His eyes were very dark. Like a shaded daemon except not scary.

"It's taken hold. How much time do we have?"

"Ten minutes until we start."

"Excellent. Mona, wait with her."

Piper stared at nothing. She blinked when Mona touched her shoulder. Her mother smiled but it was kind of sad.

"I don't think I've seen you this peaceful since you were a child." She sniffed. "But then, I've barely seen you. We belong together, Piper. I need you to stay with me and I know you need to be with me. You get in so much trouble by yourself."

Mona touched her cheek. "How do you feel, sweetheart? Calm? You shouldn't feel any fear."

Piper stared at her blankly. Mona frowned a little. "Did Walter give you too much?" She squinted. "Perhaps. But better than not enough. Tonight is going to change your life."

Mona rubbed Piper's shoulders in a soothing way while they waited. Little flickers of thought and emotion danced in the clouds in her head, nothing touching her long enough for her to feel anything.

Time passed. Piper didn't notice. Eventually other people appeared and she was pulled up to her feet and gently guided across the room. They went through a doorway and the rumble of noise made Piper stop in vague surprise. Hands prodded her forward. Up three steps. Walter stood in front of a podium. Someone turned her to face the room and she blinked.

Faces looked back at her. Lots and lots of faces. The room spun a little. The crowd looked at her curiously but didn't seem to know why she was there.

Someone nudged Piper over to one side of the dais and out of the spotlight. All the eyes shifted to watch Walter as he began speaking again. Piper stood listlessly as his words washed over her. He talked about plans for the future. Goals. Missions. Things about the Consulates. How they protected daemons instead of humans. How they were tainted by daemon favoritism.

The words spun and swirled and danced in a wash of sound. Piper stood unmoving, waiting without a thought or care, staring at the growing shadows beyond the windows as the sun disappeared.

"And when we're ready to face the remaining daemons head on," Walter declared, "we'll have a powerful ally. Do any of you know Piper's unique history? You see, Piper was born to two haemon parents."

A couple calls of disbelief from the crowd.

"We all know," he continued, "that female children born to two haemon parents always die in childhood. But do you know that daemons can save our girls? A daemon saved Piper from dying as a child by sealing away the dual magic she inherited from her parents.

"For hundreds of years, daemons have been letting our children die when they could have been saving every single one of them. Why? Because they don't want the competition. A haemon with a dual bloodline is *just as powerful* as a daemon! The daemons want to keep us weaker than them, so they let our girls die."

The Gaians jeered in anger.

"Piper's magic has been sealed away her entire life, keeping her weak. Tonight, we will remove the seal and give her full access to her magic for the first time. Witness the power your daughters could wield!"

Loud applause. Walter turned off the microphone and gestured. Hands pulled Piper to the chair in the middle of the dais and pushed her down. Other hands touched her upper arms. Magic tingled. Invisible bonds tightened around her arms, binding them to the back of the chair. Piper blinked, distantly unhappy but the feeling soon faded.

A new face appeared in front of her. An old woman. She smiled and patted Piper's hand. "Don't worry, child. I'll get that spell out of you, don't you fret."

"Are you ready, Helaine?" Walter asked quietly. The crowd chattered, a low hum behind him.

"Of course," Helaine said with a bite of impatience. "Don't be doubting me now. I've removed filthy daemon spells from hundreds of unfortunate souls."

"Begin then," he replied shortly.

"Will it be difficult?" Mona asked, crouching beside Piper. "The daemon was—"

"Hush," Helaine snapped, laying her hands on either side of Piper's head. "It's bad enough you let that devil wrap your daughter in his evil spells. He did a pitiable job anyway. I can feel the threads of it; the spell is in a wretched state. It would have lasted a year longer at most."

Piper stared at the woman's face as it scrunched in concentration. So many wrinkles. Her hands were calloused, her hold tight. Piper's head felt hot under the woman's touch. Distressed whispers skittered across her thoughts. This was a bad thing, wasn't it? She didn't want this, did she?

The woman grunted. "The devil did a fair job of it after all. The spell doesn't want to budge."

"Can you—"

"Hush!"

Piper's head felt hotter. Little flashes of fire sparked in her skull. She wanted the woman to stop. It hurt. The pain swirled through the mist, growing stronger, threatening her safe, peaceful lassitude. The fire spread to her chest. Her arms jerked and a whimper scraped her throat. Stop now. Make it stop.

"You're hurting her—"

"Quiet, Mona! Let her finish."

Hotter and hotter. Flames inside her. Little lightning bolts in her skull, shooting down her spine. The mist in her head turned red with pain. The insulating cloud thinned.

Agony blasted through her skull and she screamed.

The pain stopped, vanishing like a popped bubble. She panted in the sudden cessation of agony, struggling against the haze that immediately swept the thoughts from her head.

Helaine flung her hands wide. "It is done!" she crowed.

The crowd cheered, pressing closer to the dais. They called encouragements to Piper.

Walter gave her a pat on the shoulder before returning to the podium. He switched on the mic.

"Let us congratulate Piper—as well as the haemon race—in this historic moment! For the first time in two centuries, we have a hybrid haemon among our ranks!"

Shouts of agreement. More cheers.

"Now, before we conclude, I would like to—"

The lights went out with a pop, plunging the sprawling room into darkness.

Startled voices exclaimed in the crowd and the Council members grumbled. Power outages were regular enough not to cause a panic, but the timing was terrible. Piper sat in her chair, blinking in the darkness.

"We ask for your patience, please, everyone," Walter called. "We will have someone check the—"

With a flicker, the lights came back to life, flooding the room. The Gaians looked around, smiling in relief. Walter began to speak again but stopped as a strange hush fell over the crowd, starting from the back of the room. In a surge of movement, the haemons nearest the double doors backed away, bumping into the rest of the crowd.

One lone figure stood in the middle of the new gap, no one within twenty feet of him. He stood casually, hands in his jeans pocket, pale blond hair tousled, golden eyes flashing, catching Piper's attention even from across the room.

Euphoric delight swept through the fog in her head.

Lyre let out a low whistle as he surveyed the crowd.

"This here's a mighty big group of Gaians," he drawled, his smooth voice filling the room in a way Walter's couldn't. His teeth flashed as he grinned. "What a gathering! I didn't know murderers had a support group."

A heartbeat of silence.

"It's not murder when it's just daemons," someone shouted.

"Just daemons?" Lyre repeated. He pressed a hand to his chest. "Wow, I'm hurt. Your mothers didn't think we were *just daemons*."

Angry shouts and hurled insults.

Walter stepped up to the mic. "Restrain that intruder immediately!"

A dozen haemons pushed their way through the crowd to the open space where Lyre stood. As they rushed him, he pulled his hands out of his pockets and flicked them, a casual shooing motion as though he were swatting flies away.

All the attacking Gaians were blasted off their feet and sent crashing to the floor, stunned.

"Oooh, sorry," Lyre said with a sympathetic wince. "I was expecting you all to shield or . . . something, you know."

"Walter, that's not a random intruder," Mona hissed. "That's one of Piper's daemon friends. He's come for her!"

"Take that daemon out now!" Walter shouted. He slashed a look at Mona. "Get Piper out of here before that other one shows up. If he's here, we'll have to use Piper as a hostage to stall him until we can get the ultrasound speaker up here. Mona? Mona, are you listening?"

A moment of silence.

"Too late." The new voice shivered under Piper's skin, rubbing across her bones. She smiled, elated even through the drug haze.

Walter, Mona, and the rest of the Council retreated rapidly from the back of the dais, two of them falling down the steps in their haste. Mona pointed with a shaking hand.

"You!" she shouted accusingly.

A shadow fell across Piper. She looked up. Ash stood beside her, terrifying in black fatigues, an armored vest, and black armguards. Twin swords at each hip. A black wrap covered the lower half of his face.

Piper beamed up at him.

He kept his eyes on Walter, dark irises searing the Gaian leader.

Walter straightened sharply. "You may fancy yourself her rescuer, but—"

Breaking off mid-sentence, Walter plunged a hand into his jacket and whipped out a gun, finger already on the trigger. Ash didn't even move. His punch of magic smashed into Walter, knocking him off the dais. The gun flew out of his hand.

With a dismissive glance at the fallen man, Ash stepped in front of Piper. His gaze swept over her face before locking on her eyes. He slid his hands lightly down her arm. With a tickle of magic, the bindings holding her to the chair disappeared. As soon as she was free, she clumsily raised her arms toward him. He gently scooped her out of the chair, lifting her effortlessly into his arms as he turned. Beyond him, people were stampeding out of the room through the double doors.

"You can't have her." Mona's voice shook as she stepped in front of him. "She doesn't belong to you."

"Nor does she belong to you."

"You can't—"

"Oh come *on*," Lyre said, appearing behind Mona, making her start violently. He'd crossed the room unnoticed by the Council. "You think you have a claim to Piper? You *kidnapped* her. Now that's motherly love."

"She belongs with—"

"With whoever she wants to be with. Now get out of the way." He gave another flick of his hand and his spell knocked her on her butt.

Ash strode off the dais with Piper cradled in his arms. Most of the room had emptied, but before he could take more than a few steps, the doors banged open again. A squad of men in black uniforms rushed in, armed with short assault rifles.

Shimmers coated Lyre's body as he pivoted. His glamour vanished, one hand already pulling an arrow from the quiver hanging on his shoulder. He smoothly nocked it before letting the arrow fly. In a blink, he had a second arrow nocked. He drew the dark fletching to his cheek and loosed it.

Each arrow pierced a soldier's shoulder, pinning them to either side of the doorframe.

The rest of the squad stopped dead, their attention torn between the writhing men pinned to the threshold and Lyre's mesmerizing daemon form. The incubus drew a third arrow, and in a flash he fired it. It hit the top of the doorframe. The arrow glowed bright gold — then exploded. The doorframe collapsed in a rain of plaster and concrete.

"Zwi, lights," Ash said.

The lights went out, plunging the room into total blackness but for the dim glimmer coming off the windows of the nearest skyscrapers.

Unfazed by the darkness, Ash strode toward the wall of windows. The air crackled ominously, and then there was a boom of sound, a shocking explosion of power, and the shattering of glass. A cold wind swept inside the room through the smashed windows.

He stepped onto the ledge, a twenty-five-story drop just inches away. Lyre hopped up beside him, back in glamour, with the wind whipping his hair across his eyes. Zwi flew out of the darkness and landed on his shoulder.

A sudden flash of light illuminated the room.

"Stop!"

The two daemons glanced back as Mona ran toward them, a light spell in her hand.

"You can't have her!" Mona shouted. "She belongs with us!"

Ash looked down at Piper. She smiled. He turned to Lyre and they clasped hands. Together, they sprang into empty space and silent night.

CHAPTER

- 7 -

FLYING was cold. She absorbed little of the journey—flashes of buildings, dizzying drops to the pavement—and did her best to burrow into Ash's chest. His arms were like iron around her, warm and strong. Fear didn't touch her, even as they swooped through the city. Lyre, bent low on Zwi's back, followed along just behind, the dragon's wings beating almost lazily.

Time disappeared again, returning when Ash's wings flared wide and a building was suddenly rushing toward them. She hid her face against his shoulder as he slowed and landed lightly on the balcony railing of a top floor apartment. He jumped down and slid the door open, still holding her. Warm air rushed out.

Zwi swooped up to the balcony and grabbed the railing with her front talons. The metal creaked. With more agility than any human possessed, Lyre half slid, half sprang onto the balcony. In a rush of black fire, Zwi transformed into her cat-sized dragonet form and zipped through the balcony door ahead of them. Ash, still holding Piper, followed, and Lyre quickly shut the door once they were inside.

The tiny bachelor apartment contained nothing but a bed, table, kitchenette, and a drooping armchair with a tattered floor lamp beside it. Ash crossed the dark room in a couple of steps and gently lowered her onto the bed. She sank into the soft blankets, sighing. The cold had blown away some of the fog in her head but her thoughts were still fuzzy and distant. Carefully, she sat up, feeling clumsy and numb as Ash circled the room, trailing one hand over the dingy walls. Magic electrified the air; he was casting some sort of ward.

His wings flexed, unfurling then tightening against his back as he moved. His tail seemed to drift behind him, never quite touching the floor. She watched him, awe sliding through her muzzy brain. She'd never been able to really look at him without his glamour before. Either the draconian Nightmare Effect caused her too much terror, or they'd been busy fighting for their lives.

Thanks to the drugs, the Nightmare Effect didn't seem to be working and she stared without reservation. His movements were all power and grace. The shadows in the room welcomed him, absorbing his form even when she swore the darkness wasn't deep enough to hide him. He completed his circle and shimmers swept over him. Once they faded, he was back in glamour. He pulled the dark wrap off his face as he turned toward her.

"Brrr," Lyre said with an exaggerated shiver. He plopped down on the bed beside Piper as Ash joined them. "How are you doing, Piper?"

Ash knelt on the floor, between her knees, and peered into her eyes. "Are you hurt, Piper?"

She smiled and reached out, sliding both hands through his hair. He gently took her wrists and pulled her hands down. "I need to know if you're hurt."

It took her a moment to get a sound out. Her "no" came out as "nnnnn."

Lyre tried to swallow a laugh and choked. "Wow, she is *stoned*."

Not accepting her mumbles as a real answer, Ash ran his hands over her arms and legs, checking for injuries. Finding nothing but bruises from her fights, he sat back on his heels and studied her.

"Well, I doubt we'll find out what the hell happened until the drugs wear off."

"We should let her sleep it off," Lyre said.

Ash agreed. Lifting her ankle, he tugged her boot off. She watched as he pulled off the other. Lyre worked the blankets out from under her and fluffed the pillow. He glanced at her and paused.

"What are you so smiley about?"

She smiled wider.

"*So* stoned."

She giggled a little. When Lyre tried to nudge her onto her back, she grabbed his arm and pulled him down with her. He tipped over and landed beside her, eyebrows high. Before Ash could escape, she caught his arm, pulling him half onto the bed too.

He grunted. "The drugs aren't affecting her strength."

Lyre stretched out casually beside her. "She wants us next to her. Let her have it, Ash."

He scowled.

Lyre gave him a stern look. "Her home was destroyed, people she knew were killed, and then she was kidnapped and held prisoner by her own mother. She wants to feel safe. Get in the damn bed."

Ash sighed. He kicked off his boots and unbuckled his weapons and armor, dropping them on the floor, then he lay across the bed on her other side. She snuggled against him, still holding on to one of Lyre's arms. She quite possibly had never been so happy and content in her life. They were so warm. So close. Her two daemons.

Exhaustion slid through her, the mist returning, coaxing her into oblivion. In the darkness, Ash's hand closed around hers, warm and gentle. Her lips curved into a little smile as she slipped into silent sleep.

e e e

Her eyes flew open.

Her momentary panic vanished as her brain caught up with reality and she recognized the warmth of the two bodies on either side of her—Ash and Lyre. Ash was fast asleep on his back, one arm hanging off the edge of the bed. Lyre had snuggled up against her side, his breath warm on her neck, his arm heavy across her middle.

Amazement filtered through the evaporating haze of sleep. Her gaze wandered around the dark, unfamiliar room. Ash's apartment. Well, one of them. He probably had dozens of them scattered in the various cities he frequented—hideaways and refuges.

Ugh. Her head was splitting, dampening her elation. Ignoring the ache as best she could, she turned to look at the dark shape of Ash's face beside hers. Her rescue hadn't been a hallucination. Though that meant the rest had also happened. She battled the pain of her mother's betrayal until she had stuffed it down for later analysis.

A quiet sound—the same sound that had woken her, she realized. She looked over and saw Zwi crouched on the back of the armchair, growling very softly. Piper tensed with alarm before she saw that Zwi's attention was locked on the lampshade. Lights from beyond the window were flickering on the shade, dancing enticingly across it.

Zwi crouched a little lower, her tail lashing from side to side like a cat's. She wiggled her rump in preparation. Realizing what the dragonet was planning, Piper opened her mouth to protest, but Zwi was already in motion, leaping off the chair to pounce on the hapless lampshade. The lamp hit the floor with a shocking crash.

Ash bolted upright—and his glamour vanished in a flash of unfurling wings. He lurched forward, his claws tearing through the mattress an inch from Piper's side.

He lunged off the bed. Terror hit her like a battering ram. Lyre's hand suddenly closed over her mouth, muffling her gasp. She held perfectly still and tried to keep her breathing even.

Ash sprang into the center of the room, wings flared and tail snapping back and forth. He stopped almost as quickly as he'd exploded out of the bed. Zwi cowered beside the shattered lamp, wings clamped against her body and tail curled around her feet. He didn't move, maybe assessing the room for danger, maybe fighting for control.

Seconds dragged on before Ash finally folded his wings and straightened. His form shimmered as he slipped back into his glamour.

Fear churned inside her. She glanced at Lyre, meeting his anxious stare.

Ash's reaction wasn't right. He shouldn't have lost his glamour like that. His violent lunge out of bed could have seriously injured Piper. It wasn't like him at all to lose control. Lyre and Miysis had both claimed that Ash had the best control of any daemon they knew, and he could shade or drop glamour without losing his head the way other daemons did. But that was before he'd been tortured for weeks. Maybe Ash wasn't as okay as he'd appeared when they'd last parted.

Swallowing hard, she peeked at him again as he reached down to gently scoop Zwi off the floor. The dragonet buried her head in the crook of his elbow, mewling softly. Lyre gave Piper a little squeeze to catch her attention. He pointedly closed his eyes and relaxed his body. She did the same, though she wasn't sure how convincingly she could feign sleep with apprehension spinning in her mind.

Several minutes passed before she heard Ash move. He crossed the room and the corner of the bed dipped as he sat as far from her as possible. He didn't lie down.

Piper took a deep breath and opened her eyes, letting a yawn crack her jaw. She stretched in a hopefully convincing way and pushed her bangs off her face. When he glanced over, she gave him a small smile.

"Hey," she murmured.

Lyre stretched too, huffing out a sigh. Then his arms wound around her, pulling her close as he nuzzled her cheek. "Good morning, beautiful."

"Lyre," she complained, wiggling free and scooching away, purposefully moving closer to Ash so he wasn't all by himself in the corner. She pulled the blankets across her lap and glanced at him. He stared out the balcony doors, his expression unreadable. Zwi poked her nose out from under his arm and blinked at Piper.

She frowned slightly as she studied him, puzzling over what was different about his appearance. Then she realized what it was: a strip of blue material had replaced the strip of red silk normally braided into his hair. It was the piece of her shirt she'd given him after the battle against Samael before he'd gone underground. The fabric wasn't long enough for an end to hang down and was merely a flash of color in his dark, wine-red hair, but she had to bite her inner cheeks against a swell of emotion.

Lyre sat up, propping his back against the wall. "How are you feeling, Piper?"

Snapping back to the present, she pressed a hand to her throbbing head. "Like I have the worst hangover in history but otherwise, I'm fine. Not in la-la-land anymore."

"Good," Lyre said, suddenly intent. "Now, let's hear it. What in the Nine Circles were you doing with a bunch of Gaians?"

Ash focused on her too, turning toward her as he idly stroked Zwi's mane.

She glanced between them. "Shouldn't your first question be, 'Why aren't you a burnt corpse in the rubble of the Consulate'?"

"We already know that part," Lyre said.

Her brow furrowed. "How?"

"Kindra told us."

"*Kindra?* She got shot."

"She did," Lyre said with a nod. "But she's fast with her shields. She was only stunned."

"Seriously?" Relief swept through her, followed by annoyance. All that grief and guilt, and Kindra had been fine all along. "How did you find her?"

"She found us when we went to the Consulate to search for clues."

"About where I was?"

"No," Ash interjected darkly. "About who was responsible for killing you."

She studied him but he looked back impartially, not betraying his emotions. Maybe she had been a little hasty in imagining his anguish over her supposed demise.

She cleared her throat. "So Kindra found you guys and told you I was alive?"

"Yep," Lyre said cheerfully.

"And then?"

"Then what?"

"How did you find me?"

"Ah. Well, about that." He looked at Ash.

Ash was silent for a moment, then reached over and gave the leather band around her wrist a tug. "I followed this."

She looked at the band. "This?"

He nodded.

Her eyes widened. "You put a *tracking spell* on it?"

He rolled his eyes toward the ceiling, avoiding her stare. "Just a precaution. I needed a way to find you if Samael captured you again."

"You've been tracking me for two months?"

Lyre smirked. "Some women think it's sexy when a hot man stalks them."

Piper shot him a frosty glare.

"It only works within a three mile radius," Ash said, clearly unapologetic.

She twisted the band around her wrist. Good thing she hadn't taken it off. On the other hand . . . "Why didn't you tell me?"

"I didn't have the chance."

She grumbled under her breath, unable to argue with that. He'd left in a hurry last time, since he'd been making off with the Sahar from right under Miysis's nose.

"So fill us in," he said. "What did the Gaians want with you?"

She exhaled forcefully and raised her hands in a half shrug. "They want to tear down the Consulate system and build a new one to control and police daemons. And they want me to spearhead it."

Ash and Lyre stared at her with identical incredulous expressions.

Ash recovered first. "Well, shit."

"Not what I was expecting," Lyre said.

"I know, right?" She shook her head. "It was insane. They gave me the option to join them willingly or be sent home, but when I turned them down, they drugged me and tried to unseal my magic."

Ash's eyes widened in alarm and swept over her from head to toe. "Did they do it?"

Fear rippled through her. "Um. I'm not sure. Helaine—that crazy old lady—claimed she did, but I don't feel any different." She stared at her hands, opening and closing her fingers.

"Try to cast a spell," Ash suggested.

She gave him a long look. "And how would I do that? You might as well ask me to speak Spanish."

"Simple magic is instinctive." He pointed at a box of crackers sitting on the kitchen counter a dozen steps away. "Try to knock it over."

"How?"

"Just concentrate and gesture."

Feeling foolish, she squinted at the box and made a slapping motion. Nothing happened.

"That was lame," Lyre said. "Try harder."

Growling, she made a second attempt. Again, nothing. Magic had come easy with the Sahar once she'd tapped into it. She'd felt its power inside her, waiting to be directed. But she didn't feel a thing out of the ordinary now.

"It didn't work. I don't feel any different. That old lady was a crackpot."

Ash frowned at her. "Maybe you're right. I don't see how a haemon could undo a binding like that."

"Not that I'm arguing, but why not?"

He shrugged. "You have to be able to see what you're doing."

"Haemons can't see magic," Lyre added, "so they're limited to spells they can reconcile with something physical, like push spells, fire, bindings, that kind of thing. Really good haemons can learn simpler wards but most can't. Why the hell would the Gaians want to unseal your magic anyway? Wouldn't that kill you?"

"That's why I said no, but because of some old documents claiming other hybrid haemons survived their magic, they're convinced I'd be just fine." She quickly outlined the Gaians' plans for her and her magic.

"That's just . . ." Ash pushed his hair away from his eyes. "I can't believe the Gaians are behind the Consulate attacks."

"No kidding," Lyre said. "I never expected those bunglers to escalate to this."

She twisted the leather band around her wrist. "It'll be difficult to stop them. They have chapters everywhere. I wish I remembered more of Walter's speech." Her head had been so fuzzy with drugs that she could only recall bits and pieces of his long monologue.

"I wonder if there is something else at work here," Ash said, tapping one finger on his knee. "Why the sudden shift in methods? They were never this deliberate—or effective—before."

"Speaking of suspicious stuff," she said, nervousness swooping through her belly. "I ran into a daemon masquerading as a Gaian . . . a reaper."

Ash and Lyre both snapped to attention.

"How do you know he was a reaper?" Ash demanded.

"He teleported to stop me from escaping. The Gaians don't have any idea that he's not a haemon. I didn't recognize him as a daemon either until I saw him teleport."

Ash swore. "Samael must know your mother is a Gaian."

"That's what I figured."

Ash stood abruptly. "We need to leave. The reaper has no doubt already informed Samael that we're here. We should have immediately left the city."

"I—I guess I should have mentioned it first . . ." She trailed off as Ash picked up his gear off the floor and strode over to the table, his back to her. She quashed a surge of guilt.

Lyre patted her arm. "Don't worry. How were you supposed to tell us while you were drugged to the gills? It's only been a few hours. The city won't be swarming with assassins yet."

She hoped he was right. A thought popped into her head and she leaned closer to him, lowering her voice. "What about that note—"

He slashed a hand through the air, his eyes darting toward Ash. "Not now," he mouthed silently.

Eyes widening, she nodded. Ash must not know about it, and Lyre wanted to keep it that way. But why?

Vowing to get answers out of him later, she rubbed her aching forehead. "So . . . what now?"

"We get our asses back to Brinford. Seiya is waiting for us, and we need to figure out where your father is."

She nodded again, trying to ignore the painful twinge in her chest. Ash, Lyre, and Seiya were all together, but Piper would be handed straight back to her father for safekeeping, no longer part of the daemon trio. She was the magic-less haemon, after all. She bit her lip as she thought of Kaylee, deliriously happy with her new family, part of a group, and always belonging.

Sliding off the bed, she shook off her mood; they had more important things to worry about, like getting out of the city alive.

They got ready in record time. When she emerged from the bathroom, both daemons were standing by the balcony doors, waiting. Ash was back in full gear, his black wrap hiding the lower half of his face. Her heart pounded as she approached. It wasn't fair. She should have been intimidated—he looked downright menacing—but that wasn't why her heart was pounding. Her mind conveniently called up a vivid memory of her sitting in his lap, running her hands over his chest while he kissed her.

Slamming the door shut on that train of thought, she stopped in front of them, trying not to blush. She felt as if Lyre could read the inappropriate thoughts on her face. Ash slid the glass door open and cool air whooshed in. She shivered and followed Lyre onto the balcony. The twenty-story drop halted her one step out.

Ash, walking right behind her, bumped into her back. Mumbling an apology, she stepped sideways to clear the doorway, not wanting to move any closer to the edge. Zwi bounded out of the apartment and jumped onto the railing, wings half spread and tail lashing from side to side. Ash closed the door and warded it. Wide-eyed, she gazed at the expanse of darkness between her and the dimly lit street below.

Ash glanced at her. "Piper?"

"Huh?"

"Don't look down."

She tore her gaze away. "I'm good. I'm fine."

"Uh huh. You can ride on Zwi with Lyre, but she can't transform on the balcony. I'll take off with you, then transfer you to Zwi in the air."

"In the air?" she repeated. It came out in a squeak.

He took her elbow and guided her in front of him, her back to the railing. She stared at him as he pulled her arms around his neck.

"When I drop my glamour," he said, "you can hold my baldric."

Panic swooped through her. "You're not going to hold on to me? What if I slip and—"

He wrapped an arm around her waist and pulled her against him. She squeaked again.

"Of course I'm going to hold on to you. But you'll want to hold on to me too."

"In other words," Lyre said with a grin, moving to stand beside them, "he doesn't want you strangling him with a death grip on his neck."

"Oh."

Her heart rate kicked up as Ash hitched her up off her feet and she hooked her legs over his thighs for a second holding point. Fear of what was coming battled her untimely enjoyment of their proximity, as well as her embarrassment that Lyre was watching. Why couldn't she be drugged again?

Ash closed his other arm around her and his body shimmered. She gasped as her skin tingled wherever she was touching him. The armored vest under her hands morphed into warm black scales that protected his shoulders. She slid her hands down a little and found the strap of the sword buckled across his back. Gripping it tightly, she watched his wings unfurl. Oh God. She never realized how scared of heights she was—or that she was scared of heights at all—until this moment.

His knees bent and he jumped. She let out a brief scream but cut it short when he landed on the railing instead of plunging them into the deep darkness.

"Ow," he said. His daemon voice made her shudder.

She'd screamed in his ear. Oops. "Sorry."

His arm tightened a little more, nearly crushing her lungs, but it wasn't tight enough.

"I won't drop you," he murmured. "And even if I did, I could catch you before you hit the ground."

"You could?"

"Yes. But I won't let you fall."

Lyre climbed onto the railing and sat on it with his feet dangling over the twenty stories of empty air.

She looked at him with wide eyes. "What are you doing? You don't have wings."

"Nope," he agreed. "I'll be good though. Zwi's got my back."

On his other side, Zwi chirped affirmatively and ruffled her mane with self-importance.

"Ready?" Ash asked. Piper tightened her arms and legs around him, trying not to hyperventilate. Her breathing rate doubled when he removed one arm to clasp hands with Lyre.

"Ready," Lyre said.

Zwi chirped again and dove off the balcony.

Ash jumped.

Piper clenched her teeth against a scream as he shot out over nothingness, pulling Lyre off the balcony with him. His wings snapped wide, catching the wind. At the same time, black fire exploded just below them as Zwi transformed, her huge wings blotting out the street far below. With almost casual ease, Ash swung Lyre down onto Zwi's back, where he easily settled as though he'd done this a thousand times.

Ash's wings spread wide, locking in a glide as they banked around the apartment building. The movement was so smooth she almost started to calm down. Then she spotted the ground far below and fought another wave of panic.

"Are you ready?" Ash asked. He spoke in her ear so the wind couldn't steal his words.

She shook her head.

"It'll be fine, Piper," Lyre called up from five feet below. "It's easy."

She clutched Ash harder.

"Don't worry about it," Ash called back. "I'll carry her until we're out of the city where we can land."

Relieved, Piper buried her face against his warm neck so she wouldn't have to see the distance to the ground. They glided for a long time with only occasional beats of his wings to guide them from updraft to updraft. She saw little of the city as they passed through downtown and over a stretch of rundown residential streets. At best, she could manage a couple of seconds of the view before closing her eyes again.

By the time Ash started to descend, her arms were aching from her tight hold on him and she was frozen through. Treetops flashed by, only a dozen feet beneath them. Ash glided above the forest, slowly losing speed. Zwi trailed behind him. Suddenly, his wings flared, pulling them up short. They plunged into the trees through a gap she hadn't seen. She swallowed a frightened cry as they dropped like a rock but his wings snapped open as the ground rushed upward. It felt like getting sucked upward as they drastically slowed, and then they were on the ground.

Zwi landed seconds later, trotting a few steps as she folded her large wings. She made a rumbling sound deep in her throat as Lyre rubbed her neck.

Ash's wings folded neatly against his back and his arms loosened. She took a deep breath and unclamped her legs. Her muscles complained about the change in position and she immediately staggered back a step. As her gaze swept across him cloaked in the forest shadows, the Nightmare Effect hit her in full force.

Her knees buckled. By the time her butt hit the ground, his glamour was back in place. He didn't quite meet her eyes as he offered her a hand up. She huffed as he pulled her to her feet. She'd gone the whole flight without it affecting her but once they'd landed . . . Maybe she'd been too busy being afraid of falling to her death to be afraid of him?

"Where are we?" she asked, glancing at their surroundings. It was an unremarkable forest clearing.

"Just outside Fairglen. Brinford is a couple hours away to the west."

"Fairglen," she repeated. It was one of four cities that neighbored Brinford.

Ash gestured Zwi over. Piper let him lift her onto the dragon's back in front of Lyre. Zwi's body heat radiated off her scales, warming Piper's chilled skin. She wound her hands into Zwi's silky mane as Lyre reached around her to take a firm grip as well.

Ash stepped back. His body shimmered as his glamour fell away. Terror crushed her lungs. She gripped Zwi's mane as she fought it. He glanced at her, then turned away to face the opening in the dark canopy of leaves. His wings spread and he sprang into the air. Zwi launched forward, taking three running steps before jumping skyward. They lurched higher with each laborious beat of her wings until they'd cleared the treetops. Ash glided above them, a dozen yards ahead, his dark form almost invisible against the night sky.

Tears of shame and frustration pricked her eyes. It seemed her immunity to the Nightmare Effect, short of drugs, only worked if there was something more terrifying around to distract her. Which meant she would never get to look upon his true form with clear eyes — or without seeing that shadow of disappointment cross his face every time he saw her fear.

CHAPTER
- 8 -

ASH, she concluded, liked high places way too much.

His hideout in Brinford was also downtown and once again in the tallest building around, which made sense. Attackers could only come at him from the lower levels, making defense simpler, and he couldn't be cornered—not when he could jump out the window.

The sky was an eerie blue in the pre-dawn twilight. From her vantage point on Zwi's back, Piper watched as Ash swept around the apartment tower, searching for the right window. Unlike the last one, this building didn't have balconies. She was still puzzling over how he was planning to land when he swooped straight for a very much closed window and landed on the tiny ledge. He slid the window open and disappeared into the dark room beyond.

Zwi banked toward the same window and Piper panicked. No way was the dragon fitting through that opening. Before she could do anything more than gasp, the side of the tower was rushing to meet them. Zwi back-winged just before they crashed, and grabbed the windowsill. The talons on her hind feet scraped the outer wall as she clung precariously to the ledge with her head and neck inside the building.

Ash appeared, reached over Zwi's neck, and grabbed Piper. She squeaked as he pulled her swiftly inside, plopped her down, and spun back to help Lyre the rest of the way in. As soon as her passengers were inside, Zwi disappeared in a burst of black fire. The tiny dragonet swooped in with a happy chitter, flying straight out of the room and deeper into the apartment.

"Whew," Lyre said on an explosive exhalation. "I admit that last part always makes me a bit nervous."

"Yeah," Piper agreed, still catching her breath. Her arms and legs felt like wobbly blocks of ice.

"Ash. You're back."

Piper turned to see Seiya standing in the doorway. She swallowed a flicker of jealousy; she'd forgotten how beautiful Ash's younger sister was, though she didn't understand her resentment. She didn't usually feel envy around beautiful girls. Seiya's raven hair was pulled into a high ponytail that hung halfway down her back and her vivid blue eyes, warm with pleasure at seeing her brother, looked huge in her delicate face.

Those eyes slid over to Piper and noticeably cooled.

"Piper," she said. "I'm glad to see you're okay."

Piper blinked, seriously doubting the honesty of Seiya's words, though she didn't know why the girl wouldn't be sincere.

"Um," Lyre said in the suddenly uncomfortable silence. "Do I smell food?"

"I made stew," Seiya said. "I thought you might be cold when you arrived."

Lyre and Ash made a beeline for the door at the word "stew." Piper followed, glancing around the room. It was set up as an entry/exit point with nothing but stacks of gear along one wall and some weapons leaning in the corner. The main room was almost as barren, a shabby kitchen and living room combo. Ash was already at the stove, serving himself a bowl from the steaming pot. Seiya stood beside him, a dragonet on each shoulder as she murmured to him.

Lyre spotted Piper standing awkwardly in the middle of the room and prodded her over to a barstool at the counter peninsula. He dished out another bowl and put it in front of her. She dug in immediately.

"Well, let's hear it," Seiya said. "Where were you?"

"Let her eat first," Lyre said. "We're all starving."

Seiya scowled. He scowled back. Piper kept eating, ignoring the tension. Lyre and Seiya clearly weren't budding besties. Overall, that was probably a good thing. The first time Lyre had met Seiya, he'd seemed a little too fascinated with her. She was young and beautiful—the exact type incubi found irresistible. Piper did not want to know what Ash would do if Lyre ever seduced his sister. At best, it would be the end of their friendship. At worst, it would be the end of Lyre's life.

"This is really good," she said, pointing at her bowl with her spoon.

"Thank you," Seiya replied without warmth.

Piper went back to eating in silence, suspecting if it had been just her and not Ash, there wouldn't have been a hot meal waiting for her upon her return.

Once she'd eaten enough to sate her immediate hunger, she broke the heavy silence by reiterating the whole tale of her abduction and rescue for Seiya.

"So," Piper finished, "now I have to tell all this to my father so they can stop the Gaians from destroying more Consulates."

"I don't envy them that job." Lyre drummed his fingers on the countertop. "It's an idiotic plan though. Daemons aren't going to just shrug and leave because the Consulates are gone."

She nodded. "There's more to their plan, but they didn't share the details with me."

Seiya pushed her ponytail off her shoulder. "It's idiocy. It'll never work."

"Destroying the Consulates will create a power vacuum," Ash said, "which the Gaians think they can fill, but I doubt they have the resources to implement a new power structure. Either way, they won't get far. Once you reveal who's behind it, the prefects and Consuls will start hunting the Gaians and their plans will collapse."

"Huh." Piper poked a piece of potato in her bowl. Feeling a little better that the world wasn't about to dissolve into anarchy, she ate another bite.

Ash set his bowl in the sink. "I'm going to get a few hours of sleep."

At the thought of sleep, Piper was overcome with a jaw-popping yawn. "I need a shower first."

"Right over there." Seiya pointed to a door off the entryway. "There are towels folded on the shelf." With a brief nod, she followed Ash out of the room.

Piper blinked after them.

"Grumpy pair, huh?" Lyre commented, coming around the island to stand beside her. "I've been stuck with them for two months."

"What's Seiya's problem?"

Lyre shrugged. "She's just overprotective."

"Of Ash?"

He nodded.

"Why would that make her give *me* the cold shoulder? I'm not the enemy."

He shrugged again.

Her eyes narrowed and she lowered her voice. "Does this have anything to do with your note—"

He cut her off with a warning look. "Didn't you want a shower?"

"Yeah, but—"

He looped an arm around her waist, pulling her off the barstool and guiding her toward the bathroom. "You should have your shower."

"Lyre—"

He dragged her into the bathroom, released her, and turned on the taps. Water sprayed loudly and filled the small room with noise.

"I don't want any little dragonet ears listening to us," he said quietly, his voice almost lost to the sound of the running water.

Nervousness churned in her stomach at the extent he was going to conceal their conversation.

"Why are you being so secretive?"

He sighed, the sound full of frustration and anxiety. "I want to talk to you about Ash."

"What about him?"

"He tells you things he doesn't tell me."

"He does?"

He shrugged a little. "He told you about Seiya when he'd never mentioned a word about her to me."

"Oh right."

"I thought he might have said something to you."

"About what?"

A long pause. "About what's wrong with him."

Alarm swept through her. "What do you mean?"

"You saw it, Piper," he said, his voice roughening. He turned toward the sink and put both hands on the counter, shoulders hunched. "You saw him last night. That total loss of control. That wasn't the first time. It's been happening more and more often over the past two months."

She stared at him without seeing him, the image of Ash's wild lunge off the bed, like he'd woken not knowing where he was, filling her mind.

"There's something wrong with him," Lyre said, eyes closed, "and it's getting worse."

Forcing her hands out of fists, she said softly, "I told you a little bit about what he was like when I got him out of the Chrysalis building."

"Yeah," he said, straightening from the counter. "That's why I thought maybe you could get some answers out of him. He won't admit to me that something's wrong. But since you were there with him, maybe he'll have an easier time talking to you."

"Maybe," she whispered, though she didn't have much hope. Ash wasn't the sharing type. She let out a shaky breath. "I thought he was okay. I thought Vejovis had healed him."

"Vejovis can only heal so much, and he didn't have a lot of time."

"Maybe you should take him to another healer."

He shook his head before she'd even finished. "Healing the mind is pretty much a forgotten art. Vejovis is the only healer I can think of who would potentially know how to do it."

She twisted the leather band around her wrist. "So you think Ash is losing control of shading?"

"I'm not sure. It looks like that on the surface, but it's not . . . it doesn't quite match what I've seen of other daemons with shading issues."

"What do you mean?"

"It's just . . . I don't know. That's why I wanted to talk to you."

She closed her eyes, eyebrows pinched together. She thought of Ash when she'd first entered his cell in the Chrysalis center. Violence and rage burning in his eyes. Blind hatred. He'd wanted to kill her simply because she existed. She shivered.

"I don't know," she whispered. "I don't know what's wrong with him."

"Can you try talking to him?"

"I'll try."

"Thanks." He sighed. "All this shit definitely hasn't helped matters."

"What shit?"

"You being dead. He didn't take it well."

She went still. "Oh?"

"Well, neither did I. We felt like we'd failed you. Ash blamed himself because he hadn't insisted on taking you into hiding with us. Then we suddenly found out you weren't dead, and we had to find out where you were, who had you, whether you might actually be dead after all. It was pretty intense."

"Oh, yeah, I guess it would have been."

"You should clean up and get some sleep. I'm going to head out for a few hours and see what I can find out about your dad."

She nodded. He turned toward the door.

"Is that it?" she asked.

He glanced back, brow furrowed. "Is what it?"

"Aren't you going to offer to wash my back in the shower? Or warm up my bed for me? Or—you know—something inappropriate?"

His eyes glinted as he grinned wickedly. "Is that an invitation?"

"No." She raised her eyebrows. "Just wondering if you were feeling all right. It's not normal for you to be so well-behaved."

"I like my women feisty, so I'm waiting until you're properly rested."

She snorted. "I see. Here I was worrying for nothing."

His quiet chuckle made her smile as he closed the bathroom door behind him.

After showering and changing into a borrowed shirt and sweats — courtesy of Lyre since Seiya's clothes were too small for her — she settled on the sofa with a blanket. Ash was in the second bedroom, probably sleeping like the dead after flying around all night.

Heaving a sigh, Piper closed her eyes, listening to the quiet clink of dishes as Seiya cleaned up the kitchen. Worries spun through her head as she silently rehearsed how to bring up Ash's shading control issues. She was just starting to drift off when a weight landed on her chest. Her eyes flew open and she found a dark nose snuffling her chin. Zwi trilled a greeting, blinking her large golden eyes.

"Hey, girl," Piper whispered, stroking the dragonet's mane.

Zwi lay on Piper's stomach and chittered in a conversational way. The cat-sized dragon had once been too shy and aloof to approach Piper. She smiled, honored that Zwi now considered her a friend. As she petted the creature, her fingers encountered a leather strap over her tiny shoulders. Sitting up a little, Piper frowned at the lightweight harness. A leather triangle covered her chest — some kind of armor?

Seiya approached, stopping near Piper's feet.

"Do you need anything before I lie down?" she asked.

"I'm fine," Piper said, trying not to frown. She didn't know Seiya very well — barely at all, in fact — and her dark past made it even harder to measure her expressions and mood. Piper's overall impression of their first meeting hadn't been one of warm friendliness, but Seiya was definitely colder now than she had been two months ago.

"How have things been?" she asked hesitantly. "What's it like to finally be free?"

Surprise flashed across Seiya's face before her expression hardened. "That would depend on how you define 'free.'"

Piper blinked. "Um. What do you mean?"

"Being out from beneath Samael's thumb has been wonderful," Seiya said, the words at complete odds with her tone. "But I wouldn't call this freedom. Running, hiding, constantly looking over our shoulders. Every shadow is a potential enemy. We traded Samael's chains for the chains of fear."

"I'm sorry," she replied hesitantly. "But isn't it better than being a prisoner? Than being tortured?"

"Of course. Our quality of life is a thousand times better. I just wouldn't call it being free."

"Oh. I see what you mean."

"I'm afraid for us every day," Seiya said, ice creeping into her voice. "And now it's that much worse."

"What's worse?"

"The danger."

"What do you mean?"

"Being here," Seiya snapped. "Everything here—flying across the city, breaking into buildings, making scenes. In other words, *you*."

"Me?"

"There's a good chance that reaper spy saw Ash. If he did, it will be the first time since we've escaped that a Hades spy has come close to locating us."

"I—I'm sorry. I didn't know—"

Seiya folded her arms, towering over Piper. "That's just it. You don't know."

"Excuse me?"

"You don't know how dangerous you are. How much danger you create."

"I—"

"I'm really grateful for everything you did for us," Seiya interrupted. "You saved my brother's life, and mine. But this needs to stop."

She stared, baffled. "*What* needs to stop?"

Seiya gave her a long look. "You need to leave my brother alone."

A moment of silence.

"I need to *what*?"

"Leave him alone. Break it off. In other words, get over him."

Piper spluttered.

Her eyes like blue ice chips, Seiya leaned a little closer. "Do you think I don't know how you feel? You're obviously in love with him."

Piper sat up sharply, forcing Zwi onto her lap. "I—You—"

"You have no right to feel that way. In what world would your feelings be reciprocated? You just moon after him in your own naïve little world and make everything more complicated—and more dangerous—for him."

Piper's mouth opened and closed in soundless outrage.

"You and him," she went on, waving a finger in Piper's face, "can't be together. It won't work. My brother has dealt with enough shit as it is; he doesn't need to get tangled up with you, feeling responsible for your safety. How many times will you make him risk his life for you? Until he's killed?"

"You—" Piper began furiously.

"He already feels responsible for you and that's just as your friend. Look what your friendship has gotten him—a reaper spy on our tails."

"I didn't—"

"What's the point, anyway? You can't even look at him without glamour. You're going to move on and do whatever you haemons do. Be a Consul or whatever. Where does he fit in that future? We're going to spend the rest of our lives hiding from Samael."

Piper stared at the girl, speechless and barely able to believe what she was hearing. Zwi mewled, pawing at Piper's leg.

"There's no future for you and Ash," Seiya went on relentlessly. "But here he is, putting us at risk to save your ass. You need to deal with your own problems and leave him out of it."

Piper sprang off the sofa, unintentionally dumping Zwi on the floor. She'd heard enough. Teeth bared, she pointed a finger aggressively at Seiya.

"I didn't ask Ash to save me! I didn't even know he was out of the Underworld. And if he risks his life for me, it's because he decided to, not because I asked him!"

Seiya opened her mouth again but Piper turned and yanked the blanket off the sofa.

"Save your breath. I don't give a damn what you have to say."

She stalked across the room to the spare bedroom and slammed the door behind her. Glaring around the barren room with nothing but gear and weapons along the wall, she crossed to the opposite corner and curled up on the floor with her blanket. Pillowing her head on her arm, she ground her teeth and breathed hard through her nose.

What did Seiya know? So Piper cared about Ash. She was attracted to him. That was it. Besides, it didn't matter either way. She knew it was impossible. There was no future where the two of them fit together. And she wasn't even sure he wanted that kind of relationship with her anyway. Considering Piper had risked her life to save Seiya from imprisonment and torture, the girl seriously lacked gratitude.

She clenched and unclenched her jaw. It was a long time before she calmed down enough to fall into a fitful, uncomfortable sleep.

                                         ❂   ❂   ❂

Lunch was a tense affair.

Seiya stood on one side of the counter, nibbling on a sandwich. Piper sat on a barstool, glaring at her untouched food. Ash and Lyre stood just outside the kitchen, exchanging confused, wary looks in some sort of male Morse code as they puzzled over the problem.

Piper angrily picked up her sandwich and took a bite. No point in starving just because Seiya had made it. Her head throbbed in time with her chewing. It had been aching since she'd woken up in a stiff ball on the floor.

Lyre had returned an hour ago, unable to procure any information on the Head Consul's whereabouts. Her father and the Board of Directors had gone to ground in case unknown terrorists were targeting them. Piper figured the simplest solution was to find the nearest intact Consulate and announce her non-death to the local Consuls. Surely one of them could track down the Head Consul. Ash and Lyre both thought that was too dangerous; not only were the Gaians probably still looking for her, but Samael's spies would be everywhere in the city by now.

That meant she was stuck here until Lyre and Ash could unearth the information they needed. And *that* meant days stuck in the tiny apartment with Seiya. Seiya was in an even worse temper thanks to the continued interaction between Piper and her brother, and because Ash was taking risks for Piper again, exposing his location to the same Hades spies he wanted to keep her away from.

"Soooo," Lyre said, "will you two be okay this evening while Ash and I do some digging?"

"I should go with Ash," Seiya said. "You can stay here with Piper."

"Lyre has contacts he can tap," Ash said, frowning at his sister. "And you're better suited to getting Piper out of here if the apartment is attacked."

Piper snorted, not because Seiya wasn't capable, but because the girl was more likely to leave Piper to her fate and skip off to join her brother.

Ash and Lyre stared at her then looked at each other.

"Uh," Lyre tried again. "Can we talk about the problem here?"

"No," Piper and Seiya snapped in unison.

He stepped back. "Okay then." He looked at Ash for help but Ash just shrugged.

Her head throbbed. She pressed a hand to her forehead and stared at her sandwich, fighting nausea. Ugh. She closed her eyes as the pain intensified and expanded inside her head, an unbearable pressure that felt as though her skull was about to burst.

"Piper?"

Lyre touched her elbow, concern in his voice. She realized she was squeezing her head between her hands.

"It's just a headache," she said, a little breathless. An agonizing headache.

"Are you injured?" he asked, tugging gently at her wrist. "Let me see."

"I'm fine." The pain felt as if it were crushing her. "I just need to lie down."

"Piper—"

"I'm fine."

She tried to lower her arms but the agony swelled. She clutched her head and groaned. Ash stepped closer until they were both in front of her, filling her view. Too close. She couldn't quite catch her breath.

"I—I need space. I need to lie down."

Lyre took her wrist again, trying to pry her hand off her head. "Piper, something's wrong, let us help you—"

She couldn't breathe. She needed air. She needed space. The pain was like a steel band around her skull, around her chest, suffocating her. They were too close. Why wouldn't they give her space?

"Piper, let me see—"

"No, get *back!*" she yelled, letting go of her head to shove them away.

A crack like the sound of thunder.

Lyre and Ash flew back as if they'd been hit by a truck. Ash barely managed to catch himself, skidding gracelessly, but Lyre crashed into the kitchen table. One of the chairs broke under him as he fell.

Piper froze in place, staring at them. They stared back at her, two sets of pitch black eyes. After a moment, she slowly lifted her hands to look at them.

"What happened?" she whispered.

"Magic," Ash replied, his dark voice shivering through her.

Panic simmered in her gut. "But . . . but it didn't work. Helaine didn't break the seal."

. "It looks like she did," Ash said.

Piper shook her head stubbornly. "No. That wasn't me. I don't have magic."

The forced calm in his voice wasn't enough to hide his dread. "You do now."

CHAPTER
- 9 -

PIPER sat on the sofa with Zwi in her lap, staring at nothing. The irony was painful. The one thing she'd always wanted she now had — and wished more than anything that she didn't.

The headache was starting again, the pain of the conflicting magic inside her. She knew what to expect. She'd been through it as a child. The headaches would gradually begin, coming and going like an ever-increasing tide, growing worse and worse. Migraines would intensify to the point of nausea and seizures. That's when her parents had found the daemon healer who had sealed her magic, though she couldn't remember it; the daemon had blurred her memories at her father's request.

The rest she knew from stories about haemon children who'd died from the same affliction. The seizures would become more frequent and more violent. Eventually, the most terrible seizure would grip the child, and once it ended, she would be brain-dead. Death followed shortly after.

Piper cuddled Zwi closer, shivering. She had three options. One, she could do nothing, wait, and see what happened. Maybe she would be fine like the three hybrid women her mother had discovered. The headaches, however, suggested otherwise.

Two, she could return to Mona and search her records on those women in the hope of finding a clue as to how they'd survived their magic. But that involved putting herself at the mercy of the Gaians. She could deal with that, but the chances of finding any useful information were slim. The chances of finding useful information *in time* were even slimmer.

Or three, she could find a daemon healer to reseal her magic. She didn't know who had sealed it the first time or how to find a daemon with that kind of specialized skill; it wasn't the sort of thing any old daemon could do. She didn't even know if it was possible to reseal her magic now that it was free. Ash and Lyre were currently out in the city, searching for information on her father's whereabouts. If they could find Quinn, they could get the name of the daemon healer who'd saved her life the first time.

She lifted a hand and stared at it. Magic. There was magic inside her. She'd craved it for so long. Her first urge was to experiment with it while she had it but Ash and Lyre had warned her not to. Using magic was like working out a muscle, and the last thing she wanted was to make her magic stronger.

Sighing, she dropped her hand and watched Seiya cross the room with an armful of clothes. She listened as the draconian girl rustled in the bedroom. She reappeared, heading back to the first room. Piper briefly considered asking Seiya about Ash's control issue. She must have noticed it too, and Piper had no idea how to raise the topic with Ash.

But no, she didn't want to give Seiya another reason to be an overprotective jerk. As she watched the girl, resentment surged inside her.

"Why did you do it?" she burst out before she could stop herself.

Seiya paused on her way by. "Do what?"

Piper instantly regretted the question. "Why did you save me from Samael? You were almost killed."

Seiya assessed Piper coolly. "There's only one person I'm willing to risk my life for."

Piper narrowed her eyes. Ah, of course. Seiya had done it for Ash. If she hadn't charged in to save Piper, Ash would have done it instead, and he'd been in no condition for that.

"I'm not self-sacrificing like my brother," Seiya continued, coming over to the sofa. "I'm not noble or brave. I want to survive, and I want my brother to survive." She lifted the lock of her hair with a red silk ribbon woven into it. "Do you know why I wear this?"

Piper shrugged. "It's a symbol of your promise to Ash that the two of you would be free someday."

"No. Ash's was the symbol of his promise to free us. Mine represents a different promise." She stroked the ribbon. "It's a draconian tradition to wear visible symbols of promises from our hearts. Like humans wear wedding bands in some cultures."

Piper had thought it was just a thing between the two of them, not a part of their culture. Did it bother Seiya that Ash now wore a symbol of his promise to Piper instead?

"So what was your promise?"

"To be strong enough that Ash would never have to bleed for me again." Her eyes went distant and her voice turned husky. "He told you about our first escape attempt, didn't he? I will never forget that night. We would have escaped if I'd been stronger. But I was weak. And Ash—"

She closed her eyes. "You can't imagine what it feels like to hold your dying brother in your arms, knowing it's your fault. Because you were too slow, too weak, and he had to take a stupid risk to save you."

She opened her eyes, her blue irises dark and hard as steel. "I almost lost him that night. If Vejovis hadn't happened upon us, my brother would have died there—because of me. So I swore that I would not take our second chance for granted. I swore Ash would never bleed for me again. I would become strong enough to protect myself, so he would never have to take a stupid risk for me again."

Piper stared, caught up in the steely determination in Seiya's eyes. After a moment, she frowned. "How did you get so strong when you were locked away for years?"

"I trained every day from that point onward," Seiya said. "I learned from the other draconians—I wasn't always locked away by myself—and most of what I know I was taught by Raum. I know more lethal spells than recipes. Ash trusts me to protect myself."

Her eyes went cold again. "But just when I thought there would never again be a reason for him to jeopardize his life to protect someone weak and vulnerable, you show up. And suddenly Ash is taking risks to keep you safe."

"I didn't *ask* the Gaians to unseal my magic—"

"And yet here we are."

"You're awfully worried about him considering he's one of the most powerful daemons alive."

Seiya's expression turned from cold to subzero arctic. "There's nothing more dangerous than trying to compensate for a weak link. I don't think you understand that."

"Of course I understand that."

"Really? But you don't think he's in danger while protecting you? Are you saying he's never been hurt in a fight because of your presence?"

Piper opened her mouth but her voice died in her throat. Shortly after they'd gone on the run with the Sahar, Hades assassins had ambushed Ash in a medical center. When he'd tried to stop one of them from going after Piper, the second one had gored him. He'd nearly died. Had he not been worried about her, he could have made it out okay. And she didn't even want to think about Samael using her as a puppet to stab Ash with a poisoned knife.

Seeing her point hit home, Seiya flicked her ponytail off her shoulder. "Look, we'll get your magic sealed and then we'll get you back to your father where you'll be safe. And then we can all go back to worrying about our *own* survival."

Piper pressed her lips together. Her chest ached. That was about right, wasn't it? The strong, wise daemons would solve her problems and dump her back on some capable adults to keep her safe. It was starting to look like the only ones who wanted her around were the Gaians.

Something tickled her memory. Pressing a hand to her forehead, she stared at the wall across from her. Right. Survival. Seiya's remark reminded Piper of a comment Vejovis had made when he'd visited her cell in Asphodel. He'd admitted to almost killing her so Samael couldn't use her to wield the Sahar, "despite the effort I've invested in your survival," he'd said.

Despite the effort. She hadn't given it any thought at the time, having been more concerned with other things. But now that she thought about it, up to that point, he hadn't invested any effort into her survival. He'd never healed her. He hadn't taken any risks for her aside from sneaking down to her cell. Yes, he'd healed Ash, but not her. So what effort had he been referring to?

"How much of a coincidence do you think it is," she asked slowly, "that Vejovis has shown up *twice* to save the day at places where I've been?"

Seiya leaned back, caught off guard. "What do you mean?"

"Vejovis is a legend, isn't he? Most people never meet him even once. No one knows where he lives or where he is at any given time. Yet he's been in the same place as me twice in as many months. What if that's not the coincidence it seems?"

"Samael summoned Vejovis to Asphodel to examine Ash, didn't he? Vejovis owed Samael some kind of favor."

"Right. But Vejovis didn't have to help me after that. He even admitted he'd been tempted to kill me so Samael couldn't use me, but he didn't because of the 'effort he'd invested in my survival.'"

"What effort?"

"That's what I was wondering. But what if that wasn't the second time I'd met Vejovis? What if that was the third?"

Seiya frowned. Then her eyes widened.

"Wait, you think—"

Piper leaned forward, excitement ballooning in her stomach. "What if Vejovis was the daemon healer who sealed my magic when I was a child?"

They stared at each other.

"That would be the effort he was referring to," Piper said, her words tumbling together. "And it would explain why he didn't kill me to keep me out of Samael's hands; if he'd had no connection to me, then I'd just be some girl who was threatening the lives of thousands. What was my life worth compared to thousands of others?"

"And he waited for you too," Seiya said. "He killed the guards at the bridge. That was a big risk for him; he's always remained neutral, as far as I know."

"And the medical center—what if he'd heard about my father being there? Maybe he came to heal Quinn since he knew him. He was near my father's room."

Seiya shook her head, not in disbelief but in wonder.

"And he followed us out of the medical center too," Piper continued. "I assumed it was because he knew Ash, but maybe he was actually following me."

"Vejovis is the best healer there is," Seiya said. "If anyone can do the kind of delicate work needed to seal a child's magic, it's him."

"It makes perfect sense," Piper exclaimed. "And since Vejovis helped me before, he should be willing to help me again. All we have to do is—"

Her and Seiya's excitement vanished in the same instance.

"Find him," Piper finished in a whisper.

"How do we do that?" Seiya asked, twisting the hem of her shirt with both hands. "You said it yourself: no one knows where he is at any given time."

"I—I don't know. Maybe—"

Seiya's face slackened, her eyes distant. Then her whole body tensed. "A daemon just broke one of the wards on the stairs."

"Lyre?"

"I tied the wards to him. They wouldn't stop him, so he wouldn't have a reason to break one." Her eyes popped wide. "They just broke the ward in the hall! They're coming fast!"

She grabbed Piper's arm, hauling her off the sofa. They ran for the bedroom.

Something slammed into the front door. A second later, it exploded. Seiya shoved Piper through the open bedroom door as she flung a spell of black flames at the dark figures filling the doorway.

Piper landed on her hands and knees in the spare room. Her eyes whipped across the stacks of gear to the corner with the weapons. There were three swords, a pile of daggers, two handguns, and a shotgun. She could throw daggers with lethal accuracy but they would bounce right off a daemon's shield. She needed something more powerful.

She grabbed the shotgun from the pile and pulled the foregrip down to check the chamber. Not loaded. Damn it. A box of shells sat open on the floor. She grabbed two and loaded them, then pumped the gun as she darted toward the doorway to join Seiya, keeping low. Bracing the stock against her shoulder, she aimed past Seiya's knees and pulled the trigger.

The shot sprayed the cluster of daemons trapped in the doorway by Seiya's spell. Seiya dove backward into the room as Piper pumped the gun and fired the second shell.

"Come on!" Seiya yelled. "There's too many of them!"

Piper backed into the room and dropped the shotgun. With the flick of a hand, Seiya threw a punch of magic that blasted a hole through the wall.

"Go!"

"Go where? I don't have wings!"

Seiya spun and threw a black blade of magic at the daemon who had appeared in the doorway. He dove out of the way. Seiya spun back to Piper. Without a word, she grabbed Piper and threw her through the hole in the wall.

Piper screamed as she plummeted. Black flames erupted ten feet beneath her, and suddenly there was a dragon in her path. Piper slammed into the dragon's back, grabbing a handful of her mane as Zala—Seiya's dragonet—sped away from the building. Wheezing from the impact, she got into a more comfortable position.

"Thanks, Zala," she panted.

The dragon made a rumbling noise. Piper looked over her shoulder and saw Seiya gliding along above them, her wingspan barely half that of Zala's. Zwi, still in dragonet form with her tiny wings pumping, zoomed past Seiya and landed on Piper's shoulder. She chittered in clear admonishment.

"I didn't mean to leave you behind," Piper said. "Seiya threw me out the window."

She looked over her shoulder again as the apartment vanished behind a row of skyscrapers. Hades assassins. Samael had finally found Ash and Seiya—and it was all Piper's fault.

                                           ° ° °

Piper wrapped her arms tighter around her middle and tried not to shiver. For an early summer evening, it was damn cold.

Seiya stood nearby, leaning on the concrete wall, unaffected by the chill. They'd arrived at the rendezvous point two hours ago, but there was no sign of Ash or Lyre. Seiya said it was far too early to worry. Ash would see the damaged wall of the apartment before getting anywhere near the building, then he would go straight to the meeting point. They'd planned for this kind of emergency.

The rendezvous point was an old clock tower in the center of a sprawling park. Both the park and the tower had once been the beautiful focal point of the city, but now the park was overrun with weeds and trash, and the tower was crumbling. The metal gears of the clock had long been stolen. Only the skeleton of the tower remained. The interior stairs had crumbled, making the top level, the mechanical room, only accessible by air.

At some point, the face of the clock had fallen out, leaving a huge circular hole in the wall. Piper sat at the opposite end of the room, hugging her middle against the cool breeze as she stared out at the dark city. She wondered what rural communities were like. They couldn't be nearly as depressing as the rundown quarters of the city.

Walter's assertion that daemons were to blame for the stagnation of cities returned to her. Was she naïve to scoff at the idea that for some, running into a daemon was frightening enough to keep them out of the cities? You were more likely to get mugged by a fellow human than encounter a daemon. But cities were full of places for daemons to hide, and it was the unknown that terrified most people. To the rest of the world, daemons were very much part of the unknown.

She chewed her bottom lip. Why was it so hard to forget about the Gaians? They'd betrayed her. There was every chance she would die because of them. Because of her own mother. But though some of their methods verged on pure evil, maybe they hadn't been wrong about everything.

With a happy chirp, Zwi swooped into the room through the round opening. A moment later, the view of the city vanished as a dark shape filled the circle. With the rush of wings sweeping the air, Ash ducked inside. Lyre clung to his back, goggle-eyed with wind-tousled hair. No more immune to the Nightmare Effect than her, his face was white as a sheet. He slid off Ash's back, and shimmers swept over Ash as he slipped back into glamour. Piper let out a shaky breath as the terror waned then vanished.

"What happened?" Ash demanded, gaze darting over Seiya then Piper, checking them for injuries.

"Hades assassins," Seiya said. "They broke the wards on their way up so we had enough warning."

Ash swore. "I should have known they'd be watching."

"Watching what?" Piper asked.

"The downtown skies. Samael knows the kinds of places I'd hide in. Even before the reaper in Fairglen, he had a horde of spies monitoring the city. He must have sent them when . . ."

"When what?"

"When you were reportedly dead," Seiya snapped.

Piper flinched. Samael knew Ash cared about Piper. Of course Samael had sent spies to watch for Ash's inevitable arrival when she'd been presumed dead.

"We ran into a group camped out at your Consulate on Saturday night," Lyre said. "They were waiting for us."

Her eyes widened. "What happened?"

Lyre smiled, but it wasn't his usual teasing expression. A wolf's grin would have been less menacing. "We wiped them out."

Piper blinked, a little shiver of fright running down her spine. It was easy to forget that Lyre's playful, carefree exterior hid the deadly fighter within. Incubi weren't known for being warriors, but Lyre was most definitely an exception to that stereotype. The first time she'd seen him completely shed his role as the harmless flirt, his magic-infused arrows had killed more Hades soldiers than she'd been able to count. Where had he learned to fight like that? And why? Sometimes she wondered if Lyre had even more secrets than Ash.

"Brinford isn't safe anymore," Seiya said. "We need to leave before more Hades assassins pile in."

"We can't leave until we find Piper's father," Ash said, sitting on the edge of the opening. "We haven't found any leads yet. I'm not even sure if the Consul Board is in the city."

"All the more reason to get out," Seiya replied, shooting Piper a cold look.

"Finding my father might be a step we can skip," Piper said, ignoring Seiya and focusing on Ash. "While you were gone, I had a sort of epiphany. I think Vejovis is the one who sealed my magic when I was a kid."

She quickly explained her theory. When she finished, Ash and Lyre exchanged looks.

"If she's right," Lyre said slowly, "it would explain his helpfulness."

Ash nodded. "And even if he had nothing to do with her magic being sealed the first time, he's the likeliest candidate to seal it now."

Lyre crossed his arms. "There's just one big problem. How do we *find* him?"

"Vejovis keeps a low profile. Samael will be after him too for helping us escape. He's probably in hiding."

"As if finding him wasn't already difficult enough," Lyre grumbled.

"Vejovis is an Overworld daemon, isn't he?" Piper asked. "Is there an Overworld daemon we could ask?"

Ash and Lyre exchanged another look.

"Miysis," they said in unison.

"Miysis?"

"The Ra family knows everything about everyone in the Overworld," Ash explained. "If anyone would know—or could find out—it would be him."

Piper let out a long breath, blowing her bangs off her face. "That makes things trickier."

Miysis had acted as her ally before, but he never gave anything for free. Two months ago, they hadn't parted on the best of terms; he'd led his men to their deaths against Samael to get the Sahar back, and then she'd helped Ash vanish with it immediately after. He'd been enraged, to say the least, though he didn't know it had been her idea.

She looked at Ash. "Speaking of Miysis and the reasons he hates us, where is the Sahar? You still have it, right?"

"Of course," he said. "It's safe."

"Where?"

He raised his eyebrows and said nothing. Right. Probably best that she didn't know any details.

"So how do we get Miysis to help us?" Lyre asked. "He won't be very motivated to save Piper's life after she helped us run off with his Stone."

"It's obvious, isn't it?" Ash said, his voice a shade darker. "He won't accept anything less than the return of the Sahar."

Before she could object to giving the Sahar back to Miysis, Ash stood. "Lyre and I will keep searching for Quinn. If we can't find him tonight, we'll go to Miysis in the morning. For now, we'll get you some real clothes and a few blankets. You and Seiya will need to stay here for the night."

She looked helplessly at Lyre, who shrugged. He didn't seem to think giving up the Sahar was a problem either. She wasn't so sure, but she couldn't help being selfish. She didn't want to die. She just hoped she wouldn't live to regret giving the Stone back to Miysis to save her own skin.

CHAPTER
-10-

PIPER tugged at the waist of her new jeans, wishing they weren't so tight, and stared up at the building in front of her. Ash had stolen the clothes from some unlucky shop—hence the jeans being a little too small—and despite her guilt, she was happy with the fitted, sleeveless red top and black sweater. She was amused that he'd picked another red top for her, probably not wanting to offend her with a color she wouldn't like.

Ash had changed clothes for their outing too, giving up his draconian warrior clothes for something more familiar—dark jeans and a black t-shirt, the kind of clothes he'd worn while staying at the Consulate before their first life-changing night. The blue strip of material braided into his hair was the only color in his outfit, but at least he didn't look like he was preparing to go to war anymore.

Seiya and Lyre were out of sight down the block. They were backup. If things went wrong, they wouldn't *all* be trapped in the Ra stronghold.

Ash and Lyre's overnight search hadn't turned up any useful information. Their efforts had been cut short, well before dawn, when another party of Hades assassins had ambushed them in an alley.

Seiya had needed to heal a nasty gash on Lyre's arm once they'd returned to the clock tower. Searching the city had become far too dangerous.

Piper examined the building before her. It didn't look like a stronghold. The elegant structure rose fifteen stories and was surrounded by carved stone walls with wrought-iron fencing along the top—a pretty design with purposeful spikes that would make it hard to climb over. She doubted anyone would be dumb enough to try, though, because the chances of the grounds being unguarded were pretty much zero.

The gates in front of them were also wrought iron. Piper took another deep breath and, doing her best to ignore the throbbing pain in her head, stepped up to the intercom panel. She felt eyes watching her, though the place looked deserted. She pressed the red button beneath the speaker. A moment of silence.

"Welcome to the Ra embassy." The female voice crackled through the speaker, as perfectly pleasant and robotic as a recording. "How may I assist you?"

"My name is Piper Griffiths. I'm here to see Miysis."

"Do you have an appointment?"

"Uh, no."

"What was your name again, sorry?"

"Piper Griffiths."

A long pause. "One moment please."

Piper glanced questioningly at Ash.

"You're dead, remember?" he said.

She sighed. "I hope they believe me or this will be a really short trip."

They stood in front of the gates for nearly five minutes before the speaker crackled again.

"Thank you for your patience," the woman said. "Please proceed."

The hum of a small motor made Piper jump as the gates began to open by themselves. With another glance at Ash, she started forward down the stone pathway. She stared in bemusement at the fountain in the center of the lawn, which featured a detailed sculpture of the mythological griffin—a half cat, half eagle—about to take flight with its wings spread wide. The lion-like face of the creature perfectly captured the regal indifference so typical of cats—and Ra princes— but otherwise, the sculpture looked as much like an actual griffin daemon as draconians looked like dragons.

She stopped in front of the double doors, blinking at her reflection in the polished wood. Her gaze moved to Ash's reflection beside hers.

"You should wait here," she said. "It's too dangerous for you to go inside—"

"I'm coming, Piper."

She scowled. No wonder Seiya was so worried about him taking stupid risks. Ra daemons killed Hades daemons—and to them, Ash was a Hades daemon. And after their last encounter, Miysis had even more reasons to want Ash dead. He was walking straight into the viper's nest.

"They won't kill me," he added as he reached for the door. "Not while I'm the only one who knows where the Sahar is."

He walked in, leaving her standing on the front step. Clenching her hands, she strode in after him. Stupid, overconfident draconian. She wasn't nearly as convinced of his safety. He hadn't seen Miysis's reaction after he'd lost the Sahar.

The foyer was everything Piper had expected from the elegant exterior. Marble floors, a curved front desk, leather furniture. The center of the building was completely hollow, with unbroken rows of balconies rising over a dozen stories to a glass ceiling high above, through which sunlight streamed in. The back wall was a modern waterfall two stories tall with a glistening marble backdrop.

The building was more than just an embassy. It was also the headquarters for the majority of the businesses the Ra family ran on Earth—legitimate and illegitimate. Piper also suspected that the Ra family had a larger chunk of their military hidden in the building than was strictly allowed. Anyone who thought the empty foyer meant the building was security-free was a fool.

The receptionist—or possibly security guard—smiled pleasantly as Piper approached the desk. Her blond hair had been swept into a simple bun, not a single strand out of place, and her green eyes were bright, accented with touches of makeup. A nameplate identified her as Sara.

"Welcome," Sara greeted her. "Since you do not have an appointment, I'll have to record some basic information." Her gaze dropped to her keyboard. "Please state your name."

Since Piper was watching for it, she saw Sara's eyes darken. Definitely a Ra. She was checking the truthfulness of their answers. Before Piper could reply, Ash stepped up to the desk and leaned toward the woman.

"You know who we are," he said, his voice making Piper shiver. "And you know who we're here to see. Go get him."

Piper blinked at him. So much for niceties.

Sara paled but managed to keep her composure. She cleared her throat. "Please have a seat and help yourself to refreshments."

Ash smiled coolly and stepped away from the desk. As soon as they sat down, Piper pressed her hands between her knees, wishing for a distraction from her relentless headache. Nervousness was a slow burn in her belly. The embassy was trying really hard to look like a posh business office, but everything was strategically arranged to be defensible. Dealing with Miysis on neutral ground was dangerous enough. Going head to head with him in his own territory was frightening. He had every advantage and they had none.

"Miss Griffiths?" the receptionist called. "He's ready to see you now."

She jumped up. Ash followed at a more relaxed pace, by all appearances unconcerned with the danger. Sara gestured toward the other end of the foyer, where shiny elevator doors waited.

"Please take the elevator to the top floor. Miysis will be waiting for you." She smiled professionally. "If you need anything, please don't hesitate to ask."

"Right, thanks," Piper said distractedly. Top floor again? She was developing a serious phobia of heights.

They crossed to the elevator and Piper punched the call button. The doors responded immediately, silently sliding open. This elevator was a thousand times better than the one at the Gaians' building. She stepped inside, betting it wouldn't rattle and groan as if it would break apart at any moment.

She tapped the button for the top floor and the doors slid closed, leaving her with a final glance of Sara picking up her phone to call someone. The elevator drifted upward so smoothly she couldn't tell how fast it was ascending.

"Well, this is it," she said, turning to Ash. "Do you think—Ash?"

His eyes were closed and his arms were wrapped around himself, rigid with tension. She glanced around sharply; it wasn't a large elevator. Ash wasn't afraid of heights, but he hated enclosed spaces.

Fear prickled in her stomach. Trapped in an elevator with a draconian on the verge of a panic attack—a draconian with dangerous control issues—was not good. And, of course, being the smart person that she was, instead of getting as far away from him as possible, she stepped closer and touched his arm.

"It'll be over in a minute," she said softly. "This isn't like the cellar. You can blast the top off this thing any time you want, right?"

He didn't open his eyes. "It's not that," he said, his voice slightly hoarse. "This thing looks like . . ."

She glanced around. White walls, steel doors. A normal elevator. His hand crept up and gripped his neck—where the collar had been locked two months before. That was it. The interior of the elevator looked like a smaller version of his prison cell in Asphodel.

Her heart squeezed. Without thinking, she took his wrist and pulled his arm away from his neck. Then she stepped up to him and wrapped her arms around him. He stiffened for a moment, but then hesitantly placed his hands on her waist. He wasn't hugging her back, but he wasn't pushing her away either.

"This isn't that place," she murmured, laying her cheek on his shoulder. She could feel the tautness of his muscles, locked down against the drag of terrible memories. Some of his tension slipped out of him as he let out a long breath. She looked over her shoulder to check the display; they had to be close to the top floor. How long did it take to—

With a screech of metal, the elevator ground to a jarring halt. That was all it took to shatter Ash's fragile control.

She felt the rush of his magic as the lights went out, plunging the elevator into darkness. The dim emergency light flickered on an instant later, and Piper met Ash's black eyes, framed by the line of black scales that edged his cheekbones. He'd lost his glamour. His breathing came fast as he fought to control his panic. The elevator creaked, swaying on its cable, but she'd worry about plunging to her death later. She had bigger problems to contend with.

Her arms were still around his neck. His hands on her waist were like painful vices and his claws pricked her through her shirt. She couldn't back away. She couldn't move a single step. Shit shit shit.

His wings flared, thumping into the sides of the elevator as his gaze swung across the tiny space. Fighting for calm, she rubbed the back of his neck, gently trying to recapture his attention.

"Ash," she said softly. "Ash, look at me."

His stare snapped onto her, too intense, barely controlled savagery.

"Hey," she whispered. "You're safe, Ash. I'm here. We're safe. The power's just gone out. It'll be back on at any moment."

He wasn't listening. She knew that even before his attention darted away, searching for an escape. His hands tightened, claws piercing her skin as he forgot his strength, forgot he was holding her in his desperation to get out.

Heart pounding, she slid her hands from the back of his neck to the sides of his face and pulled gently. His fingers flexed, claws digging in a little deeper. She held her breath and firmly turned his head until their eyes met again.

"Ash," she said, keeping her tone even. "You need to calm down."

His eyes came into focus for the first time since the elevator screeched to a halt. His hands abruptly loosened their painful grip.

"Are you listening to me now?" she asked.

"Maybe," he said hoarsely.

"Good."

His face was an inch away, his eyes still black as night, his skin warm under her hands. She licked her lips, her thoughts drifting away from the danger and on to . . . other things. To the way he felt against her, their bodies pressed close. His lips so close to hers. His dark eyes locked on hers like he couldn't look away even if he tried.

His form suddenly shimmered, magic sparking against her body wherever she touched him as he slid back into glamour.

"That was stupid," he said quietly.

"What was?"

"You should have gotten away from me."

"You were holding on to me."

He closed his mouth on whatever he'd been about to say. He tensed, stepping away from her as his nostrils flared. His eyes went black again. "Shit."

"What?"

He took a step toward her—and his legs buckled.

"Ash!"

He caught himself before he fell and leaned back into the elevator wall. His eyes had lightened back to grey but had gone out of focus.

"Shit," he said again.

"What is it?" She grabbed his arm. "What's happening?"

"Drugs in the air," he muttered.

"What?" She looked around. "I feel fine."

"Must be daemon-specific. The room is spinning."

Her eyes widened. "Oh no. They're making sure you won't be a threat."

He grunted his agreement.

The main lights flashed back on. With the drone of motors, the elevator lurched into motion, ascending the last few floors to the top. Piper held on to Ash's arm, muscles tense. Damn it. She should have known Miysis would never let Ash just walk into his home base without taking certain precautions. Ash was too dangerous. She hoped whatever drugs they were pumping into the elevator's ventilation would wear off fast, and that Miysis wasn't planning something more permanent to incapacitate Ash.

The elevator dinged as it slid to a smooth stop. Piper looped her arm through Ash's. She had two daggers hidden in her knee-high boots, but she didn't dare draw them yet. Not until she knew the extent of the danger they were in.

As the doors slid open, sunlight burst in, nearly blinding her. She tensed, expecting to face a small army of Ra soldiers waiting to take them prisoner. Instead, an empty marble-floored foyer greeted her, brightly lit by sunlight streaming in through the glass ceiling. Matching glass floors let the sunlight continue straight down to the other floors and offered a dizzying view of the foyer far below. Glancing warily around, she pulled Ash into motion, guiding him out of the elevator. He leaned on her with every step, his eyes glazed over from the drugs. The "power failure" had definitely been deliberate, intended to give the drugs enough time to enter Ash's system.

She glanced back at the elevator, wondering whether they should leave. But she knew Miysis wouldn't allow it, not when Ash knew where the Sahar was.

At the other end of the foyer was a glass wall and door. On the other side, greenery flourished. A greenhouse on the top floor?

"Ash?" she whispered. "How are you doing?"

He made an incoherent sound, shaking his head. He looked as though he were trying hard to keep his stomach down. Little tremors ran through his limbs.

Since there was nowhere else to go, she pulled Ash to the greenhouse door and tried the handle. It opened. She pulled Ash inside and stopped, staring at their surroundings.

A tropical paradise filled the space, a rainforest arching two stories overhead. The entire thing was filled with birdsongs. Not a greenhouse, but an aviary. As she watched, a bright red parrot with a sweeping tail whooshed by. It landed on a branch of a nearby tree, cocked its head toward her, and let out a whistling call.

"Close the door."

Piper's head jerked around. She couldn't see him through the forest, but she recognized that melodic voice. She swung the door closed and checked that it was latched, then she led Ash down the curving path.

Around the bend was the center of the aviary: a large, circular space, paved with stones like an outdoor garden. Six carved benches with cushions formed a circle within the space, and outdoor lampposts sat between each bench to light the space at night.

Dappled sunlight streamed down through the foliage. If Piper hadn't been so tense, she would have been in awe of the beautiful, peaceful paradise.

Sitting on the bench at the far end of the space was Miysis. He reclined casually, a glass of red wine in his hand and his golden hair tousled like a magazine model's. He smiled when she appeared, his intense yellow-green eyes appraising her like laser beams.

Clenching her teeth at the sight of him, so cool after trapping them in an elevator and drugging Ash, she helped Ash to the nearest bench. His head hung forward and he was breathing hard. He barely seemed aware of his surroundings and didn't appear to notice Miysis at all. Giving his shoulder a squeeze, she turned to face the Ra daemon. He looked only too sophisticated in dark slacks and a white dress shirt, the sleeves rolled partway up. He was still smiling, looking far more pleased than the last time she'd seen him. This time, of course, everything he wanted was almost within reach.

Reluctantly, she stepped away from Ash. The thick greenery of the artificial rainforest was likely hiding a number of guards, but for now it seemed as though their meeting would be amiable. Miysis was deceptive like that. He would look serene right up until his assassin slipped a blade between her shoulder blades.

"Don't look so suspicious," Miysis told her, gesturing for her to sit on the bench beside him. "I don't have archers in the trees."

"Only in the bushes, right?" she retorted. She didn't want to sit beside him, so she dropped down on the bench nearest his. "You didn't have to drug Ash. We came here peacefully."

Miysis shrugged. "One can never be too careful." He rolled his wine in its glass. "I confess I am very surprised to see you. By all accounts, you died in the Consulate bombing. Why on earth haven't you told anyone you weren't there? Not even your father . . ." He shook his head, his disapproval clear.

She folded her arms. "Don't lecture me, Miysis. I *was* in the Consulate when it exploded, but I haven't been able to find my father to tell him yet."

He leaned forward. "Did you find out who's behind the attacks?"

"Let's not get off topic. That's not what I came here to discuss."

His eyebrows rose at her tone. He leaned back again. "Ah. Straight to business then." He tipped his wine glass toward her, inviting her to speak.

"It's pretty simple. I need you to find Vejovis for me."

"The healer?"

"Yes."

"Why?"

"Does it matter?"

"Are you ill? I have many talented healers. You need only ask."

She hesitated. "I'm pretty sure it needs to be Vejovis."

"Why?" he asked again.

She bit her lip, considering her options. She could downplay the seriousness of her situation so Miysis wouldn't know how desperate she was for his help, but anything that treaded close to dishonesty was hazardous when it came to Ra daemons. She could tell him the truth and hope it motivated him to help, especially since she was potentially useful to him. Or she could refuse to elaborate at all, but she didn't see him being very cooperative in that scenario.

When it came to Ra daemons, the truth was always the safest bet.

"My hybrid magic was sealed away when I was a child, but the seal . . . broke . . . and my magic will kill me if it isn't resealed."

His eyes widened slightly. "How did the seal break?"

"Long story. But Vejovis is more than likely the daemon who sealed my magic in the first place, and I need him to seal it again. I doubt that's the kind of thing any healer can do."

"It's certainly not within the skillsets of my healers. Applying spells *to* a mind is simple enough. Working *within* the mind, however, is nearly impossible. Most cannot do it."

"So do you know where Vejovis is?"

"I know of some likely places to look," he replied. "But his exact location? No one knows that. Vejovis is a secretive creature."

"I don't have a lot of time. How quickly can you find him?"

"I can't say. Perhaps a day. Perhaps a week. Perhaps a month or more."

She shook her head. "A week, maybe. A month, definitely not."

"I can't make any promises when I don't know where he is. We would have to search multiple locations."

She exhaled. "Okay. But you *do* know where to look?"

He nodded.

"So I suppose you want to know what I'm going to offer you in return for your help?"

His smile was so cat-like she was surprised he didn't have pointed canines to match. "I think you already know there is only one thing I will accept."

"The Sahar."

He took a sip of his wine. "Actually, I am entitled to more than just the return of my birthright. You cannot understand the damage my reputation has suffered since losing the Sahar." His expression went cold. "Do you know why I am here today and not in my homeland?"

She shook her head.

He downed the rest of his wine before answering. "Because no one in my family wants to see my face. They are disgusted by my failure."

Each word came out like spitted poison. She flinched. Yep, there it was—the rage beneath his calm exterior. Just as this sanctuary held hidden enemies waiting for her or Ash to make a wrong move, Miysis's calm façade hid a fury he could barely contain. Fear whooshed through her belly. This wasn't safe. Whatever deal she made, she needed to convince Miysis not to harm Ash. The Ra daemon was angry enough to kill.

"You offer me what is rightfully mine in return for my help," he continued, his rage transforming back into smooth confidence. "You offer me what Ashtaroth *stole* from me. I do not need to bargain anything for the Sahar. You brought him here and I can take it from him at any time, or—as I assume you were not foolish enough to bring it with you—force him to reveal its location."

She clenched her hands. She'd been afraid of this—that Miysis wouldn't be satisfied with only getting the Sahar back.

"What do you want then?"

He drummed his fingers on his knee. "Presently, you are the only person who can wield the Sahar."

She tensed.

"How quickly you paled, Piper. Calm yourself. I have no intention of mimicking Samael's crimes."

"What exactly do you want then?"

"I want you to use the Sahar to complete a task for me. Just one."

"What task?" she asked suspiciously. She wouldn't kill anyone for him.

"I need you for a minor excavation job that would otherwise take weeks. I'm sure that with the Sahar you could have it done in a few minutes."

"Excavation?"

He nodded.

"Where?"

"The details can wait until it is time for the task."

She narrowed her eyes. "This is just straight demolition, right? I won't be hurting anyone or blowing up people's houses?"

"Of course not," he said, the words clipped with offense at her insinuation.

She bit her bottom lip. It sounded simple enough. As long as she wouldn't be hurting anyone, she didn't see the harm. She let out a deep breath.

"We'll need to find Vejovis first. I can't use the Sahar like this." She pressed a hand to her throbbing forehead. "Once my magic is sealed, I'll take care of your task. However, I have one condition."

"What's that?"

She glanced at Ash slumped on the bench, nearly comatose and helpless. "You have to swear not to harm Ash or hold him against his will today or at any point while we're fulfilling either side of our deal."

Shadows slid across Miysis's eyes. She tried not to fidget as he thought it over.

Sighing, he leaned back. "I will not enact any harm against him until our bargain is complete."

"So we're agreed then?" she asked.

He nodded. "Yes, we have a deal."

"Excellent." Piper jumped about a foot off the ground at the sound of Ash's voice behind her. She spun around.

Ash was sitting casually on the bench, clear-eyed and by all appearances perfectly healthy. He was holding a dagger in one hand, nonchalantly tossing it into the air and catching it by its point. A drugged person would not have that kind of coordination, though he was barely able to walk before.

He smiled coolly at Miysis.

"Excellent," he repeated, his deep voice shivering along Piper's nerves. "But you forgot something, Ra. You forgot to get *my* promise not to harm *you*."

At the last word, a dozen daemons in green camouflage burst out of the bushes, long-handled halberds all pointed at Ash. Startled birds took to the air in a brief cacophony of flapping wings and shrieked warning cries.

Silence fell, and no one moved.

Ash tossed the dagger one more time, caught it by the tip, then pitched it into the middle of the circle. It skittered loudly across the stones. "Calm down, cat-boy. I was merely pointing out your oversight."

Piper glanced wide-eyed at Miysis, who was staring at Ash with his jaw tight and his face a little paler than normal. His eyes had gone black.

"I see your resistance to drugs is stronger than I had anticipated," Miysis said, his normally melodic voice rough with a growl. With a brief wave of his hand, he had the soldiers lift the deadly blades away from Ash.

She looked back at Ash. "How long . . .?" she stuttered.

"I was never that drugged to start with. The dizziness passed once we were out of the elevator."

"You—" She broke off, shaking her head. "Why were you pretending?"

Ash smiled at Miysis. "Because I knew the Ra would drive a much harder bargain with me rather than with you."

Miysis stood abruptly. "I have arrangements to make. Return in four hours." He jerked his chin at one of his soldiers. "Escort them out."

Without another word or glance, he strode away, through another path in the aviary.

Piper bit her lip. She hoped Miysis had bargained sincerely, because she really didn't want to find out how many loopholes the Ra prince could find in their flimsy agreement. Her life, and Ash's, counted on Miysis keeping his word—and she hoped she'd covered their bases enough to keep them safe.

CHAPTER
-11-

SITTING on the bench with her face in her hands, Piper fought the nausea churning in the pit of her stomach. Her head ached ceaselessly, the pressure in her skull almost unbearable. It wouldn't last forever. The headaches came in waves—twenty or thirty minutes of excruciating pain that died down to a dull ache for an hour before the pain level started rising again.

She couldn't specifically remember how long it had taken her as a child to reach this point, but it had been months, not days. It was happening too fast. At this rate, she would be having seizures before the week was out.

"How long?" she croaked.

Ash sat beside her on the bench, elbows braced on his knees, chin resting on his hands. "About twenty minutes before we return to the embassy."

She bobbed her head in a weak nod, but otherwise didn't move. Her body felt cold and hot at the same time from the pain, and her sides stung where Ash's claws had punctured her skin in the elevator. She'd cleaned the cuts herself and had no intention of telling anyone—especially Ash—that he'd hurt her.

The park they were waiting in, a few blocks from the embassy, held nothing more than a few struggling trees and yellow grass, with chipped, weathered cement benches for seating. Piper had claimed one shortly after they'd arrived an hour ago. They couldn't go anywhere else in the city. Brinford was no longer safe; as soon as they were done helping her, Ash, Seiya, and Lyre would flee to another city, or another world, and hopefully leave Samael's assassins behind.

Ash and his sister were back in their warrior clothes, not worried about standing out in the deserted park. Seiya stood in the long shadows beneath a tree, armed to the teeth and clothed all in black, her gaze vigilantly scouring the park. Lyre paced across the stubbly grass, unable to sit still.

Beside her, Ash stared at nothing. He'd been strangely distant since leaving the embassy. She suspected it bothered him that she'd seen him lose control again. She still hadn't figured out how to broach the subject.

"I need a distraction," she said, her voice hoarse from the pain. "Talk to me."

"About what?" he asked.

"Anything."

He thought for a moment. "I met Miysis on one of my first solo missions for Samael. A Ra aristocrat was engaging in some under-the-table dealings with a crime syndicate. They were meeting to finalize a deal, and Samael didn't want that to happen."

She tilted to her head to peek at him through her fingers. He'd never talked about his missions for Samael before.

"None of his usual reaper spies could get in. I didn't have much of a reputation yet, so he sent me undercover. The meeting place was a high-end gentlemen's club. I managed to sneak in and blend in with the crowd, though I've never felt so out of place in my life. I didn't know where the meeting with the Ra aristocrat was taking place, so I took a position near the bar where I could observe most of the room.

"After several minutes, a daemon sat down beside me. Blond, green eyes . . . I knew he was a Ra, but he was too young to be my mark. He ordered a drink and started chatting with me casually. I barely responded, not wanting to give myself away, but he kept on talking about random little things. Then he mentioned that he'd always wanted to see the secret room on the second floor but the security was too tight. Only special guests were allowed. Then he smiled, tipped his drink at me, and walked away."

Sounded just like Miysis. "Was he setting you up?"

"Yes and no. The room he described was the exact one I needed and I easily completed my objective. I escaped out the back and was heading down the street when he stepped out in front of me.

"He introduced himself, then thanked me for taking care of such an annoying problem. He appreciated not having to get his hands dirty. Then he told me to give his regards to Samael."

"Did that bother you?" she asked. "That he'd used you?"

He shrugged. "Not especially. It didn't matter how the job got done, as long as it was done."

"It sounds like things started out relatively cordial between you two," she noted. "When did that go downhill?"

"A few years later."

"What happened?"

He didn't answer.

She studied his profile. "Is it better now?" she asked softly. "Not having to follow Samael's orders anymore?"

He gave a short nod.

She hesitated. "Seiya doesn't seem as happy about her freedom as I expected she'd be."

After a long moment, he said, "The last two months haven't been easy, but it's infinitely better than what we escaped."

She sighed, pressing a hand to her throbbing head. "Everything has changed, hasn't it? Ever since losing my apprenticeship, I've spent so much time wondering what I'm supposed to *do*."

Ash looked at her sharply. "You lost your apprenticeship?"

"Oh . . . I guess you didn't know. My father cancelled it before I left for boarding school."

His voice softened. "I'm sorry."

"I don't know what to do with my life anymore, or what my future will be."

He tilted his head back, looking up at the overcast sky. "Me neither."

She gave him a questioning look.

"For as long as I can remember," he said, "Samael controlled almost every aspect of my life. Inwardly, I was consumed with not just surviving him, but escaping him. Destroying him if I could. I devoted every moment to it."

His hand closed around the hilt of one of the swords strapped to his thigh as his jaw tightened. "I have nothing to do now, nothing to work toward. I don't have a purpose."

Hesitantly, she touched the back of his hand. "I feel the same way. I'm sure we'll both figure it out."

She fell silent as the pain in her head built, squeezing her brain and pushing against her skull. She swallowed a groan. Time lost all meaning. Eventually, Lyre joined them and the two guys coaxed her to her feet. Awareness of her surroundings barely punctured the cloud of pain. The headache should have died down by now.

With Ash on one side of her and Lyre on the other, Seiya trailing behind, Piper let them lead her to the embassy. Someone else rang the buzzer; she wasn't paying attention. Then they were moving again. The rush of the waterfall in the foyer filled the echoing room. She leaned on Ash while he spoke to Sara, the words passing through her ears without comprehension. Everything was pain.

"Her hands are freezing." Lyre rubbed her fingers between his warm palms. "Piper, can you hear me?"

She gave a weak nod.

"Come on. This way."

She took a wobbly step away from Ash and toward Lyre—and suddenly the floor was rushing toward her face.

Arms scooped her up, lifting her into the air before settling her against a warm torso.

"That was close," Ash said, his voice rumbling from his chest into hers. "Piper? Say something."

"Hey," she breathed. She turned her face into his neck, trying to block out the light. Her head throbbed, the pain so intense, pounding inside her skull with each beat of her heart. Why wasn't it diminishing? The last headache had only lasted for thirty minutes.

"Hang in there, okay?" Ash murmured.

"Hanging," she whispered.

He carried her into the elevator. She closed her eyes, focused solely on enduring each passing second. Her stomach swooped as the elevator ascended. The doors dinged and Ash started walking again. She heard voices somewhere ahead.

"Bring her this way." Miysis's melodic voice came out of nowhere, suddenly beside her. "Sara called up and told me Piper was ill. My healer will be here in a moment. She's preparing a temporary treatment."

Ash carried her another dozen steps, then the world wobbled sickeningly as he lowered her onto something soft. She opened her blurry eyes and found herself on a sofa in some kind of lounge-like room. Miysis and Ash were both kneeling in front of her, side by side. And they weren't even arguing. It was a miracle.

"Piper," Miysis said gently. "Can you tell me what's wrong?"

"Pain in my head," she whispered, closing her eyes again. "It's the magic."

"What kind of pain is it? Sharp, shooting, burning, pressure?"

"Pressure."

"It's escalating too quickly," Ash murmured to Miysis.

"My people are moving as fast as possible," he replied. "Teams have already checked the most accessible locations but he wasn't at any of them."

"Piper doesn't have the time for you to search every remotely plausible hideout from here to the Overworld," Ash growled.

"I know that—"

The pain suddenly spiked, spearing her skull. Piper gasped, flinging out a hand to grab Ash's arm. She opened her mouth to speak and her stomach jumped into her throat.

Ash and Miysis sprang away as she doubled over and vomited on the floor. Her stomach heaved until she thought it might eject itself from her body. When the spasms finally stopped, she slumped backward, moaning. Ash pulled her off the sofa and back into his arms.

"Where's your damn healer?"

"This way."

Ash moved her to the other end of the room and set her on another sofa, and then there was a new voice.

"Piper." The voice was soft and motherly.

She cracked her eyes open to find a middle-aged Ra daemon kneeling in front of her, smiling gently. Miysis, Ash, Lyre, and Seiya crowded behind the woman.

"Piper, I have something that will help you, but you need to be brave, okay?"

The woman picked up a small plastic box with pin-sized holes in its sides from beside her. She opened the lid and carefully reached inside. Her hand emerged, holding a huge, hairy spider. She gripped its dark body between two fingers and a thumb, its long red legs flailing in undulating waves.

Piper's blood went cold. She jerked backward. Strength returned to her muscles on a wave of adrenaline as she scrambled away and lunged for the back of the sofa, fully intending to jump over it and run for the nearest lockable room.

Miysis and Ash grabbed her arms, pulling her back down on the sofa.

"Piper, calm down." Miysis clasped her arm tightly. "It's just a spider."

"What the hell kind of spider is that?" Lyre demanded.

"Piper, this is a rune spider," the healer said. "They are native to certain forests in the Overworld, and their venom contains some unique properties. Foremost, it affects the part of the mind tied to magic. It will numb you to your magic and cause much of it to diminish for a period of time."

"Why do you have one of those *in your embassy*?" Lyre whispered incredulously to Miysis.

"All you have to do is let it bite you," the healer said as though it were the most reasonable thing in the world, "and the pain will go away."

Piper shook her head before the woman had even finished, unable to take her eyes off the squirming spider. It was *huge*. It would fill the woman's hand were she to let it sit on her palm.

"I'm fine," she croaked. "I can handle the pain. Put it away."

"Piper—"

"I'm fine!"

"Piper," Miysis said sternly, "let her help you. It'll be over in a second."

"No!"

"She's an arachnophobe," Ash said. "She won't let it bite her. Can't you inject the venom?"

"We've tried that before. It doesn't work the same. It needs to come straight from the spider."

She tensed, prepared to fight them all. She would rather die in agony than let that spider touch her.

A moment of silence.

"It's fine," Ash finally said. "You heard her. She would rather have the pain."

"But Ash—" Lyre began.

Ash made a brusque gesture. He turned to Piper. "It's okay. You'll be fine."

He leaned closer, brushing a hand down her arm. She blinked at him, trying to think beyond the haze of panic and pain. His gray stare was reassuring as he gently touched her cheek with his fingers, wiping away a tear she hadn't realized she'd shed.

And then she felt the tingle of magic across her skin in the wake of his touch.

"No!" she cried. She jumped away from him but her knees instantly buckled.

He pulled her back onto the sofa so she fell on top of him. Mist spun through her head, fuzzing her thoughts but doing nothing to dull the pain. She slumped weakly against him, her muscles numb and listless from his spell.

"It's okay," he murmured in her ear. He ran his fingers through her hair, brushing it off her face. "You're too tough to let this beat you."

Someone took her arm, stretching it out and turning her wrist upward. She whimpered, squeezing her eyes shut.

"It's okay," Ash whispered again, his lips brushing her ear as he spoke. "You can do this. Don't you remember when we were trapped in the cellar? I couldn't think straight, but you were calm. You can handle anything. This is a walk in the park compared to that."

She took a deep breath. The edges of her panic dulled as he continued to whisper in her ear, his voice sliding down into her bones and making her shiver. She stopped hearing his words, lost in the sound of his voice alone.

A sharp prick on her wrist made her jerk, her muscles unable to do more than twitch.

"Done," the healer declared, snapping the lid back on the box. "It should start working within twenty minutes. The bite will be sore and swollen for several days, and she may have some other symptoms—brief bouts of dizziness or a mild fever. Nothing to be concerned about."

"Thank you," Miysis said. "I'll call you if we need anything more."

Ash brushed his fingers across her cheek again, lifting his spell. Feeling crept back into her muscles, but she didn't move. His arms were around her, his cheek resting against her forehead. He was warm, strong, and his delicious scent of fresh mountain air surrounded her. She closed her eyes and burrowed her face into the side of his neck, blocking out the world as she waited desperately for the pain to stop.

"How long will the effects of the venom last?" Ash asked.

"It depends on the person's metabolism," Miysis said. "For daemons, only a few hours. For haemons, a day or two."

"Can we give her more after that?"

"It's not wise. It's still a poison, even if the effects are working in her favor right now. We found each subsequent exposure had less effect on magic and more adverse effects on the victim's health, especially with back-to-back injections."

"That sounds ominous," Lyre remarked, not quite managing a flippant tone.

"We need Vejovis," Ash said.

"Obviously," Miysis replied. "As I started to say before, I suspect I know where he is."

"Where?" Ash demanded.

"I believe he's gone home."

"Home? Where is 'home'?"

Miysis let out a deep breath. "Kyo Kawa Valley in the Overworld."

A heartbeat of silence.

"Is that," Lyre asked, dread clear in his voice, "the valley of . . ."

"The ryujin," Miysis finished. "Yes. Vejovis lives in the heart of their territory."

"But how?"

"He must have some kind of truce or deal with them."

Another moment of quiet.

"But *how*?" Lyre repeated.

"I have no idea. But that is where he lives, and it's the safest place for him. Vejovis was instrumental in your escape from Asphodel. Samael will not allow that to go unpunished."

"Well, he should definitely be safe in the ryujin valley," Lyre muttered.

Piper lifted her head from Ash's shoulder and glanced across the group. Lyre stood beside the sofa while Miysis sat on the arm. Seiya stood a few feet away, her arms folded and her expression dark.

"What's a ryujin?" The name was familiar but her pain-hazed brain couldn't pull up the information.

"The ryujin are an Overworld caste," Miysis answered. "Aquatic quasi-amphibians related to water dragons. They are not a friendly people. In fact, they generally kill any other daemons they catch in their territory—Vejovis being the exception. Over the past centuries, various families have attempted to absorb the ryujin's lands into their territory, but none have succeeded in spite of the ryujin's relatively small numbers."

She rubbed a hand against her forehead. It was subtle, but the pain was definitely beginning to wane.

"So what's your plan then?" Lyre asked. "How will you get a message to Vejovis telling him we need him?"

Miysis's eyes turned to Piper, intense and analyzing. "To be blunt, I doubt Piper can afford to wait for messengers."

"What do you mean?"

"We need to take her straight to Vejovis. She doesn't have time to wait for him to come to her."

"You want to take Piper *through* Kyo Kawa Valley?" Lyre exclaimed. "Are you insane?"

"The ryujin stay in or near water. We can cross their land to Vejovis's residence without travelling too near to the river." Miysis turned to Ash. "I can send a team to find Vejovis, but by the time they reach him and bring him back, it could be too late. I believe our only option is to take Piper straight to him. If we can get her to Vejovis before the rune spider's venom wears off, there will be no risk of her condition deteriorating to dangerous levels, which I expect will take, at most, forty-eight hours once the venom is no longer protecting her."

"Forty-eight hours?" Lyre repeated. "But—her magic has only been unsealed for two days! It takes haemon children months to—"

"I didn't expect her to worsen this quickly, even from this morning," Miysis said. "I would have expected at least six weeks, probably closer to ten, for her to reach this point. Her magic should require time to develop, like unused muscles that need to be strengthened . . ."

"The Sahar," Piper muttered.

Miysis looked at her. "Pardon?"

"I think . . ." She swallowed. "I think the Sahar damaged the seal on my magic. When I used it to break the gold collar Samael made me wear, the Stone's magic felt like it was tearing me up inside. And . . ." She pressed her lips together for a moment. "I've been having headaches for weeks. The whole time I was at Westwood. I thought it was just stress."

Miysis nodded. "That would explain it then. Your magic started developing two months ago when the seal was damaged. The remains of the seal were protecting you from the worst of it, but now that the seal is gone, your magic is nearing lethal levels."

She flinched at the word "lethal."

Ash's arms tightened. "Then we take her to Vejovis—now," he said. "We can't chance waiting."

"You don't even know if he's there," Seiya snapped, speaking for the first time.

"'We'?" Miysis repeated to Ash, ignoring Seiya. "You can't possibly intend to come."

"He's right," Seiya said, her voice cutting. "We're from the *Underworld*. What use will we be there? It's ridiculous!"

"We won't be walking through an Overworld city," Ash replied calmly to Miysis. "The valley will be deserted except for the ryujin. And if we do encounter them, you will need my help."

"My team and I will be perfectly capable of handling anything we encounter."

"Good for you. But I'll be there anyway to make sure you don't screw it up."

They scowled at each other, but Piper wasn't watching them anymore. She pressed closer to Ash, fear rushing through her at the pure hatred on Seiya's face as she glared at her.

CHAPTER
-12-

PIPER tightened the strap over the armguard covering her left forearm and checked that the band Ash had given her was secure. Miysis's embassy had three basement levels, and two of them contained nothing but supplies and gear. It was an armory stocked for war. She definitely suspected he had a good chunk of his military scattered throughout the building.

She'd been outfitted with new clothing and gear. Thankfully, it wasn't in the Ra military colors of red and gold. Just regular browns. Fitted pants of a tough material that could take a lot of wear and tear, and a tan button-down shirt. She'd passed on a leather vest, not liking how it would restrict her movements. Speed and flexibility were her biggest strengths.

What pleased her most was that, finally, she was armed again. A row of throwing knives was attached to her belt, two long daggers were strapped to her right thigh, and a sword was on her left hip. No gun though. The Overworld was, apparently, a gun-free zone. They didn't manufacture firearms there at all, relying instead on simpler weapons and magic.

Brushing her hands down her front, she nodded to herself. She was as prepared as she could be considering she had no idea what she was walking into. The Overworld. She'd been to the Underworld, though she'd seen very little of it. Asphodel, Samael's estate, had been beautiful, with old-world elegance and an ancient style of architecture with interconnected buildings and courtyards. Only one building had had electricity: Chrysalis, where they developed products that crossed magic with technology.

Outside the estate, she'd seen mountains and forests with strange species of trees and plant life, but by far the most shocking sight had been the sky, where a massive planet drifted by for large portions of the day, and two suns and three moons arched above both day and night.

What would the Overworld be like? An entirely different planet in some other far corner of space? Seventy years ago, before the Third World War, space travel had been a thing. She'd heard that humans had gone to the moon, but not to other planets. According to Raum, she was the first non-daemon to go to the Underworld and back. Now she would be the first to go to both daemon worlds and back again.

Assuming she made it back alive. If Vejovis wasn't there . . .

She really didn't like the idea of Ash and Lyre coming with her. Both had been insistent, even though they were Underworld daemons; they didn't know any more about the Overworld than she did. Aside from moral support, she didn't see how useful they'd be.

Sighing, she pressed her thumb to her armguard over the hidden spider bite—an ugly swollen lump the size of a walnut. Ugh. She would have been angry at Ash for putting a partial sleeping spell on her, except it had been the right thing to do. The bite was a hell of a lot better than the pain of her headache, but she'd been too panicked to see that. Her record for keeping her composure lately was abysmal.

She was already counting down to when the venom would wear off. Two hours of her precious forty-eight were already gone.

Unable to hide in the small room any longer—the others were probably already waiting in the larger room down the hall—she turned toward the door, only to see someone already opening it. She was expecting it to be Ash or Lyre coming in to see what was keeping her. When she saw who came through the door, her face paled.

Seiya, the very person she'd been hiding from, stalked straight for Piper with icy fury in her black eyes.

"After everything I've said," she snarled, bearing down on Piper. "After everything I've told you."

Piper held her ground as Seiya stopped practically on her toes.

"I can't believe you," Seiya hissed. "Why are you doing this?"

"I—"

"You don't need Ash! You don't need his help! Why are you trying to get him killed?"

"I'm not—"

"You're bringing him with you into one of the most dangerous territories in the Overworld. *The Overworld!* We're Underworld daemons. What use will he be in the Overworld? Are you too selfish to leave him behind?"

"I didn't ask him to come!"

"You're not stopping him either!" Seiya yelled.

"How am I supposed to stop him?" she shouted back. "I already told him he didn't need to come, that I'd be fine with Miysis and his guys. He won't listen!"

"You aren't trying hard enough!"

"What else am I supposed to do?"

Seiya leaned in even closer. "You told him he didn't have to come. You didn't tell him you don't *want* him to come."

"What difference—"

"It makes all the difference!" Her eyes went from midnight blue to pitch black. "You say, 'Don't come, Ash, don't come,' but your body language says, 'I want you with me so badly. I can't do this alone. I *need* you with me!' Of course he'll listen to that instead of your half-hearted protests!"

"I did not—"

Seiya threw up her hands and turned away. She stalked two steps then spun back again. "You don't even realize the signals you're sending. God, humans are stupid."

Piper balled her hands into fists, fury from the insult nearly choking her. "You—"

"Do you actually care about him?" Seiya demanded.

"Of course I—"

"Then convince him to stay behind!" Seiya pointed at the door. "Go out there and convince him. Tell him you don't want him to come. That you can't stand the sight of him. Tell him he terrifies you and you never want to see him again. Whatever it takes. *Stop him.*"

Piper stared at her. After a long moment, she shook her head. "No."

"What?"

"I won't manipulate him. He can make his own decisions."

Seiya bared her teeth. She was shaded—really shaded. Seiya would protect her brother from any danger, and right now, Piper was that danger.

The draconian girl took a step toward Piper, magic making the air around her sizzle. The door to the room opened a second time. Seiya whirled around, hands raised and ready to cast lethal magic.

Lyre leaned on the doorframe, as cool as ever. Shadows gathered in his golden eyes as he assessed them.

"Afternoon, ladies," he said calmly. "Must you fight? You're both far too lovely for scars." A half-smile curved his lips and his voice took on a purring note. "If you're feeling so feisty, perhaps I can help you expend your energy in a more pleasant manner."

Piper inhaled deeply as tingles ran across her skin and warmth gathered in her belly. Aphrodisia. Lyre was using aphrodisia to diffuse Seiya's anger. That didn't seem like a smart idea, but at least Seiya wasn't on the verge of attacking *her* anymore.

Seiya dropped her aggressive pose and folded her arms across her chest. "Mind your own business."

"I am. But everyone is waiting, so . . ."

Casting a killer glare over her shoulder at Piper, Seiya stalked out. She deliberately slammed her shoulder into Lyre's on her way by.

Piper exhaled shakily once she was gone.

"You okay?" Lyre asked, crossing the room to her. "You're white as a sheet."

"I'm fine," she mumbled.

"Do you want to talk about it?"

"Maybe later. Everyone is waiting." She flapped her hands like she was shaking water off them. Her skin was tingling in a very delicious sort of way that really made her want his hands on her body. "Wow. Could you have gone a little easier on the aphrodisia?"

"Ah, well, didn't want to take any chances."

Piper stilled. "Was Seiya really going to attack me?"

Lyre's eyes were somber. "I think she was. You need to be more careful around her."

Exhaling, she took his arm and led him to the door. "Let's go visit the Overworld."

"I've always wanted to see it," he said, cheerful again in a blink. "I don't have any spray paint though."

"Spray paint?"

"I've always wanted to paint 'Overworlders Suck' on the side of a mountain and see how long it took them to notice."

She rolled her eyes as they joined the others in the main room. Seiya was skulking behind Ash, Zala in her arms. Zwi sat on Ash's shoulder, watching the room with alert golden eyes. Ash absently stroked her side, looking vaguely disconcerted as he glanced at his sister. Piper was suddenly struck by the thought that, though they loved each other as profoundly as any siblings, Ash didn't actually know Seiya that well. They'd been apart for years, seeing one another only from a distance. They'd probably been very close before their separation, but he'd spent only the last two months with the grown-up Seiya, who might very well be a completely different person from the child he once knew.

Miysis stepped into the middle of the group as soon as Piper and Lyre had joined them. He'd changed from his business chic outfit into gear very similar to the rest of theirs—neutral colors and light armor. He wore a sword and several wicked curved daggers.

"We'll be travelling to the ley line shortly. Once we're in the Overworld, it will be about twelve hours of hard travel to reach Vejovis's home. We will stay there for the night, then travel back to the ley line.

"Before we go, there are some rules I need to establish. First, we stay together. No wandering off. No adventures. The ryujin territory is not a place where you would want to find yourself alone.

"Secondly, if you do get separated from the group, stay where you are. We'll find you.

"And lastly, don't touch anything. Some plants in the Overworld are poisonous and we can only carry antidotes for the most common. Some don't have antidotes. Keep your skin covered and don't touch any plants, flowers, or fungi."

Lyre nudged Piper with his elbow. "And watch out for spiders."

She scowled at him.

"We will be accompanied by four of my men." He gestured to the four Ra daemons standing off to one side—all blond, green-eyed, and very muscular—before turning to Ash and Seiya. His expression hardened. "By coming, you put Piper and the success of this mission at greater risk. Do you still insist on accompanying us?"

Seiya shot Piper a threatening look, and Piper knew she was supposed to jump in and tell Ash she didn't want him to come. But she wouldn't lie; she did want him to come. Besides, she didn't fully trust Miysis and definitely didn't want to be alone with him.

"We're coming," Ash replied.

"Fine," Miysis said flatly, turning away. "But I am not responsible for your fate. Let's get this done."

He strode out of the room, toward the elevators, his men following behind. Piper fell into step beside Lyre, glad she would have him as a buffer between her and Seiya during the trip. When she'd first met Seiya, she'd thought maybe they could be friends. But now the feel of Seiya's eyes on her back made her skin prickle with nervousness, and she honestly wondered what the greater danger was: their upcoming journey, or Seiya's fierce determination to eliminate any threat to her brother.

◦ ◦ ◦

The cars dropped them off at what looked to Piper like a random spot along the highway. She watched as the drivers turned the vehicles around and drove about fifty yards back to a small opening off the side of the road where they parked. They would wait there until Miysis and the rest of them returned.

Lyre stood beside her. He'd kept close to her since her confrontation with Seiya, not leaving any openings for another argument to erupt between them. Perhaps by mutual agreement with Lyre, Ash was staying close to Seiya, doubling the buffer.

Piper gave her head a little shake. During her two months at Westwood, she'd frequently doubted her decision to go to the school instead of staying with Ash. But if this was what it would have been like, she was glad she had made the responsible decision.

"This way," Miysis said, leading them straight into the trees.

At first, Piper thought he was walking right into the bushes, but after a few steps into the shady undergrowth, she recognized the faint trail he was following. As they walked, her nervousness grew, but at least she didn't have a blinding headache to deal with. She hoped Miysis's guess was right and Vejovis was actually at home. If he wasn't, they'd be making this long, dangerous trip for nothing. It was too bad telephones didn't exist in the Overworld. It was travel to talk to someone, or don't talk to them at all.

Ahead of her, Ash walked behind Seiya, Zwi riding on his shoulder. The dragonet usually hid when there were strangers around, but he must have told her to stay close. Otherwise no one in the group would have been able to spot her.

Ten more minutes into the forest and the trees thinned out, allowing the group to break single file. Lyre trotted up beside her, flashing her a grin when she glanced at him. Her stomach did one of those inevitable swoops; he was just that gorgeous.

"Hey, beautiful. Stop looking so glum. Aren't you the one who loves adventure?"

"I prefer my adventures to be a little less life-and-death, you know."

"All my adventures are life and death," he replied with a shrug.

She studied him, again remembering the deadly black stare in his stunning face when she'd glimpsed him without his glamour. He was only too happy to let everyone think he was a pushover. Samael's soldiers certainly hadn't had any idea how deadly he was. She would never again make the mistake of assuming he, or any daemon, was an easy foe.

He grinned mischievously. "All your adventures lately have been life and death too. Maybe secretly, that's how you like it."

She snorted.

"Is there anything else you secretly like that you want to share with me?" His tone left no question as to what sort of undisclosed preferences he was asking about.

She rolled her eyes. "*Lyre.*"

He chuckled, and they walked in silence for a few minutes before he spoke again. "So . . . want to tell me what's going on between you and Seiya?"

Piper glanced at the two draconians. They were speaking quietly and far enough ahead that they probably couldn't hear her or Lyre.

"Seiya is blaming me for Ash putting himself in danger to protect me," she whispered.

"Ah. I thought it might be something like that."

"Lyre . . ." She took a deep breath and forced the words out. "I'm afraid she might kill me to protect him."

She'd expected Lyre to scoff. Panic plunged into her belly when he nodded.

"You should be afraid."

"Are you serious?"

"Very." He leaned his head closer and lowered his voice. "Seiya isn't like Ash. They fight their battles in completely different ways."

"What do you mean?"

"Ash faces every challenge head on. If he can't plow directly through his enemies, he'll sneak up on them from behind. But when he wants something done, he goes straight for it. Although he's capable of subtlety, he's not a subtle guy."

"No, not really."

"Well, Seiya is the opposite. She learned how to get the results she wants at Samael's feet. Think about what that means."

Piper licked her lips. "She doesn't attack problems head on like Ash."

"No, she doesn't. She circles the problem and snips bits out here, cuts out bits over there, then stands back and watches as the whole thing implodes. She may be a draconian, but she is a daughter of Hades."

Piper exhaled shakily. Seiya had done a very good job of cutting the ground out from under her. First driving home that Piper and Ash didn't belong together. Then preying on Piper's desire to protect Ash from danger. Then threatening Piper's life when it became clear the first two hadn't worked. What would Seiya do next? There wasn't much left short of actual violence.

"Shit," she whispered. "Does Ash know she's so dangerous?"

Lyre's face hardened with quiet pain. "I don't know. He won't talk to me. He keeps shutting down, closing off . . . slipping into this state like . . ."

"Like Raum."

They exchanged anxious looks.

The last time Piper had seen Raum, he'd been on the floor in a pool of blood from the wounds she'd given him using the Sahar. She wasn't entirely sure whether he'd survived, but since Vejovis had been there to heal him, she was hoping he had.

Raum had been Samael's slave for his entire life, and his spirit had been broken a long time ago. He was cold, detached, and unswervingly obeyed Samael's every command. It was like his soul had died, leaving just a body to obey and a mind bereft of emotion. The thought of Ash dying inside like that terrified her.

Lyre's fingers closed around her hand, squeezing it gently. "What Seiya doesn't see," he whispered, "is that you're good for him. Since we got you back, he's been more animated and engaged than I've seen him in weeks. Have you had a chance to talk with him yet?"

She shook her head, enduring a stab of guilt.

"Don't worry. This probably isn't a good time anyway. The only thing he's worrying about right now is getting you through this."

Ahead of them, Miysis had stopped. She and Lyre joined the group in what appeared to be a random spot in the forest. Lyre kept her fingers in his, his thumb rubbing the back of her hand comfortingly as her nervousness increased.

To get to one of the other worlds, a daemon first had to enter a ley line—one of the invisible rivers of power running across the Earth, the Underworld, and the Overworld. From there, he had to jump into the Void, the empty nothingness between worlds. If he survived the Void, he would come out into another world.

Piper couldn't cross the Void on her own, so someone would have to put her to sleep and carry her through. Raum had carried her the first time. Ash had done it the second.

"Can you feel it?" Lyre whispered to her as Miysis discussed something with Ash and one of his men. "The ley line? You have magic now. You should be able to sense it."

"Me?" she whispered back in disbelief. Her? Sense a ley line?

"Close your eyes. What do you feel?"

She closed her eyes, trying to blank her mind, but she didn't have to try hard. As soon as the visual distractions around her were gone, she felt it; like an invisible canal rushing past, the ley line was impossible to ignore, a combination of the spark of magic in the atmosphere and an indescribable presence in her mind. It called to her, urging her closer. She couldn't see it or picture it in any way, but she knew it was right in front of her, just a few steps beyond where Miysis stood talking with the others.

"Wow," she whispered to Lyre, opening her eyes. She squinted at the boring stretch of trees. "Should I be able to see it too?"

"If you were a daemon, you could, but haemons can't."

"What does it look like?"

"Like a band from the northern lights running across the ground."

Her eyes widened. "Wow. Wish I could see it."

"Well, you know, they say that when two people are as one, they can see through each other's eyes. I'm totally willing to try if you want—"

"Not *now*, Lyre."

"So later then?"

Miysis looked past Ash and caught Piper's eye. He motioned her over. Her anxiety levels shot up. Lyre gave her hand one more squeeze before letting go. She warily approached Miysis. Ash stood beside him, his expression unreadable. An icy drop of fear hit her stomach as she searched his eyes. Too much like Raum.

"Piper," Miysis said, "Koen will carry you through first. My men will partner with Ashtaroth, Seiya, and Lyre to make sure they come out in the correct spot."

The ley lines on Earth and the other worlds didn't correspond geographically. You had to know what exit point you wanted, but since the Underworld daemons had never been to the Overworld before, they would need guides.

Her eyes darted from the Ra daemon beside Miysis to Ash. "Can't Ash take me through?"

"He's only done it once and my man is trained in this," Miysis said.

Ash nodded his agreement.

Her hands shook a little. She'd felt a lot better when she'd assumed Ash would take her through. She trusted him a lot more than a daemon she'd just met, even if he were more experienced than Ash.

Ash stepped closer and leaned down to put his lips to her ear. "You'll be safe with Koen. Don't worry," he whispered, his breath tickling her ear. "It would drain my magic to carry you through, and I don't know where I'm going. It's not worth the risk."

She nodded. She hadn't considered the drain on his magic stores; it would be a very bad idea for him to go into the Overworld already weakened.

She caught his wrist before he could pull away. "Ash . . . could you do the spell to make me sleep? I—I don't want anyone else messing with my head."

With a glance at Miysis for confirmation, he slid one arm around her waist to catch her when the spell took hold. His other hand cupped her cheek, warm and gentle.

"Ready?" he murmured.

"Yes," she whispered.

Her cheek tingled under his touch as soft magic spiraled through her head. Her eyelids grew heavy and slid closed. The next time she opened them, she would be in another world, but that wasn't where her thoughts lingered.

Instead, as she slumped forward and he pulled her against his chest, she wished he would hold her in his arms again, and that by holding him in hers, she could fix the damage Samael had done to his heart and soul before it was too late.

CHAPTER
-13-

PIPER sat on a rock and stared. Just stared.

The ley line Miysis had chosen in the Overworld was on the side of a mountain. Behind her, grassy slopes rose steeply before giving way to craggy rock. High, high above, the snow-tipped peak of the mountain challenged the sun in the sky.

Five yards beyond her feet, the flat stretch of grass ended. The sheer cliff dropped a hundred feet to a fast-flowing river below. She'd taken one peek over the edge before the vertigo had forced her away. She'd decided sitting was her best bet and had parked her butt on a rock.

Beyond the cliff, on the other side of the river, two more mountains rose. Miysis had already pointed out the suspected location of Vejovis's residence—at the base of the third, most distant mountain. It was a long distance to travel on foot, but there were no ley lines any closer.

The shapes of the mountains and valleys were familiar, but nothing else in this place reminded her much of home.

She felt as if she were looking at the world through blue-tinted glass. The grass had a bluish tinge, and each waxy blade was decorated with tiny bright blue dots. The rocky peaks of the mountains were veined with blue stone, some of it glittering in the sunlight and sparkling like lines of blue ice through the rock. In the valleys, she could see the tops of trees, their wide, pale leaves scattered through with azure orbs—some kind of fruit or flower? She was too far away to tell.

She looked up, squinting at the bright morning sky. Directly above, a second sun beamed down on her face. Her gaze dropped to the horizon. The curve of a planet rose beyond the farthest mountains, just breaching the horizon as it rose into the sky. It wasn't quite as large as the planet in the sky in the Underworld, but big enough. If the Overworld hadn't had two suns, it would've been dark for much of the day due to regular eclipses from the planet orbiting them. Or perhaps it was this planet orbiting the other.

Ash sat beside her, his eyes also on the slowly rising planet.

"The first time I saw it," he murmured, seeming to be reading her thoughts, "I wondered if it was the same planet. What if the Underworld and Overworld are both moons of Periskios? But there's no way to know for sure."

"Daemons have never tried to figure it out?"

"Underworld daemons don't normally visit the Overworld and vice versa. In fact, we deliberately avoid such a thing. And we don't talk to one another either. Philosophers and scientists we are not."

She squinted at him. "So you've been here before then. Why didn't you say so?"

"I didn't think it was wise to mention it around Miysis."

"Why not?"

"Because it was Samael who sent me here."

She quickly schooled her expression. Whatever Samael had sent Ash to the Overworld to do would have been something bad for the Overworlders. Definitely not a good thing to mention.

Lyre stood a half a dozen paces away, a lot nearer to the cliff's edge than Piper was willing to go. He stared across the landscape, silent with awe. Seiya stood beside him, also gazing at the beautiful world they'd found themselves in.

Miysis strode over to them. "My last man just came through. He'll stay here until we return in case we need to separate for some reason."

He turned to the valley. "We'll follow this mountain around, staying on the east side of the river. It only runs north for a few miles before bending toward the west."

He pointed, his finger tracing the path of the river. "The mountainside eventually grows too steep for travel, but there's an easy crossing where the river goes underground. We can cross without getting wet then continue through the west side of the valley. The river exits the caves a mile downstream. Beyond that is Two Dragon Falls. We'll have to rappel down along the west side; there's no other way into the valley."

Piper let out a long breath. Staying dry was a good thing on two levels: it kept them out of the ryujin's element, and she wouldn't have to admit to anyone that her swimming skills were limited to a clumsy dog-paddle. Rappelling down a mountain didn't sound all that fun though.

"After that, it should be easy travel through the base of the valley to the north end where Vejovis resides."

"The river goes under the mountain?" Piper asked. She'd been squinting at it for several minutes already, trying to figure out where the water flowed.

"Yes. There are dozens of major rivers and hundreds of smaller ones in this stretch of mountains, and most of them flow in and out of the extensive cave system beneath the mountain range. It's made mapping the valley rather difficult."

Lyre turned away from the valley. "I have a question. Why are we walking there? We have more than enough wings to fly. It would take, what, an hour or two to fly across? Versus an entire day to walk?"

Piper blinked, then remembered that Ra daemons were griffins— and griffins had wings. She and Lyre were the only members of the group who couldn't fly.

"About two centuries ago," Miysis replied, "a warlord of questionable intelligence decided that an aerial raid was a surefire strategy to exterminate the ryujin in the valley, which is sitting on the borders of five different territories. Since then, the ryujin keep close watch on the skies. They have become quite adept at shooting moving targets out of the air."

"Ah," Lyre replied. "In that case, I really don't mind walking at all. Good exercise."

"Speaking of wings," Miysis said, turning to the draconians, "I strongly recommend you keep your glamour in place while we're here. You know the consequences of releasing it."

"What consequences?" Piper asked in alarm.

"Our magic is different from Overworld magic," Ash said with a shrug. "It would attract too much attention."

"Oh."

"Definitely something to avoid," Miysis remarked. He focused on Ash. "If you do die, should we be concerned about searching your body for the Sahar?"

"Do you really think I would walk around the Overworld with the Stone in my pocket?" He looked Miysis straight in the eye. "I don't have it and I didn't bring it here."

Shadows passed across Miysis's eyes as he checked Ash's truthfulness. "A smart decision. Are we ready to begin then?"

Miysis and one of his men went first. Lyre followed, Piper trailing behind him, Ash behind her, then Seiya and the last two Ra daemons. The fourth one stayed on the narrow plateau. Piper kicked at the gravel-scattered path, watching the stones tumble down the gradual decline ahead of her. The trail was decorated with blue and brown stones in all shades, with the occasional ice-green pebble mixed in.

The track soon narrowed and grew steeper as they followed it along the side of the mountain. The slope rose steeply on her right and dropped away a few feet to her left. She tried to keep her eyes off the cliff, with the river—a shimmering, ocean-like blue distinctly different from an earthly river—rushing below. Instead, she watched Lyre's back. The sunlight glinting off his hair made it look as pale as ivory.

They walked for nearly an hour, the pace as fast as was safe on the rocky ground, before the slope gentled somewhat. A few trees had taken root among the grassy patches, with thick, twisting trunks and wide, bluish-green leaves. The azure orbs she'd seen from a distance looked like some sort of seedpod, with long trailing vines—roots, perhaps—dangling from the branches. She stared as they passed the first tree growing a dozen feet up the slope. Its roots coiled and twisted at the base, only half submerged in the turf. The trunk was covered in greyish blue moss.

The next tree, an even larger one, hung over the trail, the tendrils from the azure pods swaying in the breeze. Miysis and his man walked off the path for the first time, trudging through the calf-high grass so as to not pass under the branches. Lyre followed their route and Piper stepped off the trail too.

The ground suddenly tilted as dizziness swept over her.

Hands flying up to clutch her head, she stumbled backward, fighting for balance as the ground tried to throw her off her feet.

"Piper!" Ash's voice was sharp with warning but she couldn't even see where he was.

A hand grabbed her arm and yanked her to the side. Someone else's grip tightened on her other arm, pulling her back the other way, all while the world whirled crazily.

As quickly as it had come, the spinning stopped. Free from the dizziness, she looked up, swallowing her stomach back down. Ash held her arm, leaning away from her as though he didn't want to get too close. His grip was almost painful. She turned to see who was holding her other arm and felt the blood drain out of her face.

No one was holding her other arm. Instead, hundreds of root-like tendrils from the tree's pods were coiling around her arm, in her hair, and over her sword. Her mouth dropped open in horror. Little roots wiggled under her clothes and tickled her skin. She jerked backward and felt her feet nearly leave the ground as the elastic-like tendrils tugged her back again.

"Don't move, Piper." Miysis stopped beside Ash, his three men joining him. He assessed the tree, calm as if foliage attacked people every day.

"Keep a tight hold on her," he said to Ash. "We'll have to cut her loose."

Piper tried not to hyperventilate, her face scrunched against the burning pain in her arm where Ash was holding her back from the slow but powerful pull of the tendrils, and also against the violating touch of the roots wiggling under her shirt.

Miysis and one of his men drew their swords. Positioning themselves as close as they could without getting tangled in the tendrils too, they raised their blades, and on some silent signal, simultaneously slashed down. The blades sliced through the roots.

Ash pulled at the same time, heaving her away from the tree. A few roots clung on tenaciously, trying to drag her back. Miysis quickly cut them. Piper staggered, abruptly free. Ash helped her straighten, then began plucking the severed roots off her. She looked down, saw they were still moving, and had to choke down a horrified squeal.

Miysis sheathed his sword and started pulling roots off her back.

"Get them all," he said. "They can take days to die."

Hands shaking, she stood with her arms out while the two daemons plucked all the roots off her. While Miysis was untangling a dozen from her hair, she untucked her shirt and reached under it to pull some out of her bra. Ugh. She was never going near a tree in the Overworld again.

"I think that's all of them," Ash said, flinging the last one into the grass. "Are you okay?"

She nodded. "What the hell was that? Why did the tree tangle me up?"

"It wraps up anything that touches it." Miysis shrugged. "Dead things make good fertilizer."

She looked at him, then at the tree, eyes wide with horror.

"Well done," Seiya mocked, appearing behind Ash. "Jumping right into the tree. Are you suicidal?"

"This huge dizzy spell hit me," Piper said defensively. "I didn't mean to stumble into the tree. I didn't even know which way was up or down."

"A side effect of the rune spider venom," Miysis said. "You'll likely have recurring periods of dizziness for the rest of the day."

"I'm fine now." She shot Seiya a nasty glare. "We can keep going."

They started out again, returning to the same order. This time, Ash stayed right behind her, nearly stepping on her heels. The path narrowed and grew steeper as they descended deeper into the valley. Luckily, as there was no room to detour, no more trees hung over the path. On her right was a steep slope, nothing but grass and small, struggling plants. A foot beyond the edge of the trail on her left was a straight plunge into the raging river.

The sound of the water grew louder and louder until it was a ceaseless roar. Piper trudged after Lyre, her steps heavy. What she wouldn't give for a ten-minute break. Not that there was anywhere to stop. The adrenaline from the tree incident had left her legs shaking, but dizziness no longer threatened her balance.

Ahead of them, the mountain filled their path, curving across the river. Water boiled and frothed where it met the barricade of rock. The water had carved a small pool and the current violently swirled inside it. She could just make out the mouth of the cave where the water funneled in. The river fought the inevitable, the current whirling and crashing among the rocks as though trying to claw its way back upstream.

She didn't have a clue how Miysis intended to get them across. The path they were following meandered lower and lower down the mountainside as they approached the insurmountable obstacle of the sheer cliff blocking their way forward. She followed Lyre as they filed down the path toward the cliff face. The trail dipped until the raging current was only a dozen yards below.

They were nearly at the end of the path before Piper saw how they would be crossing. Etched into the side of the mountain was a narrow trail—little more than a crumbling ledge—that crossed the face of the cliff a few yards above the mouth of the cave. They were going to cross *there*? On that tiny ledge?

When they reached the end of the trail, Miysis turned back to face the rest of the line. The mountain rose behind him, casting its shadow across the entire valley.

"Be careful here," he shouted over the roar of the water. "The rocks are wet and slippery. Single-file. Take your time."

Piper turned to Ash. "Wouldn't it be safer to fly across this part?"

He shook his head. "Not this close to the water. Dropping glamour now would be like a beacon to the ryujin."

She swallowed hard.

"The ledge isn't as narrow as it appears from here." He took her shoulders and turned her back toward the cliff where Miysis had started across. He walked normally; he didn't have to sidle along with his back pressed to the stone wall.

"See?" Ash said in her ear. He squeezed her shoulders. "I'll be right behind you."

"Okay," she said. No one else was freaking out. She would be fine.

Pushing her shoulders back, she followed after Lyre. The rocky path turned smoothly to join the ledge. She stopped to watch Lyre take his first few steps. It wasn't that bad. The path was almost a foot and a half wide. Easy, right?

Glancing at Ash to make sure he was right behind her, she stepped onto the ledge. Resisting the urge to press her back to the cliff wall, she kept one hand on the rocky surface for balance and concentrated on putting one foot in front of the other. She kept her eyes on Lyre, who was several steps ahead of her and by all appearances unconcerned by the fifteen-foot drop to the raging waters below. She could probably survive dropping fifteen feet onto rock, but no one could survive that river.

Halfway there, she relaxed a little. Directly below her was the mouth of the cave. Weird suction noises pierced the roar of the water as it splashed against the opening. She glanced down, awed by the power of the water as it tore in swirling spirals around the small pool before vanishing beneath the mountain.

And that's when the dizziness hit.

The world spun. She didn't know which way was up or down. Her balance vanished and she pitched forward with no idea where the cliff was—or the drop to the deadly waters below.

Ash's hands clamped around her waist and he yanked her back into him. On his other side, Seiya grabbed his arm, making sure he was firmly balanced as he steadied Piper. She pressed a hand to her head, waiting for the dizziness to pass. Her heart pounded. That had been close. Taking a deep breath, she opened her eyes and found the world was steady again.

"Thanks," she said.

Ash's grip loosened. "Let's get you to the other side. Take it slow."

She cautiously stepped away from him. He kept one hand lightly on her waist as he followed directly behind her. She kept her eyes off the river and watched the ledge. Mist sprayed her face, carried by the breeze, and settled on the glittering, blue-streaked rocks in a slippery sheen. Lyre waited a few steps ahead for her to catch up before continuing toward safety. Ten feet to go.

She stepped again, and with a sudden crack of breaking rock, the ledge crumbled.

Seemingly in slow motion, she pitched sideways as the rock vanished from under her left foot, her sudden motion tearing her out of Ash's grip. Her eyes met his as she fell backward with nothing but air below her. Her mouth opened to scream.

Ash lunged for her, reaching out over empty space to grab her outstretched hand. Seiya grasped his other arm to keep him from falling over the ledge.

Ash's hand swung toward hers. She could see the perfect trajectory as though someone had drawn a diagram over the scene: her hand swinging toward his, his arching down toward hers. His hand would close securely around her wrist, her grip locking around his in turn. In the slow motion bubble of time in her head, relief swept through her.

And then Seiya yanked Ash back from the ledge.

Horror filled his eyes. His fingertips brushed hers as their hands swept past each other's.

Her bubble of slowed time popped and her scream filled her ears as she plunged into the icy river.

CHAPTER
-14-

IF PIPER had been lucky, she would have landed in the pool in front of the cave's entrance and been caught in the swirling current that spun around the bowl. It would have whisked her in a violent circle, spinning her past rocks and shattered bits of trees and other debris that had been beaten to pieces by the current. As dangerous as that would have been, it would have given Ash time to drop his glamour and sweep down on agile wings to pluck her from the water—but if she'd had any luck, she wouldn't have fallen in the first place.

She hit the water, plunged beneath its surface, and was instantly sucked into the cave.

Pitch darkness swallowed her. The current was like a giant beast all around her, throwing her one way, tossing her another. She spun in the freezing water, tumbling over and over as it whipped her around. Her head broke the surface and she gasped a panicked breath before the river pulled her down again.

Pain exploded through her thigh when she hit the first rock. The water dragged her along as it raced recklessly through the winding, night-black cave. The second rock broke her arm. A scream burst out of her, echoing off the cave walls before the current dragged her under and water filled her lungs.

Spinning, tumbling. Her head popped above the surface and she fought to keep it there as she hacked up water and gasped for air. Her stomach swooped as she was dropped over a small waterfall and pushed down to the riverbed. The current grabbed her again, whipping her downstream. Another rock, the same arm crushed. She nearly blacked out.

Another drop. Faster and faster. More rocks. Pain everywhere, chest burning. Water in her mouth, in her lungs.

She jerked to an agonizing stop.

Water pounded against her back, trying to beat her back into motion. She hacked and coughed, fighting to breathe as she clutched at the object that had stopped her. Her sword. It had caught crosswise between two rocks, too long to fit between them. She hung on to it despite the pain, the sheath digging into her hips as the water fought to push her through the gap.

She couldn't see anything. There was no light. No sound but rushing, roaring water. She had no idea how far the current had carried her.

No one could save her. The cave system was over a mile long. No one could get in the entrance without sacrificing themselves to the river as well. Even if she could get on top of one of the rocks, there was no way out.

No way out but to ride the current for a mile until she reached the other end.

"No," she wept, the roar of the water swallowing her voice. She couldn't do it. She couldn't let the water take her again and—

Her sword slipped on the slick rock and she plunged back into the current.

It whipped her into motion. She hit another rock. Agony exploded in her hip. Another drop over a small waterfall. Swirling, tearing water. Burning pain in her chest. Water in her lungs, mouth, stomach, eyes. Freezing cold. Her limbs had gone numb.

She spun and spun. It went on forever. Every time it seemed as though she would surely drown as the water summersaulted her beneath the surface, spinning and whirling, the current would push her back up at the last second and she would gasp in a few precious breaths before another current pulled her down, another rock smashed her body, or another waterfall plunged her into its depths.

Whirling, spinning, tumbling. And then, suddenly, sunlight blasted her face. The echoing roar of the water in the caves changed as fresh air swept into her lungs. The swirling current smoothed, rushing forward in a straight path. No more rocks. No more deadly twists and turns or boiling, frothing currents.

She was out of the cave. Somehow her head was above water. Rocky shores sped by on either side. She tried to move her limbs, to swim for the shore, but her arms and legs wouldn't work. Numb from the icy mountain water, she couldn't feel them. She spun slowly, not understanding why she wasn't sinking.

As she turned in the racing water, she saw it. Ahead of her. Closing fast.

The horizon.

The river ended at nothing.

And then she heard it—the waterfall. It must be Two Dragon Falls.

The water rushed toward the cliff, carrying her helplessly along with it. She couldn't escape. She could barely keep her head up. The current spun her in another circle, turning her away from the terrifying sight that awaited her. The mountain rose behind her. Somewhere on the other side, Ash and the others were probably heading back to the ley line. They had no reason to continue their journey without her.

She stared at a black blot in the sky for several seconds.

Wings.

Black wings pumping fast. The spot grew larger. Impossible. Ash? It had to be him. Then she remembered the leather strap around her wrist, the buckle infused with Ash's tracking spell. He'd flown *over* the mountain to find her—probably expecting to pull her battered body from the cave's exit.

Instead, he would be fishing her broken body from the bottom of the waterfall.

He shot toward her. The river carried her toward the cliff. She tried again to kick her legs but dull pain met her efforts. The current continued to spin her, turning her again to face the fast-approaching drop. The water picked up speed. The roar filled her ears, filled her head. Ash was too far. Whatever lingering willpower had kept her head above water finally failed her. She slipped beneath the surface, sinking into icy darkness.

Ash plunged into the water and his arms closed around her. He heaved her up. Her face broke the surface. They swirled together in the river. The edge was right there. Ash couldn't take flight from the water. He clutched her to him as the world turned to roaring white.

They plunged over the edge.

Ash's arms crushed her. Freezing air hit her soaked clothing as they free fell alongside the plummeting water. Then Ash's wings opened, catching the air, and they were soaring away from the waterfall.

She hung in his arms with no will to move. He was safe. He hadn't died with her. She was so happy he was safe.

Cliff walls disappeared. Ash descended toward the valley floor—toward the forest of blue-green things. He swept into the first clear spot, a little opening beside a quiet pool off the main flow of the channel. He landed and immediately knelt to lay her gently on the soft moss. He shimmered back into glamour, his wings disappearing.

"Piper?" he said hoarsely. His chest heaved as he fought to catch his breath. "Piper?"

His hands touched her face, so very gentle. "Piper, say something."

She tried. All that came out was a wheeze. Even though she was out of the water, it was hard to breathe. She still felt as though she were drowning. Her body wouldn't move. There was no strength left in her limbs. But she felt no pain. Just cold.

He ran his hands over her shoulders, checking for damage, then grabbed her shirt and pulled, popping buttons off to reveal her stomach. His hands hovered over her without touching her.

"No," he moaned.

Faint pain in her middle as he lightly pressed on her ribs.

"I—I can't heal this," he whispered. "I don't even know where to start. You—you're—" His voice broke. He returned to her face, his hands gently touching her cheeks. "I'm sorry. I can't fix you. I'm so sorry."

She wanted to tell him it was okay. It wasn't his fault; he wasn't a good healer and so many things in her were broken. But her voice wouldn't work. It was so hard to breathe. Each weak inhale gurgled in her lungs. A rasp escaped her as she tried to find her voice.

He stroked her cheek. "Shh. I'm here. I won't leave you."

She managed to smile, trying to tell him it was okay. It didn't hurt.

He sucked in a breath and bent over her, eyes squeezed shut against his inner agony. It wasn't fair. Why did he have to endure so much pain when she felt nothing? She couldn't stand to see him suffer. Her eyes slid closed, dimming the painful light of the sun.

"I can't believe you made it through the caves," he whispered, thumbs stroking her cheeks, his forehead lightly touching hers. "When I saw you come out the other side, I thought maybe you were—you were okay—but—" He broke off, the words strangled in his throat. "I'm sorry. I'm so sorry."

A weak, wet breath sighed from her lungs.

"Piper," he whispered brokenly. His lips touched her forehead, then brushed across her mouth.

If she could have captured one feeling to take with her, it would have been the touch of his lips on hers.

Darkness closed in, pulling her gently into its embrace. If this was dying, it wasn't that bad. No pain. Ash's fingers were warm on her cheek. He would stay with her. She wouldn't be alone. She could slip peacefully into sleep—

Ash jerked, the sudden movement jarring her body. Pain ricocheted through her limbs. She gasped, her lungs gurgling. Her eyes opened.

Ash leaned over her, a hand still on her cheek, but his gaze was on something beyond her—on the river. His eyes had gone black.

With the last bit of strength she had, she rolled her head to one side to look.

In the deep, calm pool, sheltered from the rushing river and shaded by overhanging trees, something moved in the water. Ripples disturbed the surface, then a pale flash just beneath.

A creature rose out of the pool, a head first, followed by a long, snake-like neck. The reptilian head was delicate and graceful, large sea-blue eyes framed by fins on either side of its head. Pale scales covered its body, shimmering with every shade of blue, teal, and green imaginable.

A water dragon.

Its back arched out of the water, a spiked fin running along its spine. Its head tilted as it studied them. Two foot-long tentacles—she didn't know how else to describe the long, sinuous appendages that swept back from it forehead—undulated slowly as though it were thinking. It was without doubt the most beautiful creature she'd ever seen. She wanted to run her fingers over those iridescent scales. It seemed so close to them, but it really wasn't; it was just large—and deadly.

The surface rippled again. A second dragon raised its head, shaking the water off in a spray that sprinkled Piper's face. Ash tensed further. He was in danger. He needed to get away. But he wouldn't leave her, not while she still drew breath—but that wouldn't be for long.

Once more, the water rippled. A third creature broke the surface and rose, dripping, in front of the two dragons. But this one was not a dragon.

Long hair of an impossible deep bluish green fell to his waist. Fins in place of ears. Dark eyes with no discernible whites. His shape was largely human, but his pale skin, almost white, shimmered strangely. Over his shoulders, down his arms, in a line down the center of his belly—all over him were iridescent scales that glimmered like mother of pearl, greens, blues, teals, purples.

There was only one thing the creature could be: a ryujin.

And still Ash crouched protectively over her. Fool. Idiot. The ryujin studied him with strange, dark eyes. Three scales shaped like teardrops glowed on his forehead. He was going to kill Ash. Ash was an Underworld daemon in the territory of a fiercely aggressive Overworld caste. The ryujin and his dragons would rip him apart.

But Ash wasn't moving.

The ryujin took a slow step closer. Piper tore her eyes from the creature to look at Ash, adrenaline slightly clearing her head. Ash leaned over her, but his expression had gone blank. Empty. He stared ahead, eyes out of focus, no longer seeing the ryujin in front of him.

The creature reached across Piper and grabbed Ash's chin, pulling his head up to peer into his face. Ash didn't react, lost to some kind of trance. He just knelt there, unseeing eyes looking right through his enemy.

Still holding Ash's chin, the ryujin's other hand came up. Blue magic gathered in his palm, crackling dangerously. A lethal spell. The ryujin was preparing to kill him. Trapped by the creature's hypnotizing magic, Ash didn't even know it.

Panic surged through her but her limbs wouldn't move. The ryujin drew his hand back to strike.

"No!" The scream burst out of her, tearing her brutalized throat as though a knife had been shoved down her windpipe.

The ryujin jolted, startled eyes dropping to her. At the same time, Ash gave his head a rough shake, the trance broken either by her scream or the ryujin's interrupted concentration. Her outcry had used up the last of her strength. Blackness closed around her vision, forming a dark tunnel as her fear disappeared in a numb haze.

The ryujin raised both hands, blue magic crackling over his fingers. Ash surged to his feet, black magic dancing across his palms as he called up a spell of his own.

Darkness closed over Piper, and she knew nothing more.

o   o   o

Air swept into her lungs. It whooshed out. Inhale. Exhale. Her lungs expanded, deflated, expanded again with each flex of her diaphragm. It felt wonderful.

Insistent little thoughts poked at her sleeping brain, telling her to wake up. She felt as though she were coming out of the deepest slumber imaginable, sleep still clinging to her like an impossibly heavy embrace. Groggily, she listened to her own breathing, quietly amazed. She remembered struggling to breathe and the suffocating feeling that there was no room left in her lungs for air. Then she remembered the surging, crushing current of the river, the utter darkness of the caves, the terror and pain.

Adrenaline sparked in her blood and her eyes popped open.

Someone was leaning over her.

Dark eyes with no whites. Pale skin. Patterns of iridescent blue and green scales. The ryujin. She pressed into the mossy ground, unable to move away. Her hazy thoughts tried to untangle themselves, to sort out her last pain-obscured memories, but all she knew for sure was that she was in danger.

He studied her, by all appearances utterly calm. She could almost feel the serenity radiating off of him—but that made no sense. The ryujin were vicious and violent. Why hadn't he killed her yet? Was he waiting for her injuries to finish her off?

She drew in another deep breath. No gurgle in her chest. No numbness in her limbs. She flexed her fingers. No pain. She looked at her hand and remembered the deadly sphere of magic in the ryujin's palm as he prepared to kill Ash.

Ash! Panic flaring, she rolled away from the ryujin, intending to spring to her feet. Her muscles didn't cooperate and she ended up on her hands and knees as the world whirled in a dizzying circle. As soon as it steadied, she scrambled up and staggered back a couple of steps. She turned, searching, and came nose-to-nose with a water dragon.

She gasped and lurched back. It watched her with its sea-blue eye, the strange appendages on its head undulating slowly. It had been so still and silent that she hadn't noticed it, even though it was huge. Not as heavy as Zwi in dragon form, but lithe and long-bodied. Even lying down, its head was at the same level as hers. Its forehead had the same three-teardrop pattern of darker scales as the ryujin. Its snaking tail ended in a beautiful, elaborate double fin.

She looked past the dragon and to the little clearing beyond. A dozen feet away, Ash lay half on his side, unmoving, eyes closed.

Two huge silvery dragons lounged on either side of him, the tear-drop scales on their foreheads glowing.

"Ash!" she cried. She ran around the nearer dragon and rushed to his side. She dropped to her knees. "Ash, can you hear me? Are you okay?"

She shook his shoulder. He didn't so much as stir. She ran her hands over his head, searching for an injury—nothing. He didn't appear hurt at all, so why wasn't he waking up?

Fighting terror, she turned. The ryujin was walking toward her, unhurried, almost casual. He moved like water, flowing from step to step, his body shimmering as the sun danced across his pearly scales. He wore almost nothing, just a fitted garment similar to shorts, decorated with uncut stones that glittered in the sun. A long tail ending in a double fin, just like the water dragons', trailed behind him. And like the water dragons, he had the same strange appendages, not really tentacles but something similar, that drifted like decorative feathers, four long ones starting from the base of his tail and one behind each fin-like ear.

He was coming toward her and Ash—to finish Ash off? She grabbed the hilt of her sword, but the blade had been bent when she'd hit the rocks; it wouldn't come free from the sheath. With no better option, she pulled a dagger from the sheath on her thigh and raised it threateningly as the ryujin approached.

He walked up to her, reached out, and plucked the dagger from her hand.

She stared at him, dazed. A strange buzzing had filled her head, drowning out her thoughts. Sluggishly, she wondered what her plan had been. She'd had a plan, hadn't she? She needed to defend Ash, but she couldn't remember how. She couldn't remember how to make her muscles move. All she could do was stand there, staring at the daemon.

The buzzing in her head disappeared and panic swept in to take its place. She stumbled away from the ryujin and tripped over Ash's prone form behind her. She fell backward, landing on her butt with her legs on top of Ash.

The ryujin calmly tossed her dagger into the bushes.

Piper tried to slow her breathing. He'd done it to her—the same thing he'd done to Ash. The trance. That inexplicable hypnosis that had made them both freeze in place, unresisting. She and Ash had both been helpless. She glanced at Ash, who was still mysteriously unconscious.

"W-what did you do to him?" she demanded, her voice high. Demanding answers from a creature that was probably planning to kill her—was she insane? She thought about pulling another dagger but was certain he would just put her in another trance.

The ryujin tilted his head to one side. "He merely sleeps."

His voice was soft and husky, the deep tones tinged by a strange accent. She tensed as he crouched beside her and looked down at Ash then back to her. The teardrop scales on his forehead glowed faintly with his magic.

"He's sleeping?" She was shocked that he'd actually answered. She looked nervously at the two dragons lying on either side of them like silver sentinels. "Are they forcing him to sleep?"

The ryujin didn't answer. He studied her for several long seconds. "Is he yours?"

"Is he—what? Ash? Yes, he—he's my friend," she stuttered. "Will—will you wake him up?"

Again ignoring her question, the ryujin flowed to his feet.

"Wait, you have to wake him up!" She hurried to get up as he turned away from her. "Hold on!"

The ryujin moved toward the river. Piper rushed after him. What if the sleeping spell on Ash was permanent? What if he never woke up?

"Wait!" she yelled.

The ryujin stepped off the rocky shore and into two-foot-deep water. The water in the pool suddenly stilled, the current vanishing. Instead of sparkling ripples, he walked through a sheet of glass, a perfect mirror reflecting the sky above.

She stopped on the last of the rocks. "Did you heal me?"

He stopped. Pivoting to face her, he tilted his head to the side.

"When you are ready, we will be waiting for you."

He turned and dove into the water. He barely disturbed the surface as he disappeared beneath it. She stared at the faint ripples, then jerked in surprise as the three massive dragons appeared out of nowhere, flowing past her on either side, and splashed into the pool. With fluid, flexible bodies and graceful flicks of their finned tails, they too vanished into the water.

She stared at the spot where the ryujin had disappeared. It had to have been him. Who else could have healed her? And why hadn't he killed her or Ash? She was sure he'd been about to kill Ash when she'd screamed. Shaking her head, she spun away from the quiet pool and ran back to Ash.

Dropping to her knees beside him, she touched his shoulder. "Ash? Ash?"

His eyelids flickered and slowly opened. Hazy grey eyes met hers. His gaze darted over her face, brow furrowing. She gave him a trembling smile as relief rushed through her.

"Ash, are you okay?"

He lifted a hand and touched her cheek. She went still as he stared at her.

"You died," he whispered.

She let out a shaky breath. "No, I *almost* died. But I'm fine now. All healed. See?"

She held out her arms. Her shirt, held closed over her bra by two remaining buttons, hung open, baring her unharmed stomach. She didn't know what Ash had seen when he'd pulled her shirt open the first time, but judging by his reaction, it must have looked gruesome.

His gaze slid down to check her torso for injuries before flashing back up to her face. The haziness was fading from his eyes as they sharpened—and darkened. His hand was still resting against her cheek, the muscles in his arm taut.

She frowned. "Ash, I'm fine, I swear," she insisted, trying to sound soothing. "I'm not dying and the ryujin is gone and—"

His hand slid from her cheek to the back of her neck and tightened. He pulled her down with inescapable strength, and then her mouth was on his.

The kiss wasn't the carnal, aggressive kind they'd shared before. It was slow, intense, gentle but somehow challenging. Her hands found their way to his face, fingers tracing his jaw as his lips moved against hers. He held her in place with one hand, not giving her the option of pulling away—not that she tried—while his other slid over the small of her back, hot against her skin.

Only when dizziness threatened from her shortness of breath did he allow her to raise her head and gasp for air. She brushed her fingers over his cheek and stared into dark eyes that weren't quite shaded to black.

"Stop doing this to me," he whispered, voice husky. "I can't take it anymore."

"Take what?"

"You dying. How many times are you going to die on me?"

She huffed. "I'm not doing it on purpo—"

He pulled her back into another kiss. She sprawled across his chest, weak from the warmth rushing through her. He kissed her, slowly, precisely, with the same intense determination she'd seen him take into battle, until her body tingled with leisurely tides of heat.

Their prior intimacy had been all passion and hunger, driving desire that made her pant with desperate need for him. But this was different. Deeper. More powerful. This wasn't lust. This time, the heat came from within her, from within him, intense and passionate but so much more. This time, the need to just hold him, touch him, kiss him without ever moving again overwhelmed her.

An animal squeal erupted above them.

Jarred out of her dreamlike obliviousness, Piper jerked her head up in time to see Zwi swooping in. She landed right on top of Piper's head, wings flapping against her face as the dragonet chittered ecstatically. Piper sat up and Zwi jumped into her lap, nuzzling her stomach and squirming in delight. Grinning, she pulled Zwi close and petted the dragonet's back. Zwi cooed, tail flicking all around as if she couldn't keep still.

Ash pushed himself up. "Zwi is happy you're okay," he murmured. He looked around at the clearing. "How *are* you okay, actually?"

"Now you ask?" she asked with raised eyebrows.

"I was getting around to it."

Her smile faded as confused wonder whispered through her. She looked toward the water. "The ryujin healed me."

She turned back to find him staring at the water as well.

"But . . . why?" he asked.

"I don't know. But he didn't seem to want to hurt me."

"He sure seemed intent on hurting *me*."

She cleared her throat. "I think he *was* planning to kill you, and then . . . I don't know. He must have changed his mind. He put you in some kind of trance, and then put you to sleep."

He slowly nodded. "I remember the trance, and your scream, but nothing after that."

"He did the trance thing to me too. What kind of magic is that?"

"I'm not sure. It wasn't a paralysis spell; he would have had to touch me first, and I know how to defend against it." He paused. "I think it was some kind of telepathy."

"Telepathy?" she repeated in disbelief.

Telepathy as a caste ability was nothing more than a rumor. The closest thing she'd ever seen was the draconian/dragonet bond, and that was a limited connection between each pair. As far as she knew, no caste in either the Overworld or Underworld had been confirmed as having telepathic abilities.

"Do you think he can read our minds?"

"I have no idea. Either way, that hypnosis ability will be hard to fight."

"I'm not sure we need to fight it—or them," she said. "Maybe they only have bad reputations because other castes keep trying to steal their territory. Why else would he have healed me? He had no reason to. What if he read my mind and knew we weren't here to harm them?"

Ash shook his head. "Either way, you're damn lucky. Your injuries were so severe . . . Vejovis himself would have been hard pressed to heal you in time. I have no idea how that ryujin did it."

As he spoke, his eyes travelled over her face with a desperate sort of hunger—not desire, but the need to reaffirm she was really alive.

Slowly, hesitating, she leaned toward him. Yes, they'd just kissed. Yes, she'd kissed him before. But aside from that first kiss in the Styx's ring, he'd been the initiator, and she wasn't sure about anything anymore. The ground beneath her feet was crumbling away, and all she knew was that she desperately wanted to feel his mouth on hers again.

She hesitated just shy of touching him, his breath warm against her lips. Half-expecting to be rejected, she brushed her lips over his. His hand came up to cup her cheek, and he gently pulled her mouth back onto his. Another light brush of lips. Then he pressed his mouth harder, deepening the kiss. Heat rushed through her and she reached to wind her arms around his neck, pressing close to him. Zwi let out an angry squawk.

Piper jerked back. Zwi shook her mane out and rustled her wings, giving them reproving glares for having squashed her.

"Sorry, Zwi," she said contritely.

Zwi chirped, though Piper wasn't sure whether the sound meant forgiveness or a warning not to do it again.

Ash rose to his feet and stretched, then held out a hand. Scooping Zwi up to her shoulder, Piper took his hand and let him draw her up off the ground. As soon as she was on her feet, she swayed dangerously, the world tilting strangely. Ash wrapped an arm around her waist to steady her.

"What's wrong?"

She opened her mouth to answer and a huge yawn overcame her. "I'm suddenly so tired I can barely stand." Her legs felt like jelly in the aftermath of all the adrenaline.

"That's normal after major healing. Are you up for walking?"

"Ah. Not really. I'd be back on the ground if you weren't holding me."

"I see. In that case . . ."

He turned and crouched, presenting her with his back. She put her arms around his neck, and he hooked his arms under her legs and stood. She laid her head on his shoulder and let out a long sigh. His clothes were still damp from the river but his back was warm.

Closing her eyes, she relaxed as he walked, his steps smooth and his strong arms holding her in place with no effort on her part.

The ryujin's parting words whispered through her head. When she was ready . . . Ready for what? And why would they be waiting? Maybe the problem with the ryujin wasn't that they were vicious, but that they were crazy.

Putting the whole thing out of her mind, she snuggled against Ash and let the motion of his stride lull her to sleep.

CHAPTER
-15-

EXHAUSTION lay over her like a heavy blanket. She drifted in and out of consciousness, returning to fuzzy awareness only to drift away again. Healing major injuries was a huge drain on the body. After his near-death experiences and subsequent healings, Ash had slept for an entire day each time. It was no wonder she couldn't fully wake up.

The first time she remembered stirring awake was when Ash had found the others. The shouts and disbelieving exclamations had been unpleasantly loud, though they'd soon died off. She came around several more times just to reassure herself that Ash was still carrying her, his back warm and his mountain-air scent comforting. Then she would go back to sleep again.

By the time the exhaustion finally began to lift, she sensed a significant amount of time had passed. Ash was still walking, the motion rocking her gently. Her eyelids fluttered, letting in the dim evening light from a setting sun beyond the tree line. She let out a silent sigh, still limp and weary.

"It just doesn't make sense," Lyre's voice murmured from somewhere to her left. "Why would a ryujin heal her?"

"I don't understand it either," Ash replied, his voice low. Either they were trying not to wake her, or they didn't want anyone to overhear their conversation.

Too tired to move, she listened to them talk.

"He was going to kill me," Ash continued. "He would have succeeded too. I was defenseless." A growl crept into his voice on the last part.

"Why didn't Miysis warn us about the telepathy? Unless he didn't know?"

"I suspect he knows more about the ryujin than he's letting on," Ash murmured, that hint of a growl still roughening his voice. "He's far too knowledgeable about their territory for casual study. He mentioned mapping it. You know the Ra territory shares a border with ryujin land."

"Do you think they're planning an invasion?"

"I'm not very familiar with Overworld geography, but I believe the ryujin territory is the key to controlling trade between the northern and southern halves of the continent. No doubt the Ras want it."

Lyre snorted. "That would explain why the ryujin are so damn territorial." A pause. "Which, again, makes me wonder what the hell that one wants with Piper."

"Maybe they want her for the same reason as everyone else."

"The Sahar? But how would they know about that?"

"No idea. But nothing else makes sense. Maybe he saved her—and didn't kill me—to win her over. I'm just glad I was there. He could have disappeared with her without us ever knowing she hadn't drowned."

"Speaking of that . . . I gotta ask, man," Lyre said hesitantly. "When Piper fell . . . have you considered that Seiya—"

"She didn't."

"Those rocks broke away *right* when Piper stepped—"

"It was a coincidence."

"A coincidence that the ledge broke under Piper and not any of the heavier men who went across before her? Seiya has—"

"I would have sensed her magic," Ash snapped. "She was right behind me. And how would she have set a spell beforehand? She was with us the whole time."

"You have to admit it's suspicious."

"Suspicious or not, it isn't possible. I would have noticed. It's more likely that one of the Ras set a trap."

"Why would a Ra want Piper dead? Seiya is the only one who has a problem with her."

Ash made a sound of anger and exasperation. "*Why* does she have a problem? Nothing I say makes a difference."

"Well, I already told you my theory."

"Yes," Ash said acidly. "I know."

"I warned you something like this might happen."

Ash growled.

Lyre pressed on. "Seiya is too strong for Piper. If you let this go on, Piper might not survive."

"Seiya did *not* make Piper fall."

"Maybe she didn't," Lyre said softly, "but you know it's her fault you weren't able to grab Piper in time."

"She was just trying to keep me from falling in too. She overreacted."

"You have wings, Ash. You can't fall anywhere."

The silence stretched between them.

"I know she's just trying to protect you," Lyre finally murmured, sympathy in his voice, "but you can't protect Piper from her."

Ash grunted.

Lyre lowered his voice. "You know what you have to do, right?"

A heartbeat of silence. "Yeah."

"I'm sorry, man."

They walked in silence. Wide-awake by this point, Piper did her best to feign sleep. Anxiety churned in her stomach at the things she'd overheard—mainly the possibility that Seiya had tried to kill her, and would keep on trying until she eliminated her as a threat.

Lyre's voice broke the silence again. "You should go talk to Seiya. Do you want me to take Piper?"

"Yeah, I guess."

Piper had to work to hang limply while the two guys switched her from Ash's back to Lyre's. Once she was settled, she cracked her eyelids open and saw Seiya a dozen yards ahead, walking alone. Beyond her, Miysis and two of his men were leading them through a lush forest. The murmur of the river was nearly lost to the rustle of leaves in the breeze.

Ash strode ahead of Lyre and caught up to his sister. Piper saw him bend his head toward her, mouth moving with unheard words.

She licked her lips, nervousness churning inside her. "What does Ash have to do?" she whispered.

Lyre jumped about a foot in the air, nearly dropping her. "Holy crap, Piper!" he yelped. "I thought you were asleep."

"Sorry."

He took a few deep breaths. "Trying to give me a heart attack? Jeez."

"So? You told Ash he knew what he had to do. What's that?"

Lyre grunted. "That conversation was none of your business. You shouldn't have pretended to be sleeping."

"It's my business if Seiya is trying to kill me." Betrayal burned in the pit of her stomach. "How can Ash defend her?"

"One, because she's his sister and he loves her. Two, there's no proof and of course he doesn't want to think the worst of her. And three, she's been the prisoner of a violent, sadistic madman for her entire life and only escaped two months ago. That's not a fast or easy adjustment. She came from a world where *everything* was life or death and you had to kill to survive."

"Ash was a prisoner too and he's not trying to kill people left and right."

"He has his hang-ups too. I'm sure you've figured out why he can't stand enclosed spaces. You were in those cells yourself."

She shuddered. The cells of the bastille in Asphodel were small, dark, freezing cold, and underground. She wondered how many days Ash had spent down there.

"Ash got out of Asphodel way more often than Seiya did. He saw other places and other worlds where not everything was a threat to be destroyed and not everyone was out to get him. Seiya is still learning the difference. It's going to take time to retrain her instincts."

"But—"

"She's alive right now," Lyre said firmly, "because she was tough enough and hard enough to destroy those who threatened her and Ash. Do you really expect her to just ignore things she perceives as threats because she's outside of Asphodel? In Asphodel, she knew the rules. Now, she doesn't know. She's going to do everything she can to make sure she and Ash can live to enjoy their freedom. My suspicions aside, we don't actually know if she did anything to cause your fall."

Piper scowled but didn't argue. Put that way, she could kind of understand where Seiya was coming from. The girl didn't know any other life than one where she had to destroy her enemies before they destroyed her—not that that made trying to kill Piper okay. And even if Seiya hadn't made her fall, it was Seiya's fault that Ash didn't catch her.

"So what does Ash need to do?" she asked again.

Lyre sighed as though he'd hoped she'd forgotten. "Isn't it obvious? He can't be around you and Seiya at the same time. As soon as we're out of the Overworld, he needs to take Seiya far away from you. He's talking to her now. If he can convince her to calm down until we're out of here, you might live to see Earth again."

Piper's heart squeezed. Ash was going to leave her. He was going to take Seiya and leave again. The memory of his kiss, its slow burning intensity, rose in her mind. The hoarse pain in his voice when he'd promise not to leave her as she lay dying. The look in his eyes when he'd woken and seen she was alive.

And he was planning to walk away . . . again.

Her hands clenched around fistfuls of Lyre's shirt. Rejection lanced her, leaving burning lacerations across her heart even as she berated herself for such a reaction. What choice did Ash have? Nothing he said could change Seiya's mind; if she had to betray Ash to protect him, she would. He had to leave for Piper's safety. Piper didn't expect, and would never ask, him to abandon his sister to stay with her. Of course not. She would be furious with him if he tried. What did he owe Piper over his flesh and blood sister?

Again, the memory of that kiss filled her mind.

She tugged Lyre's shoulder. "I can walk now."

He loosened his arms, letting her slide down. She landed on her feet and steadied after a moment of wobbly weakness. Stretching her arms over her head, she leaned back until her back popped.

"Mmm," Lyre purred. "You should do that again."

She dropped her arms, blinking, then realized her shirt was hanging open, baring a long strip of her stomach. She grabbed the bottom ends of her shirt and tied them in a knot, hiding half of her stomach. Nothing she could do about the rest.

"That's a good look too. Or you could just take it off."

"Not happening."

He gave a long-suffering sigh.

She fell in step beside him, trying to ignore the sight of Ash and Seiya conversing ahead. Ash was still bent toward her, and he gestured angrily as he spoke. Seiya flipped her ponytail over her shoulder and made an equally irate gesture in Piper's general direction. Looking away from them, Piper silently took in the forest around her. High above, the thick canopy of leaves blocked the remaining sunlight, covering the forest floor in shadows, but it wasn't entirely dark. Scattered throughout the trees, those azure pods with the deadly tendrils glowed faintly in the dim light. Tiny insects, glowing their own shades of purple and violet, fluttered around the glowing orbs, drawn by the light.

The roots of the huge trees crawled along the forest floor, creating barriers across the path and bridges that arched over them. She was amazed she'd slept as long as she had, given how the path went up, over, under, and around the twisting roots, some as thick around as her shoulders. The pale moss she'd seen before was everywhere here, and though it didn't quite glow, it shimmered in the faint light. This was a forest that would never truly be dark.

As they climbed over a gnarled cluster of roots, she looked at Lyre again. "So you guys think that the ryujin wants me for the Sahar?"

"Is there *any* part of our conversation you didn't eavesdrop on?"

She shrugged. "Don't have private conversations while I'm right there then."

He scowled. She smiled.

Rolling his eyes, he shoved his hands into his pockets. "We're just guessing. I really don't see how the ryujin could know about that. They don't have spies or communication channels outside of their territory—not from what I understand, anyway."

"Huh." The ryujin's comment about waiting until she was ready didn't offer any clues either.

"How are you feeling?" he asked.

"Still kind of tired, but not too bad." She glanced at the sky, looking for the glow of the sun above the tree line. The forest seemed to go on forever all around them, with shadows stretching across their pathway. She frowned.

"If this territory is so dangerous, why are there walking paths?"

"I wondered the same thing," Lyre said. "Koen said there are a few brave smugglers who'd rather risk the ryujin than pay the Ra taxes for transporting goods across their border."

"Must be some serious taxes. I wonder what the Ra territory is like."

"A lot less wild than this one, I imagine."

Someone up ahead whistled. Ash and Seiya had joined Miysis and his men, who'd stopped where the trail curved to the northwest. Piper and Lyre broke into jogs at the same time, rushing to catch up. As they joined the others, Piper accidentally caught Seiya's eye. The draconian girl looked at her coldly, but her expression was unreadable. Swallowing hard, Piper turned to Miysis.

"Vejovis's cabin is about half a mile northeast of here through the forest," he said quietly, green eyes glinting in the dim light. "There's no trail, but Koen went ahead and scouted the surrounding area. There are signs of multiple people entering and exiting the cabin."

"What?" Piper shook her head. "Why would there be other people here? Isn't the location of his home a secret?"

"It is."

"Could it be some ryujin?" Lyre asked.

"Ryujin don't wear boots."

A long moment of silence as they all looked at one another.

"It could be a trap," Miysis finally said. "We'll have to approach carefully. Koen and—"

"Me," Ash interjected.

"Koen and *Ash* will go in while the rest of us wait here. Koen will give a signal if it's safe to approach."

Ash and Koen nodded to each other, quickly signaled their intended directions, and split up, disappearing into the trees. Piper squinted through the foliage but couldn't make anything out. Vejovis's home was well hidden. She bit her lip. If Samael had found it, the healer might have gone somewhere else to hide and they would never find him in time.

They stood in tense silence. The minutes ticked by. Piper pointedly ignored Seiya, feeling the girl's icy glare burning the back of her head every minute or two. Ash was taking risks again for Piper, volunteering to scope out a possibly booby-trapped cabin; Seiya's anger saturated the air.

Piper was just about ready to demand they go look themselves when Ash and Koen appeared out of the trees, Ash a step behind the Ra daemon. There was no one else with them.

"Well?" Miysis asked tersely.

Piper stared at Ash, his eyes black and jaw clenched.

Koen answered, his voice heavy.

"Vejovis was there. He's dead."

CHAPTER

-16-

PIPER sat on a thick, moss-covered root, her face in her hands. Lyre sat beside her, a hand on her shoulder. Ash leaned against a nearby tree, staring off in the darkness as his jaw flexed.

Dead. Of all the possible outcomes in their search for Vejovis, that was one she hadn't considered. Vejovis was a legend. Immortal, or close to it. He'd probably been around at least as long as the Sahar had. He couldn't be dead.

Koen had explained that they'd found the interior of the cabin destroyed by a fierce struggle. Vejovis's body had been sprawled in the main room, showing distinct signs of brutal violence, and he'd been dead for at least three weeks. Ash had refused to let her anywhere near the cabin to confirm for herself. Not that she wanted to see the body, but she just couldn't believe that Vejovis had been murdered. His home hadn't been as safe from Hades assassins as he'd thought.

Although she hadn't known Vejovis well, sorrow still weighed on her. But far more prevalent was the choking, twisting anxiety that bordered on panic. Vejovis had been her best chance at resealing her magic. Possibly her only chance. The rune spider's venom would wear off within the next day, and the horrific pain would return. The seizures would begin shortly after. Maybe another few days before the seizures did permanent damage. She would be dead within a week.

"Miysis is going to call in his best healers," Lyre murmured. "They'll be able to help, I'm sure. Maybe not fix your magic, but at least delay it until we find a solution."

Piper nodded numbly, glancing toward the unseen cabin. Miysis and his men were digging a grave to lay Vejovis to rest with dignity. Well, Miysis's *men* were digging. Miysis was probably supervising. He wasn't the manual labor type.

"We'll figure something out," Lyre went on, the comforting words ruined by the note of desperation in his voice. "We'll get you through this."

She nodded again. Ash didn't move, his jaw clenching and unclenching. It had to be driving him crazy that there was nothing he could do to help her. He couldn't even fly her back to the ley line to get her home faster; her next best bet was Miysis's healers, so beating Miysis back wouldn't do her any good.

She wished they could leave. Just sitting here made her want to scream, but the last rays of sunlight were disappearing behind the mountains. According to Miysis, it was too dangerous to travel at night. The path was treacherous, and lighting their way would attract all sorts of unpleasant attention, from both the natural predators of the area and the ryujin. No one, not even Piper, trusted that a second encounter with the ryujin would go as well as the first. There was no way to know if the one ryujin she'd met had been the norm or an exception to the caste's violent reputation. Miysis had decided they would camp among the trees for the night. Piper didn't expect to sleep.

A little ways away, Seiya reclined against a tree, Zala in her lap. She'd taken Piper completely by surprise by saying how sorry she was that the healer wouldn't be able to help her. Piper didn't know whether she believed Seiya's apparent sincerity.

She rubbed both hands over her face. So many emotions were jammed inside her that none of them could get out, leaving her outwardly calm while panic whirled around in her head. Her chances of survival had dropped to single digit percentages now. And the most painful wound of all came from knowing that it was her mother's fault that she was probably going to die. She'd been planning to find her father and uncle as soon as she got back; they still thought she'd died in the Consulate explosion. But maybe it would be kinder to let them continue to believe that she was dead. She couldn't even imagine their reactions to the news that she'd died because of her mother's crazed ambitions.

The first tears welled in her eyes at the agony of the betrayal. She blinked them back.

"We should start planning," Lyre said, still trying to hide his apprehension. "You know the names of these hybrid women, right Piper? I can search for records on them while you go to the Gaians for information."

She pulled in a deep breath and let it out. "Yeah, there were three. Calanthe Nike—no, Nikas. And Raina . . . G-something. Umm. Golkin? Glovin?"

"Golovkin?" Lyre guessed.

"Yeah, that's it."

"And the third?"

"Um, Natania something. Natania . . . Roth."

She fell silent, staring at nothing. Natania. The name was familiar—really familiar. She tried to push away the spinning urgency so she could think. How did she know that name? It had seemed familiar when Mona had first mentioned it, but she'd had more important things on her mind at the time.

Natania. She heard the name in her mind, spoken by a male voice like music, beautiful and crystalline. *Natania.* The name again, this time murmured by a voice like silk, deep and powerful.

And the connection she should have made when she'd first heard the name clicked.

"Oh," she breathed, eyes wide.

"What?" Lyre demanded. Ash straightened, turning toward her.

"Uh—nothing. Nothing. I was just thinking. So, Natania Roth is the third one. Do any of the names sound familiar?"

Lyre shook his head. "I'm sure we can find something on them though."

Piper rather doubted it. There hadn't been a method for storing information since before the Third World War, but maybe daemons had their own record-keeping systems. She hoped so. Her thoughts returned to Natania and she bit her lip.

Miysis and Koen appeared from the shadows, stepping out from the trees and onto the trail. Koen was dirt-smudged but Miysis looked as perfect as ever — as she'd suspected.

"It's done," he said, green eyes catching the last of the sunlight. "Does anyone want to say some words?"

Piper shook her head. She didn't know Vejovis well enough, and it wouldn't feel right knowing she was far more upset that he couldn't save her life than she was about him being dead. Maybe the ryujin would bless his grave, though she doubted it. Whatever his agreement with them had been, they hadn't noticed — or hadn't cared — about him being killed.

"We might as well set up camp here," Koen said, his voice nearly as musical as Miysis's. "There likely aren't any better places nearby, and we're far enough from the river, I think."

Miysis nodded and Koen turned to the stack of packs that he and his fellow bodyguards had been carrying for the group. After passing out blankets and rations, he and Miysis sat on a mossy root, talking quietly about the journey back. The last light of the sun vanished, plunging the forest into even darker shadows with abrupt speed. The glow of the blue pods brightened noticeably, though the light was too dim to do more than create strange, swaying spots of light in the black forest.

Piper stared upward at the unseen treetops. The river murmured its song somewhere in the distance, and the breeze whispered through the leaves. The night was beautiful, peaceful, but she sat as tense as a pole, hands clamped between her knees.

Lyre shook out his blanket with a sigh. "Sleeping on the ground," he grumbled. He cast a sideways glance at her and shifted closer until their hips touched. "It'll probably be cold during the night. We should really share a blanket, just to be safe."

"You think?" she said dryly.

"Definitely. You need to keep up your strength. In fact, we can share our body heat more effectively without our clothes on."

She snorted. "I think I'll be fine."

"Well, if you change your mind—"

"Don't worry, I'll let you know."

Lyre sighed rather wistfully and stood, searching for a flat spot to lay his blanket. Piper watched him move away, then glanced toward Ash. In his dark clothing, he was nearly invisible. He still leaned against a tree, eyes turned toward the distance, folded blanket tucked under one arm.

Leaving her blanket on the root, she rose, and with a quick glance to see Seiya spreading her own blanket out, she tiptoed over to Ash.

"Hey," she whispered. "Can we talk?"

He glanced toward the others.

"Privately?" she added.

He nodded and tossed his blanket over with hers. With a similar glance toward his sister, he took her hand and pulled her down the path. He could see—or sense—the trail far better than she could. She walked after him, trying to be quiet. A little ways away, he turned into the trees, the soft moss completely absorbing their footsteps.

He stopped. She looked around, unable to see or hear the others. Or see much of anything, in fact, except for the glowing spots of blue among the trees.

"Um," she said, blinking at him. All she could see was the outline of his body, a darker shadow against the rest. His hand was still holding hers, fingers warm and reassuring.

A tiny light appeared, glowing in the palm of his other hand, too dim to be seen beyond the tiny circle of space in which they stood. It lit his face from beneath, casting harsh shadows over his jaw and cheekbones. For a moment, she forgot what she'd been going to say, transfixed by his dark eyes looking into hers, sliding right down to her soul.

He lifted his hand, tossing the light into the air. It stuck in place, hanging there as if suspended by an invisible wire.

"Ah," she tried again, keeping her voice low without actually whispering. "I, uh, need to tell you something."

He nodded again. She wished he would speak. Her voice sounded so loud in her ears, even though she was barely murmuring. She held his hand tighter.

"And it's going to sound crazy, but bear with me, okay?"

He sighed. "Just spit it out, Piper."

She shivered, his voice caressing her down to her bones.

"Right," she said breathlessly. Gathering herself, she cautiously began, "You remember how I used the Sahar to break that gold collar Samael made me wear, right?"

Surprise flickered across his face—not the topic he'd been expecting. "Yes."

"Well, when I broke it, I passed out for a few minutes. And while I was unconscious, I . . . had a vision."

"A vision?" he repeated blankly.

"Yeah. Keeping an open mind, remember? This vision was from the perspective of another person, like I was reliving someone else's memories. Her name was Natania."

His eyebrows rose.

"Natania was meeting with two daemons," she said quickly. "Her, ah, lovers. One was a draconian and one was a Ra and she called them Nyrtaroth and Maahes."

His eyes widened slightly and he gestured for her to continue.

"So Natania meets with the two of them, and Maahes asks her if she'll help them complete their special lodestone. After she agrees, he surprises her with a spell that puts her to sleep, but she resists long enough to overhear their conversation." She let out a breath. "They discussed how they were going to kill her to make their lodestone, because the strongest emotion comes from a human soul while the strongest magic comes from the soul of a daemon, so they needed the soul of a hybrid haemon to complete their lodestone."

Ash rubbed a hand through his hair. "You saw this in a vision? Like a dream?"

"Sort of, but it wasn't nonsensical like a dream. It was more like a flashback, except it wasn't my memory."

"So you think," he said carefully, "that the Sahar was made by imprisoning this Natania woman's soul inside it, and your vision was one of her memories?"

Piper licked her lips and nodded. "Pretty much, yeah."

He frowned. The silence stretched, but she waited, knowing he was weighing her words carefully. Her fingers involuntarily closed tighter around his. He always took her seriously; she couldn't think of a single person who wouldn't have gone ten rounds with her about whether it was just a dream before actually considering the possibility that it wasn't.

"The name coincidence is too much," he finally muttered. "The girl in your vision is named Natania, and there's a famous hybrid haemon from hundreds of years ago with the same name. You didn't find out about the haemon woman until your mother told you a few days ago, right?"

She let out a relieved sigh. He didn't think she was crazy. "Yes. I didn't mention the vision before because I was afraid it was just a vivid dream, but the name made me realize that it probably wasn't. And the thing about the Sahar being made from a person's soul . . ."

He nodded. "A soul would make sense. It's utterly abhorrent, but it makes sense. We siphon emotional energy from humans to charge lodestones. An unlimited lodestone would need *some* kind of power source."

Piper shivered, disturbed for a moment by how much Ash sounded like Nyrtaroth.

"I can't deny I felt something alive in the Sahar," he continued. "I thought it was ancient magic that had taken on a life of its own, but maybe the Sahar started out as something—someone—who was truly alive."

He focused on her again, eyes sharp. "That can't be all you wanted to tell me."

"Well, Natania was like me. A hybrid haemon. But *she* clearly wasn't dying. In fact, she was as powerful as a daemon. That means she must have figured out the secret to surviving her magic."

His eyes lit with a sudden spark of hope. "So if she knew the secret—"

"And her soul—her *memories*—are inside the Sahar, then maybe I can find out the secret from her." She squeezed his hand. "I already relived one of her memories. If I can see into her memories again, maybe I can find the answer."

"Do you know how you saw the first memory?"

"I lost consciousness while tapping the Sahar's power. That's all I know."

He frowned. "That's a risk. You know what happens when you use the power. And I can't take the Stone away from you without . . ."

She nodded. She had no desire to see him driven mad by the Sahar's violent power ever again. He'd almost killed her the last time.

"We'll have to figure out a safe way to do it," she said. "When we return to Earth, you can get the Stone from wherever you—"

"Actually . . ."

"What?"

He rolled his eyes toward the sky, avoiding her gaze. "Ah, well. We don't have to wait until we're back. The Sahar is here."

"You brought it? But you—you told Miysis—"

"I don't have it *on me*. But I couldn't leave it behind unguarded."

She spluttered. "Why didn't you tell me?"

"I didn't tell anyone."

"So where is it?"

He gave a low whistle. With a quiet rustle, Zwi dropped out of the darkness, wings flared, and landed on his shoulder.

Piper stared. "You mean—you mean *Zwi* has it?"

Zwi fluffed her mane with satisfied self-importance.

"No one can catch Zwi if she doesn't want to be caught. And I always know where she is, so the Stone is perfectly safe."

"Huh."

He released Piper's hand and pulled Zwi into his arms. He unbuckled the leather armor on her chest and flipped the breastplate over to reveal a leather bag sewn into it. Zwi hopped onto his shoulder. Tearing off the bag, he dumped the Sahar into his palm. The oval stone shone silvery blue in the dim light hovering above their heads. Piper clenched and unclenched her hands. Memories of the Sahar's limitless power—and limitless rage—swirled through her head. She really didn't know how she felt about seeing it again.

"We need to figure out a safe way to do this," he said. "Not only to keep you from losing control, but also to make sure these visions are safe. This is completely uncharted territory for me."

"Well, I don't have a lot to lose at this point."

His eyes darkened, his expression going tight. She remembered again the look in those eyes when he whispered that he couldn't take it anymore, thinking she was dead.

"We can't put anyone else at risk if I go crazy with the Sahar's power," she added. "But if you can't take it away from me . . ."

"That won't be a problem."

Ash and Piper both jerked in surprise at the unexpected voice. Zwi screeched angrily, her scales turning red with menace. Piper whirled around and her jaw dropped as alarm rushed through her.

Miysis leaned casually against a tree, a few steps away.

"You—where did you come from?" she stuttered.

"This is my world," he said coolly, a purr touching his melodic voice. "I know how to hide here far better than you."

"How long were you there?" she demanded.

"The entire time."

Ash swore. He held the Sahar in one clenched hand, his eyes black. He was ready to fight for it, but Miysis didn't move.

"I'd hoped, despite your earlier assertion, that you had brought the Sahar with you. It makes matters so much simpler."

Piper pressed her lips together.

"Piper needs to be unconscious to tap these memories," Miysis continued. "So I don't see why we need to be concerned about stopping her from going on a rampage. The moment she taps the Sahar, hit her with a sleep spell. Simple."

Piper and Ash exchanged a quick look.

"Between the two of us," Miysis said, "we can put her down before she causes any trouble."

"You're going to help?" she asked hesitantly.

"Of course. I don't want you to die." He flicked a glance at Ash's hand, where the Sahar was hidden. "And that is already mine. Our agreement was for you to give it to me after I found Vejovis, which I have done. But I will loan it to you for your experiment."

Piper quashed a scowl at his arrogance. She could use all the help she could get, so no point in arguing.

After a moment's discussion, they sat down with Piper in the middle, Ash behind her, and Miysis in front. Ash handed her the Sahar, then lightly touched his fingertips to her temples, ready to put her to sleep. Miysis kneeled in front of her, green eyes intense, ready to call out the exact moment for Ash to spell her.

"Try for a light connection first," Ash murmured. "Whenever you're ready."

She swallowed hard. "Are you guys sure about this?"

"Go ahead, Piper," Miysis said. "You're sitting between two of the most powerful daemons of our generation. I think we can handle you."

Not bothering to hide her scowl this time, she looked down at the Sahar in her hand. It was heavier than it looked, cool in her palm, and tingled against her skin with a strange kind of alien life—a soul trapped inside a stone prison.

"Okay," she said on a heavy exhale. "Here I go."

Closing her eyes, she mentally reached for the Sahar's power. When she'd first begun using it consciously, she'd had to think violent thoughts to trigger the Stone. But with all the practice she'd gotten while escaping Asphodel, it was now as easy as turning her thoughts toward the waiting power and letting it rush in.

And rush it did. It exploded inside her on a wave of burning rage and poisonous hatred. The power lit her blood on fire, electricity under her skin, ready to strike.

"Now," Miysis said.

Tingles rushed across her skin where Ash touched her. Darkness instantly closed over her.

CHAPTER
-17-

SHE SAT on the cushioned stool and methodically pulled the brush through her golden hair, humming softly. Her reflection smiled mysteriously in the mirror, cheeks flushed a pretty pink, blue eyes large and sparkling with contentment. She pulled the brush through another lock. There were no tangles; she simply enjoyed the motion, the soft pull of the brush, the silky feel of her hair.

Her gaze drifted across the mirror to the reflection of the bed and to the one who reclined in it.

Dark hair and commanding grey eyes. He was in glamour, a rare choice for him, but it was not often she saw him so relaxed. He lounged atop the quilted blankets, propped on a pillow, his hair tousled. He wore only casual slacks, his muscular chest cast in sharp relief by the dim lamp on her dresser. In his hand was a handful of papers, his eyes tracing the notes he and his partner had detailed on their last meeting.

She smiled as she watched him in the mirror. Her magnificent dark moon. She missed his wings though. It was such fun to tease him when he was out of glamour. A light touch on his wings was all it took to make him shiver and retreat. She knew it was a pleasant sensation, but he didn't like it. Still, she teased him anyway. Exploiting that simple weakness—that small power she could claim over such a powerful man—always delighted her.

Sliding the brush through her hair again, she turned on her stool, angling her body in the way she knew was most flattering.

"My love," she cooed softly, gently drawing his attention.

His gaze lifted from his papers, drifting across her body clad only in a silk dressing gown, before rising to her face.

"Nyr, my love," she said, "shouldn't you ready yourself? Maahes will arrive at any moment."

He murmured an agreement but didn't shift, gaze sliding over her again, eyes darkening. She knew that look, and desire heated her belly. A night of pleasure had not fully sated his appetite. Setting her brush down, she slid from the stool and moved toward him, hips swaying. His eyes darkened a little more with each step, each sway.

She stopped beside the bed and trailed her fingertips up his abs, then plucked the papers from his hand. She set them on the bedside table with care, knowing he would be angry otherwise. With that done, she turned back to him and again brushed her fingers over the smooth muscles of his torso.

"You look at me with the eyes of a man unsated," she whispered. "Do I not satisfy you, my love?"

"Always," he replied, deep voice caressing her as his hand curled around the back of her knee and slid up over the bare skin of her thigh. Her breath hitched. "But I always hunger for more."

He pulled on her thigh, guiding her onto the bed. She surprised him by swinging right over him and straddling his hips. His eyes went entirely black and his hands found her thighs again, gliding over her skin as he pushed her dressing gown up. She leaned down and brushed her lips over his, very lightly, then kissed him hard. He kissed her even harder, his natural aggressiveness triggered. She was in the dominant position. Any moment now he would pull her onto the bed and roll on top of her, and his deliciously talented hands would remove the barriers of clothing between them, and—

"Am I interrupting?"

She jerked up and twisted around with an embarrassed gasp.

Her glorious sun stood in the threshold. His eyes were black, jealousy hardening his beautiful face. She froze in place, not knowing how to react. This had never happened before. That she was lovers with them both was an unspoken secret they all knew but never acknowledged, a truth they never allowed the light of day to touch.

"Maahes," she stuttered.

His glare slashed over them. She dared not look at Nyrtaroth, at his reaction. If he challenged Maahes for her now . . .

Maahes's jaw clenched. He strode into the room and she thought he was coming at her. But he merely snatched the papers from the table.

"I will begin in the parlor." His words were like ice, razor sharp and arctic cold. "When it pleases you, perhaps you will join me for our discussion, as planned."

His gaze raked across her, fury bordering on hatred in his eyes. Jealousy was a fierce, consuming beast. She couldn't let him leave to seethe in solitude, nursing his jealousy into a hatred that would destroy their love.

Without thinking, she grabbed his wrist before he could turn away. Hostility lit his eyes at her daring. She instantly lightened her hold, caressing his hand. She couldn't let him leave by himself, but neither could she abandon Nyr. There was no solution where irreparable damage would not be inflicted on her relationship with one or both of them.

She licked her lips.

"My love." Her gaze flicked to Nyr. "My loves. I cannot bear to be parted from either of you. You know my love for you both is unrivaled and immeasurable."

Nyr's gaze began to darken with anger as well.

She stroked his chest at the same time she caressed Maahes's hand. "My dearests, I need you both. I . . ." She pulled his hand to her and kissed his inner wrist. "I need you both now. Right now."

Nyrtaroth's hands tightened where they still held her thighs. She continued to stroke his chest and kiss Maahes's wrist, hoping against hope that this was not the day they killed her.

Maahes held tense for a long moment, then melted into motion. His hand gripped her hair, forcing her head up. His mouth closed over hers, rough, demanding, fierce. His other hand grabbed her arm and dragged her off the bed. She scrambled to get her feet under her as he pulled her hard against him, still kissing her relentlessly.

And then Nyrtaroth was off the bed and pressed against her back, crushing her between them. His mouth closed over the spot where her neck and shoulder joined, teeth grazing, hands pushing up her dressing gown as he rubbed against her from behind. Aggressive. Possessive. Demanding.

Heat rushed through her. Fear. Adrenaline. Pleasure. This would either be the best day of her life—or the last.

c　c　c

Piper's eyes flew open as she gasped. She could still feel Maahes's mouth on hers, the fierceness of his kiss—if something that carnal and aggressive could be called a kiss. Fear and desire mixed with adrenaline in a cocktail that had her panting.

The moment her eyes had opened, Maahes's cold green eyes had filled her vision. She lurched back, only to discover she was leaning against Ash, cradled in his arms. She blinked and Miysis's face came into focus. But the eyes . . . the two Ra daemons had exactly the same eyes.

"Piper?" he asked. "Are you all right?"

"I—I—" She took back-to-back deep breaths, trying to clear her head.

Holy crap, Natania was insane. There was every chance those two could have torn her apart in their antagonistic competition. But she'd survived long enough for them to kill her for their lodestone, and if Piper correctly recalled from her first vision, Natania had been very fond of the memory.

"Did it work?" Ash asked.

Piper shivered. His voice was so similar to Nyrtaroth's. Not quite as deep, but with the same tone and inflections. She looked around to confirm it really was Ash behind her and met his worried grey eyes.

"Um, well, yes and no." She swallowed, trying to sound casual. "I got another memory, but it wasn't useful."

"Your heartrate really picked up, so Ashtaroth lifted the sleep spell," Miysis said. "What was the memory?"

"Ah, um." She shook her head, hoping they couldn't see her blushing in the dim light. "Nothing important. But I'm going to be doing this all night if all I get are random memories. Is there any way to control what I see?"

"Probably not," Miysis replied. "Unless . . ."

"Unless what?"

"What if you reach into the Stone instead of merely touching the power and letting it flow into you? It would be more in line with charging a lodestone, though of course this one has never needed to be charged."

"That's dangerous," Ash said. "Reaching into a lodestone with a soul inside it? We have no idea what might happen."

"How do I 'reach into the Stone'?" Piper asked.

"The simplest way is to follow the power from the Sahar back to its source," Miysis said. "It should be easy enough. I don't see how it could harm you, even with the soul inside."

"You should try what you just did a few more times," Ash said. "You only did it once. Maybe you'll gain more control with practice."

She dropped her eyes to the Sahar in her hand. Miysis disagreed with Ash and they began to argue, beautiful voices wrapping around her, and she felt as though she were sliding back into Natania's memory of Nyrtaroth and Maahes. How strange was it that she was sitting with the likely descendants of those two daemons, holding their weapon, and discussing their lover, who had been a hybrid haemon just like Piper? The parallels were freaking her out.

Of course, there were some major differences. The first and most important one being that she wasn't sleeping with either Ash or Miysis. And definitely not both at the same time.

She really didn't want to relive any more of Natania's R-rated memories. She let out a deep breath.

"Okay, I'm ready to try again."

Miysis nodded and Ash once again touched his fingertips to her head. She closed her eyes and called on the Sahar. The hate-infused power rushed into her, but she resisted the wave of rage and imagined the magic as a river flowing into her. And then she imagined herself flying down that river and into the Stone in her hands.

"Now."

Darkness snapped over her.

●   ●   ●

She opened her eyes. Heavy, embroidered canvas stretched above her, hanging from the tall bedposts of a deliciously soft bed. Pillows and blankets under her. Soft, warm light. Deep shadows. She slowly propped herself up on one elbow, her gaze travelling over the shapes of the familiar bedroom.

Against the wall was a mirrored dresser, and sitting on the stool in front of it was a woman with long, wavy blond hair.

Piper looked around sharply. This was definitely the bedroom from the last memory but was now devoid of daemons. Instead of seeing the memory from Natania's perspective, she was looking *at* Natania. Miysis's theory had proven correct—somewhat. Piper wasn't stuck inside Natania. But she didn't feel any more in control of the memories.

Natania slowly pulled the brush through her hair one last time. She set it gently on the table and turned on the stool, just as she had when she'd greeted Nyrtaroth in the previous memory. Piper tensed. Natania's gaze moved toward the bed as she smiled mysteriously.

She was beautiful. No wonder the two daemons had put up with sharing her. Her blue eyes were huge and expressive, and seemed to naturally exude a seductive heat without any effort. Her creamy skin was flawless, perfect cheekbones, full lips. She sat with her legs crossed at the knee, all womanly curves and perfect angles.

Piper was so distracted by her beauty that she didn't immediately realize Natania was looking at her—as in, *right at her.*

"Hello, Piper."

Piper's breath froze in her lungs.

Natania pushed her hair off her shoulders, smoothing the locks. Her smile grew. "You know who I am, don't you?"

Piper swallowed twice and still couldn't find her voice. She nodded.

"Do you like it here?" Natania lifted her hands, taking in the room. "My bedroom. So many memories of this room. Most of them would make you blush, I am sure."

Piper cleared her throat. "Um. I'm sorry to—to intrude. I didn't know . . ."

"You didn't know I was here? You thought I was merely a disembodied collection of memories and emotions roiling forever within a prison of stone and magic?" Her smile was ice and her blue eyes glinted strangely—the gleam of madness. "No, I am quite aware, as I have been for a very, very long time."

Horror closed Piper's throat. Had Nyrtaroth and Maahes understood what they were condemning Natania to when they'd sealed her soul in the Sahar?

"No one has ever visited me before," Natania continued pleasantly, even as the glitter of insanity in her eyes grew. "I've had only my memories as company for so long. Memories of my stolen life and my heartless lovers who betrayed me."

Her smile widened. "One of them paid dearly, did he not? I destroyed him. My dark moon, my deadly dragon. He thought to use me, the power he had created me to be, but I would allow no such thing. He paid the price for my power in madness. And they killed him. Did you know that?"

Piper nodded woodenly.

"I do wish I could have destroyed my glorious sun as well, but he was ever the cautious one. He wisely did not attempt to wield my power. So few have. So many long years of silence. Until . . . you." She hummed a few notes of a song.

Piper licked her lips, transfixed by Natania's eyes, which were slowly paling closer and closer to the shimmering blue-silver shade of the Sahar.

"And there was the other one too. The dragon. The one who is so *very* much like my Nyr. His mind has the same taste. Not as intelligent, not quite as cunning, but oh my, the rage. He has such rage. Such hatred. So very fragile. I almost had him. He was easy to claim but hard to control." She smiled. "Next time I will have him. I know where the cracks are now. I will shatter him with a single touch."

Hands clenching, Piper leveled Natania with a glare. "You won't get anywhere near him. He'll never use the Stone again."

"Won't he? He wants to. He craves me. His rage and mine. His hate and mine. With me, he can unleash it all." Running her tongue over her upper lip, Natania smoothed the front of her silk dressing gown. "He wants me more than he wants you."

"Why would he want *you*?" Piper snapped.

"I am power. And you have none."

Piper flinched.

Natania smiled again, madness oozing from her. "I will have him soon. He can't resist me—just like my Nyr. And once I have him, I will destroy him—just like my Nyr."

Fear trickled through Piper. She straightened, crossing her arms. "I came to ask you something."

"I know."

"I—you do?"

"Yes. I have been inside your head, dearest Piper. I have crawled through your thoughts and shuffled through your emotions like playing cards. I know *exactly* why you came to me."

Her eyes narrowed. "Why then?"

"You don't want to die."

Piper bit the inside of her cheek and reluctantly nodded.

"You are like me. You have two strains of magic and they are like fire and oil, growing hotter and hotter as they feed each other and devour each other until your mind burns away with them." She raised her hands in a shrug-like gesture. "And you want me to tell you the secret to surviving this inevitable fate, correct?"

"Yes, that's exactly what I want."

"That's a shame, really."

Piper clenched her hands. "Why?"

"We all want so many things we can't have."

"But—you know the secret."

"Yes."

Piper bared her teeth. "You're not going to tell me, are you?"

"No."

"Why not?"

"It's so wonderful to have company," Natania sighed. She uncrossed her legs and leaned toward Piper. Her irises had turned completely silver. "Isn't it lovely? It's been so long since I've had a real conversation."

"I'm not here to keep you company."

"Aren't you?"

"No!"

Another smile. "You think I will tell you what you need to know? How simple of you. Perhaps you thought to force answers from me? Please do try. I would enjoy that."

Piper gritted her teeth.

"This is my mind, Piper. I control everything."

"So you're refusing to help me?" she demanded. "You'll just let me die?"

Natania shrugged. "Should I care? The only pleasure left to me is death. I care not whose."

"So you're no better than *them*, are you? Maahes and Nyrtaroth. You're just as evil."

"If it soothes your childish view of morality, then believe what you will." Natania traced a finger thoughtfully across her lips. "The mind is a strange thing, is it not? You exist here as your mind perceives your body. And this place? It is a memory, a strong one. Weak memories are like dreams, unstable and unpredictable. But this is far more than a dream."

Sliding off her stool, the woman sauntered toward Piper, silver eyes gleaming as she smiled. Piper tensed, but Natania merely reached out a fragile-looking finger and touched a lock of Piper's hair in an almost maternal way.

Faster than the blink of an eye, Natania's hand closed around Piper's throat.

Natania shoved her back onto the bed and used one knee to pin her down. Piper grabbed Natania's wrist, but she couldn't budge the woman's grip. Mouth open for a breath she couldn't take, she tried to throw Natania off her but nothing she did made the slightest difference. Natania was as solid and unmovable as stone.

"Fascinating, isn't it?" Natania purred as she continued to choke Piper with one hand. "You have no power at all here. Our bodies reflect our minds. Your body is powerless because your mind is powerless against mine."

Piper dug her nails into Natania's hand but couldn't break the woman's skin. Her lungs screamed for air.

"You don't need to breathe, of course, but your mind doesn't know that. In this place, your mind is your body and your body is your mind." She hummed a thoughtful note. "What do you think will happen if I kill you?"

She leaned close, smiling into Piper's eyes as her vision blurred. "I'll give you a hint: you won't be waking up again."

Piper stopped struggling. Wake up. Yes. She needed to wake up before Natania killed her. Squeezing her eyes shut, she willed herself to wake up in her body—willed it as hard as she could.

Natania hissed.

Piper's eyes flew open. The walls of the room were wavering. For a brief second, she thought she heard a voice calling her name—a distant, muffled male voice. Gritting her teeth, she willed herself again to wake up. The room shimmered, the edges softening like ice in the summer heat, but she didn't know whether she was waking up or passing out.

With a flip of her hair, Natania let her go.

Piper gasped and coughed, sucking in air desperately. Natania stepped away from her and circled back to her dresser to pick up her hairbrush. Holding one hand to her aching throat as she stared at Natania, Piper sat up, debating whether she should continue to try to awaken before Natania attempted to kill her again. But she would die regardless if she didn't get the information she needed.

"What the hell was that about?" she asked hoarsely.

Natania drew the brush through her hair. "I reconsidered," she said lightly.

"Reconsidered what?"

Setting the brush down again, Natania turned to face Piper and her voice lost all inflection. "My prison is stillness and emptiness, the unweathered and unaging stone untouched by external elements — except another mind. You cannot imagine the tedium. Silence upon silence with nothing but my memories. And then . . . you." She spread her hands in a wide gesture as her silver eyes lit up again. "My existence has been far more interesting since you touched my power. You have a gift for destruction, Piper."

Piper pressed her lips together. Natania hadn't killed her because she was entertaining? She rubbed a hand over her forehead, swallowing against the ache in her throat. She could almost still hear the faraway voice calling out to her.

Natania sat down on the stool and crossed her legs. "Do you know why your magic will soon take your life?"

Piper blinked, caught off guard by Natania's sudden business-like tone. "Because I have two kinds of magic that are incompatible."

"Yes. And what solution can you imagine for this dilemma?"

"I—well—" Getting rid of one would be the easiest solution, but her mother had said that the other hybrid women had possessed both strains of magic. "Separating them, I guess—"

"Exactly."

"But—but how would I do that?"

"You can't."

Trying to control her temper, Piper squeezed her knees with her hands. "Are you just taunting me?"

Natania turned back to her dresser and began tidying it. "Do you know what a daemon's greatest advantage is over a haemon in magical ability?"

Piper almost said "raw power," but Lyre's voice murmured in her memory, a conversation from just days ago.

"Daemons can see magic," she said. "Haemons can't."

"Correct."

Piper stared at Natania's reflection in the mirror, her eyes narrowed. What game was Natania playing now?

"Do you know how daemons create glamour?"

Piper scowled. If Natania knew everything in Piper's head, then she knew perfectly well that Seiya had explained how glamour worked when they were escaping the Underworld. As though the thought conjured it, for a second, Piper thought she could hear Seiya's voice, muffled and far away.

"They create a new form when they cross the Void," she answered shortly. "It's not an illusion but a sort of twist of reality. What's with the quiz?"

"Close," Natania replied, arranging some jewelry in an elaborately carved wooden box. "However, *they* do not create their shape. The ley line of Earth shapes their new form, choosing it for them the first time they enter an Earthly ley line."

Piper's brow furrowed. "I don't understand."

"Ley lines are the planet's magic. It is not sentient, but neither is it inert. When daemons come to Earth, Earth's magic tries to shape their alien forms into something familiar, something that belongs there. The ley line gives them a form, sometimes one quite close to human, sometimes not. It is the only glamoured form they can take.

"Maintaining a glamour is easy on Earth; Earth's inherent magic tries to hold it in place for them. In the Underworld, a daemon must work harder to hold the glamour, because the Underworld prefers that they be what they are."

"How do you know all this?"

Natania smiled, mysterious mien turned on full force. "My sun and moon shared many secrets with me. Satisfied men are like open books."

"Why are you telling me?"

Natania picked up a necklace, studying the shimmer of the rubies. "Do you know why haemons, though they have both human and daemon blood, look entirely human?"

"No."

"No?" Natania glanced over her shoulder, her look scathing. "After what I just explained to you?"

Piper shook her head. She didn't have a clue and her patience with Natania's question game was waning fast.

Natania dropped the necklace into her jewelry box. "Most haemons are born on Earth."

Straightening, Piper stared hard at Natania's back. "You said Earth's magic makes daemons look more human. So you're saying . . . Earth's magic also makes haemons look human?"

Natania nodded.

"No way. I didn't suddenly turn into a half-daemon mutant when I went to the Overworld—or the Underworld."

"Of course not. You didn't traverse the Void. You were carried."

"Wait, you mean—"

Natania snapped the jewelry box's lid shut. "I do hope you survive, Piper," she said pleasantly. "We could have such fun together."

"Survive—"

"Try not to perish in the Void. It would be a most unpleasant way to die."

"What—"

Natania turned on her seat and smiled. Piper's blood chilled at the cold, calculating glitter in the woman's eyes.

"Should you successfully yield your humanity to the daemon within, we will then see just how strong you truly are. I look forward to it."

Piper opened her mouth to demand an explanation, but the room blurred. The faint, nearly inaudible voices grew louder in her ears, shouting words she couldn't make out. The world dissolved into impenetrable darkness.

CHAPTER
-18-

GROGGY awareness filtered in. Voices. She could hear voices—angry, shouting, fearful voices.

Her eyes flew open.

She was lying on the mossy ground, a folded blanket acting as her pillow. The forest was no longer pitch black but tinged with the pale light of dawn. Her body felt weak and wobbly, muscles simultaneously feeble and stiff—but a flood of adrenaline was already filling them with strength as she took in the scene before her.

Miysis, Koen, and another Ra stood on one side of the tiny clearing, eyes black, swords drawn, tensed for battle. Lyre and Seiya stood out of the way, wide-eyed with hands outstretched in placating gestures. Lyre spoke quickly but in a soft tone, though Piper didn't bother to listen to his words.

Her attention was locked on Ash.

He faced Miysis—and he was no longer in glamour. Black wings rose off his back, half-spread in preparation to attack, tail lashing behind him. A massive black-handled sword was in his hand, point resting on the ground, almost casually, but there was nothing casual about his stance.

She could only see his face in profile, but it was enough. Black, black, black eyes. Face twisted. Teeth bared. Rage burning off him like heat from a fire.

Miysis was about to die.

"This is your fault," he snarled, his sepulchral daemon voice barely human. "You caused this."

Piper's terror doubled in an instant. Rage. Feral fury. She'd seen this before—first in the Chrysalis building, then when he'd used the Sahar to destroy Samael's army. Shading so complete and encompassing that it bordered on madness. Fueled by mindless rage and hatred so deep it went beyond thought or logic.

Cracks, Natania had said. Ash was full of rage and cracks.

"Ash," Lyre tried again, hands stretched toward the draconian, though he didn't dare move any closer, to step between Ash and the target of his bloodlust, "just listen, okay? We don't know that Piper won't wake up—"

Ash's weight shifted slightly. It was the only warning.

Piper lunged to her feet in one powerful move. Ash sprang for Miysis. He was impossibly fast, but she was in just the right spot. She flung herself at him and grabbed his sword arm, yelling his name at the same time.

He spun with unreal grace, channeling his forward momentum into a sharp spin that yanked her off her feet, but she didn't let go. His free hand flashed toward her as his black eyes slashed in her direction. His hand locked around her throat, claws sinking into her flesh, the talon on his thumb dangerously close to her jugular.

"Ash!" she screamed.

He froze. Black eyes on her face. Teeth still bared. She saw no signs of recognition, but he wasn't moving.

"Hey," she whispered. Thankfully, he wasn't choking her; he was merely an instant away from ripping out her throat. "It's me. I'm awake. I'm fine."

She waited, holding as still as possible. His eyes gradually focused, the mindless rage quieting. His hand on her neck loosened, talons retracting from her flesh with sharp shocks of pain that she didn't allow to show on her face.

He pulled his hand away and glanced at it, at her blood smeared on his fingers. For the briefest instant, a bare fraction of a second, his face crumpled with an agony beyond words—and in the next instant, his expression had emptied, closed, turned to impenetrable stone. He stepped back.

And then he walked away.

Her heart clogged her throat as he strode past them all without a glance, wings folding tightly against his back as he disappeared into the shadows of the forest. Piper lurched forward a step, intending to follow, but a hand closed on her arm. She looked around to find Lyre holding her.

"Don't, Piper. He needs time to cool off."

She looked back at the spot where Ash had vanished. Her instincts said he shouldn't be alone. Lyre hadn't seen that moment of agony, that moment where all his walls had crumbled and she'd glimpsed his soul. Hatred as poisonous as the hatred within the Sahar boiled up inside her, threatening to overwhelm her. She would kill Samael. Kill him slowly for what he had done to Ash.

Lyre took her chin, distracting her from her murderous fantasies as he checked both sides of her neck.

"He missed the vital spots," he said with a relieved sigh.

Miysis approached, looking pale as he sheathed his sword. "Your bravery is admirable, Piper," he said quietly.

She wasn't sure whether he was being sarcastic.

"Very brave," Lyre agreed. "And very stupid. But brave."

"Thanks," she muttered.

Miysis also checked her neck. "Koen can heal this. It will only take a few minutes." A pause. "I feared you would never wake."

"I was a bit worried too." She rolled her shoulders, stretching the tight muscles. "What the hell happened to set all this off?"

Lyre grimaced. "You'd been down for hours—most of the night. Nothing could wake you. Ash and Miysis kept arguing over whether to take the Sahar away from you to see if that would break the connection and allow you to wake up. Ash was afraid it would trap you inside and seal your fate." He shot the Ra heir a cutting look. "Miysis tried to take it anyway. That's when Ash lost it."

Piper glanced past him and saw Seiya slip into the trees in the direction Ash had vanished. At least he would have someone to comfort him, someone who probably understood his state of mind far better than she did.

She focused on Lyre as he spoke to her again. "You shouldn't have done that."

"Done what?"

"Grabbed Ash in the middle of an attack. He almost ripped your throat out."

"But he didn't, did he?" She waved a hand. "Let's not start the what-if game. I'm fine. Miysis is fine. Ash is—"

She broke off. Ash clearly wasn't fine.

Lyre's face tightened.

Miysis touched her elbow, drawing her attention to him. "What happened with the Sahar? Do you remember?"

"Oh yes," she said. She let out a long breath. "I didn't realize so much time had passed. I guess it took a while for Natania and I to get to the bottom of things."

"For—sorry?"

"Didn't you know?" she said bitterly. "I thought you knew everything about the Stone."

His expression cooled. "Know what?"

"That Maahes and Nyrtaroth didn't just lock Natania's soul inside the Sahar. They locked away her mind too. Her whole, conscious, thinking mind."

His eyes widened slightly. He hadn't known. She felt a little better. If he'd known . . .

"Did she tell you?" Lyre asked. "How to survive your magic?"

She nodded as fear prickled through her. "I think so."

"What do you need to do?"

She swallowed hard. "I need to go into the Void."

●　　●　　●

While the others packed up their supplies for the return journey, Piper picked her way through the tangled roots of the trees. The sky beyond the mountains was pale blue, the sun only a few minutes away from cresting the horizon. In the opposite direction, the massive curve of the distant planet was completing its slow slide out of sight below the jagged mountains.

She glanced up at the trees, strange while at the same time so familiar; there was something about forests that transcended geography, even on different worlds. Birds were just beginning their morning ritual of song, filling the cool air with life and noise. She carefully circled the dangling tendrils of an azure pod.

Rubbing a hand against her forehead, feeling the dull ache of a sleepless night—or was it the return of the magic-fueled headache?— she moved toward the murmuring sound of water. She didn't know where Ash had gone, but he preferred open spaces, so the river was her best bet.

The shore was only a few minutes away. She stepped between the last two trees and onto the rocks. The water drifted by, calm, deep, murmuring gently. Her eyes drifted across the crystalline, blue surface. It seemed almost welcoming, the current lazy and smooth, the sparkles of the sun on the ripples dancing with carefree abandon. Fear curled in her stomach as memories of the cave flashed through her head.

Pulling her eyes away, she looked down the shore and saw him.

He was sitting on a large rock that jutted out over the water, with one knee propped up and his elbow resting on it. So casual at first glance, calm and safely back in glamour, but she didn't trust his outward appearance one bit. There was no sign of Seiya; she must have already returned to the others.

Picking her way carefully over the rocks, Piper closed the distance until she was standing several steps behind him on the far end of the rock where he sat. He didn't turn or acknowledge her.

She swallowed to moisten her tongue. "Ash?"

No response.

Biting her lip, she walked out onto the rock. She stopped beside him, looked down at the top of his head, then sat next to him. He was staring at the water.

"Ash . . ."

He spoke without looking at her. "How badly are you hurt?"

She shuddered. That tone. She knew it—and hated it.

Death is easy. Living is difficult.

It was Raum's voice, Raum's tone. Empty, distant, inflectionless. Dead.

"I'm fine. Just a couple scratches," she replied quickly, forcing lightness into her voice. "Already healed. It was no big deal."

He finally looked at her, but his gaze was like a knife slashing across her skin. Eyes still too close to black. He made a noise that was half cold amusement, half disgust.

"No big deal," he repeated, again toneless. "Do you think you're invincible?"

"What? Of course I don't—"

"A heartbeat. One heartbeat's difference and you would have been dead."

"But I'm not," she said firmly. "You didn't kill me, Ash. You barely scratched me, and—"

"Next time I might."

"There won't be a next time."

His gaze returned to the water, his eyes empty. "There will be. I can't control it anymore. It's like the Sahar has me all over again. All I feel is rage and hatred until I can't think anymore, until all I want is to see blood."

His rage and mine. His hate and mine. Piper brushed away Natania's insidious whisper from her mind.

"It's only been a couple of months," she said. "You can't expect to get better in so short a time after everything that's happened."

"I'm not getting better. I'm getting worse."

"Ash, I'm sure—"

He made a sharp, angry noise, the first sign of emotion since she'd approached.

"What do you know?" he snapped, his anger breaking free. "You don't understand anything."

He abruptly stood, and for the second time that morning, he walked away from her.

She sat on the rock, stunned. Aching. She looked down at her hands and saw they were shaking. A quiet, slightly hysterical laugh escaped her as she thought of Lyre's request that she talk to Ash about what was wrong. Yeah, that had gone well.

He was upset. He'd injured her. He was afraid he would kill her. She got that. But that didn't mean his words hadn't left her hurt and bleeding—especially since he was right. She didn't understand—couldn't understand—what he was going through. What he'd been through.

She pressed her hands to her face, blinking away tears. None escaped to wet her cheeks. She dropped her hands, clenching them into fists. Part of her wanted to slink away and lick her wounds. The other part of her wanted to punch him for being such a jerk.

Huffing and sniffing, she pushed herself up and turned.

Seiya stood at the edge of the trees, watching her. Piper stilled, wariness flaring.

"Last warning, Piper," Seiya said. Calm. Lethal. "Let him go."

She turned and strode back into the trees.

Piper's hands clenched as she fought down the irrational wave of fear. She glanced back at the water then hurried into the forest. Her morning just kept getting better, didn't it? Chances were she'd be dead before the day was over anyway. Wouldn't that solve everyone's problems?

Shaking her head, she hurried to join the others, knowing her time was slipping away far too quickly. If she survived, she would figure out what to do about Ash and Seiya. But until then, she could only worry about what would happen when they reached the ley line.

◦　◦　◦

Piper panted, struggling to keep up with Lyre as they climbed the steep path. The ledge loomed, closing with painful slowness, though she dreaded the moment they would reach the top. She did her best to ignore Ash, far ahead, Seiya on his heels. He'd avoided Piper—everyone, in fact—since they'd headed out. He hadn't even asked if she'd gotten what she needed from Natania, though she assumed someone must have told him what the plan was.

She bit her lip, remembering that look in his eyes when he'd grabbed her throat. *All I feel is rage and hatred until I can't think anymore, until all I want is to see blood.* No matter what Seiya threatened, Piper would get to the bottom of whatever was wrong with him. But not yet. First she had to survive the next obstacle, and she really didn't know how well that was going to go.

Though Piper hadn't realized it immediately, Natania's question game hadn't been the frivolous waste of time that it had first appeared to be. The woman's questions had provided Piper with a clear roadmap of what she had to do if she wanted to survive. The problem was successfully doing it.

Assuming she'd understood correctly, Piper couldn't separate her two magic lineages until she could see what she was doing, and only daemons could see magic, which was why she had to unlock her daemon side. She needed to do the opposite of what daemons did to create a human glamour. They went through the Void and into an Earth ley line in order to be "given" a human glamour. She needed to go from the Void into an Underworld or Overworld ley line in order to be "given" a daemon form.

The thought terrified her.

First, the Void was the embodiment of the most frightening thing in existence: the unknown. No one knew what the Void was, and even though Miysis and Koen had spent the better part of the day coaching her on how to survive it, she still didn't understand what it was or what it would do to her—only that it was insanely dangerous and she probably wouldn't survive.

Second, the idea of, as Natania had put it, *yielding to the daemon within*, was almost as frightening. In her mind, the only difference between a haemon and a human was magic—nothing else. And since Piper had never had magic, the only difference between her and humans had been her attitude and knowledge. She'd never thought of herself as a half-daemon. The very notion that there was dormant daemon blood inside her waiting to be brought to life freaked her out.

And that didn't even address the whole "daemon glamour" aspect. Miysis surmised that she would look like a diluted daemon — though his overall doubtful state that it would work gave her little confidence in his opinion. For all she knew, she would survive the Void only to discover that she'd turned into some kind of hideous hybrid mutant. After all, she had *two* daemon bloodlines, not one. Again, Miysis had a theory. He explained that there were no true hybrid daemons because one bloodline was always dominant, so she should come out looking like only her dominant bloodline. But he was only guessing.

She was doing her best not to worry about it. None of it would matter unless she survived the Void.

Her heartrate kicked up to double speed when they reached the small plateau where they'd first come through on the ley line. She could feel its power sparking in the air, the soft call of magic, Mother Nature's voice whispering words of welcome in her ears. For a moment, she didn't feel so scared. Then she thought about the Void and her terror came right back.

Miysis rested one hand on his sword as he surveyed the ley line that was invisible to her. He turned toward her. "Are you clear on what to do?"

Still breathing hard from the climb, she sat on a rock. "One of you will take me into the Void and let me go. I'll have to pull myself back out and into the Overworld ley line, where I'll let the magic create my . . . daemon glamour."

"You should take your clothes off beforehand," he said. "There's no way to know what your form will be. Constricting garments could be painful."

She tried not to blush. "Okay."

"Hold on a minute." Lyre folded his arms across his chest and scowled. "How come when *he* tells you to take your clothes off, you're all, 'Sure, no problem'?"

"Are you certain you want to do this?" Miysis asked, ignoring Lyre.

"If I don't do it now, I won't get another chance." She pressed a hand to her head, which throbbed painfully in time with her heartbeat, like a hammer striking the inside of her skull. "The rune venom is wearing off and the pain is coming back quickly. If it gets any worse, I won't be able to concentrate on anything."

"Reduced pain means reduced magic."

"I'll take the risk."

"Why don't you take the Stone instead?"

She looked around, surprised to hear Ash speaking to her after his daylong silence. His voice was again toneless.

"Take the Sahar?" she repeated. "Yeah, that would work. Emergency magic if I needed it."

"No," Miysis said. "That would be an even greater risk. You can't be distracted by the Sahar's rage. It would undo you in the Void. You must stay calm."

Piper's eyes narrowed. Was his concern for her, or for his precious Sahar getting lost in the Void?

"Fine, no Sahar." She swallowed. "Who will take me in?"

"Koen can—"

"I will."

Again, she looked at Ash. "You—you want to?"

He nodded shortly.

"Ashtaroth," Miysis said, voice clipped, "Koen is trained—"

"I want Ash to do it," Piper interrupted.

Seiya's glare flashed in her direction, but she ignored it. Yes, she was being selfish, but she needed Ash for this. Her hands were already shaking. She needed his strength, his steadiness, not a stranger she didn't trust.

She stood up. "Let's get this over with."

Face tightening, Miysis turned to Koen and muttered something. Koen reached into his pack and pulled out a blanket, which he handed to Piper.

"Good luck," Miysis said.

She accepted the blanket and turned.

Lyre gave her a tight smile. "You're the toughest haemon I've ever met. You can do this."

She nodded, unable to speak from the fear sweeping through her. She was going into the Void—the mind-shattering nothingness between worlds that the majority of daemons feared too much to ever enter.

Ash stepped up beside Lyre. The two daemons shared a strange, silent look before Ash touched the small of her back. He guided her up the trail. The soft murmurs of the others disappeared as the path curved around an outcropping of rock. On the other side, the ledge widened, offering some breathing room between the side of the mountain and the cliff's edge that dropped to the rushing river a hundred feet below. A dozen scraggily trees had managed to sink their roots into the rocky mountainside, thankfully free of strangling azure pods.

She held the blanket against her chest and tried not to hyperventilate.

Ash led her to the trees and stopped. She could feel the rush of the ley line beside them. Panic swirled in her head like a whirlpool, sucking in all her attempts to think calm thoughts and leaving her shaking.

"Piper."

She turned to him, trying to breathe normally.

He touched her chin with light fingers. The stoniness was gone from his face, replaced with fire and determination. "Are you ready to do this?"

Was she ready? Miysis and Koen had gone over everything. Every step, every little thing to expect. How to hold her mind together. How to get back to the ley line. She knew what to do. It was just doing it that terrified her. What if she wasn't strong enough?

Her head throbbed. The pain was getting worse. She couldn't wait. It would only get more difficult.

She looked at him, eyes wide. "You'll be here when I get back? Waiting for me?"

"Right here. I'll be right here."

"Okay." Inhale, exhale. "Okay. Yes, I'm ready."

His thumb lightly brushed her cheek as he lowered his hand.

She glanced down at her clothes. "I—I just need to . . ."

He turned around and moved away a few steps. Biting hard on her bottom lip, she quickly stripped down, removing every last stitch of clothing, then wrapped the blanket around herself like a towel, the edges dragging on the ground.

"Okay."

He returned to her, shadowed eyes searching her face.

"What if—" she began in a whisper.

He stepped close and gripped her upper arms with warm hands. "You'll do this, Piper."

"But—"

"I'll be right here when you get back. It'll be over in five minutes."

She blinked quickly and nodded, letting herself lean against him. She took a deep breath.

"Just in case—"

"Piper—"

"Just listen! Just in case I don't make it back, I want to tell you something."

She felt him tense. He slowly nodded, his hands still on her arms. She looked up at him as a thousand things rushed through her head. She could tell him she knew he cared about her. She could tell him she cared about him too—a lot. But then, he already knew those things.

Maybe she could tell him instead that she loved how his grey eyes looked right into her, seeing down to her soul. That she loved the feeling of his arms around her. That she loved the touch of his lips on hers. That she loved his rare smiles, all of them, from the contented ones to the "I'm going to kill you now" ones that, thankfully, he'd never directed at her.

All these things boiled up inside her until she couldn't say any of them. So instead, while holding the blanket in place with one hand, she reached up with the other. Grabbing the side of his face, she yanked his head down and kissed him hard.

His hands tightened and he kissed her back just as fiercely.

She pulled back. "That's what I wanted to say."

"I see."

"And I want another one when I get back."

"Whatever you want."

"Good." Inhale, exhale. "I'm ready."

He nodded. Eyes dark, movements just a little edgy, he pulled her back a couple of steps. They were in the ley line now. She could feel it all around her, sparking against her skin and rushing by her like a breeze that touched only her soul.

"We'll step together," he said, moving behind her, hands on her upper arms. He turned them around so she was facing the length of the ledge, the mountain range spreading before her, and the arch of the planet rising above the jagged peaks. "One step backward. I'll pull you in and then let go. You'll be right on the edge. All you have to do is step forward again."

She nodded tersely, heart pounding.

"I'll be right here. Right beside you."

She nodded again. Squeezing her eyes shut, she did as Miysis had instructed, imagining a bubble of fire around her head—her magic—protecting her mind. There was no special spell for going into the Void. You just had to have enough magic, and enough concentration, to create an impenetrable shield around your mind.

"Ready," she whispered.

His hands on her arms tightened. She felt the tingle as he wrapped magic around his own mind to protect himself. Then the tingle rushed over her as he tied them together so she would be pulled into the Void with him.

Panic exploded inside her. Insanity. Madness. That's what this was. Why was she trusting Natania?

Ash's lips brushed her ear. "You can do this."

Yes. She could. She would.

"Now," she said.

He stepped back, pulling her with him. The world disappeared into screaming black oblivion.

CHAPTER
-19-

SHRIEKING, tearing oblivion.

Silent, crushing nothingness.

It tore her apart, shredding her into a thousand pieces. Thoughts, memories, emotions ripped away from her, vanishing into the emptiness. Agony. Numbness. Burning heat. Or was it searing cold? She didn't know, couldn't tell. The Void was everything and nothing, both trying to destroy her.

She fought to hold herself together. Her entire being tried to expand to fill the vacuum, stretching in every direction at once. She couldn't think, couldn't process. Every sense she possessed screamed from sensation overload and deprivation at the same time. She was breaking, splintering, shattering into infinite particles of madness.

She had to move. She had to take a step. One step. Where was her body? Where were her legs? The oblivion tore everything away, ripping her to pieces. *Take a step!*

It all stopped.

She crouched barefoot on the hard dirt. Chest heaving. Arms clamped around her middle. Eyes squeezed shut.

Her entire body trembled as she rocked back and forth, tears leaking down her face. Very slowly, one by one, the torn pieces in her head slipped back into place. She hadn't lost everything, but so much of it had been scrambled, cast about like puzzle pieces in a tornado.

She let out a shuddering breath. Memories drifted back: The beautiful forests of the Overworld. The soaring mountains. Kissing Ash beside the river. Finally, thoughts shivered through her torn mind.

I am alive.

I survived.

I did it.

She cracked her eyes open, blinded by the low afternoon sun. Her rocking slowed, then stopped. She was back. She was free from the soul-sucking nothingness. She didn't remember stepping out of the Void, but she must have. Sluggishly, she looked around. Mountains. A trail. An empty trail.

Ash wasn't here.

Panic clenched around her chest. He'd promised. He'd promised he'd be here. Why wasn't he? She was alone, broken and shattered inside, and *he wasn't here.* Her breath came fast, speeding toward hyperventilation. She was alone. Alone, alone. Just like the Void. He'd been there, his hands on her, holding her against the tearing nothingness, and then he'd let go. And now she was alone, and it was ripping her apart, and she was shattering into a thousand pieces again.

Gasping for air, she looked from one end of the ledge to the other. Looked back. Looked again. It came to her, oozing through the cracks in her memory: this wasn't the same spot.

She was in a different place on the mountain. She'd come out of the ley line farther up the trail. It looked higher here, the river a rushing echo far below at the bottom of the cliff. She shuddered, clamping her arms tighter around herself. She was lost, alone, still alone.

He would find her. He'd promised.

Gulping, she loosened her grip and realized she was rocking again. She stopped. She was okay. She was alive. The Void hadn't destroyed her. It had tried. She'd almost lost. She didn't know how she'd managed to take that step back, how she'd done it with the Void ripping her open and tearing out her insides. But she'd done it.

Her head throbbed, pain growing worse with each drifting minute. More memories slipped into place. More thoughts formed, coherency gradually returning. And she remembered *why* she'd gone into the Void.

Heart pounding, she raised her hands. Over each of her knuckles, a shiny oval scale glittered, bright as a gem, shimmering like mother of pearl. Blues and greens and teals. Her fingernails and the first joint of her fingers were decorated with the same kind of scales. Her nails were pointed. Stretching her arms out in front of her, she discovered large, shining, shimmering scales plating her elbows and running partway down her forearms and up the backs of her upper arms, even across her shoulders.

Her breath came faster and faster. She struggled to breathe.

Scales covered her knees and ran partway down her shins, tapering away halfway down. Large, plated, almost jewel-like. The scales curved over her hips too. Her frantic fingers slid over her belly and found three flat, teardrop scales forming a triangular shape at the base of her ribcage beneath her breasts. She lifted a shaking hand to her forehead and touched the same three-teardrop pattern in the center of her forehead.

Trembling even more violently, she looked down over her body, at the strange scales, like delicate armor. And she saw the rest.

Drifting around her hips were four long appendages—thin, lightweight, the ends flattened and widening into an almost leaf-like shape with shiny teardrop scales. She recognized them, had seen them drifting about the water dragons' heads.

Tentacles. She had *tentacles*.

Horror engulfed her. Shame. Disgust. *Tentacles*. Why couldn't she have been pretty? Or at least cool-looking? Instead she'd gotten tentacles. Her hands shot to her head. A short tentacle-thing sprouted from behind each of her ears, curving toward the back of her head.

A freak. She was a goddamn tentacled freak.

The blanket had slipped from her grip. She grabbed it, swinging it around herself, pulling it tight to hide the awful sight of her body. The material brushed against the tentacles around her hips, making her cringe. It felt like someone was rubbing sandpaper inside her skull. The damn things were sensitive on top of being hideous—weak points. A vulnerability.

She gulped in air. It was fine. It was okay. She would learn how to see magic with her daemon eyes, fix her competing magic, and go back to being human. She would never have to revert to this monstrous form again. Her head throbbed.

"Piper!"

Ash's voice. Calling her. Frantic.

"Piper!"

Distant. Coming closer. Coming fast.

She pulled the blanket tighter, still crouched in a ball. No. She didn't want him to see her. She couldn't bear it. But he was coming and she couldn't stop him. She withdrew a hand from the blanket and yanked out her ponytail, roughly pulling her hair over her ears to hide the tentacles. It felt awful, more sandpaper scratching inside her head, but she ignored it. Flattening her bangs over her forehead to hide the three scales, she wrapped the blanket up to her neck.

He appeared, running full tilt around the bend in the path. He saw her and didn't slow—just charged straight to her, somehow managing to stop and drop to his knees right in front of her despite his speed.

"Piper!" he gasped. He reached for her but she flinched away, afraid he would feel the hard scales through the blanket. He pulled his hands back. "Are you okay?"

She nodded, head ducked, unable to meet his eyes.

"When you didn't come out again, I was afraid you'd . . . but then I thought maybe you slipped a little down the line. Are you sure you're okay?"

"I'm fine," she whispered. "It was tough but I—I made it out."

"Did it—" She felt his gaze sweeping over her. "Did it work?"

She nodded again.

He was silent for a moment. Then his fingers touched her jaw. She tried to pull away but his hand followed, forcing her chin up. She looked away from his eyes, unable to bear seeing the inevitable judgment in them. With his other hand, he brushed her bangs away from her forehead.

She squeezed her eyes shut, humiliation choking her.

"I don't believe it," he breathed. "How is it even possible? You're part *ryujin*."

His fingers slid into her hair, pushing it aside to reveal the tentacle thing.

"I don't believe it," he whispered again.

Her brow furrowed. He didn't sound disgusted. His voice was filled with . . . wonder? Her eyes opened of their own accord.

Ash stared at her with amazement etched on his face.

"Piper, this is—it should be impossible. Ryujin never leave the Overworld. How could you have a ryujin grandparent? It's—it's astounding. It also explains *a lot* about your encounter yesterday." He brushed a thumb across a scale on her forehead. "You have the blood of one of the rarest and most powerful Overworld castes. You couldn't have been luckier."

"Lucky?" she croaked, anger filtering through her shame. "*Lucky?*"

He blinked.

"I'm not lucky!" Tears filled her eyes. "I'm hideous."

He blinked again. "What? No, you're—"

"Don't lie to me!" She turned her head away. "I'm a freak. I have goddamn *tentacles*."

He grabbed her arms and stood abruptly, pulling her to her feet with him. She clutched her blanket with every bit of strength she had, head turned away.

"You are not a freak," he growled.

She looked back at him, startled by his sudden anger.

"You're beautiful."

"No, I'm—"

"Do you think *I'm* hideous?" he demanded. He waved a hand over his body, safely in glamour.

"No!" His daemon form was frightening and alien, but not ugly. There was a clear beauty to his dark, interlocking scales, the way they followed the curves of his body and muscles. The grace of his wings. The mesmerizing way he moved.

"Do you know how many times I've been called a monster?" he asked her.

"But I'm—you—you haven't seen—"

"Show me, then."

She shook her head, shrinking away.

"*Piper*," he said in exasperation. With a dart of his hand, he grabbed one side of the blanket and gave it a hard yank.

Squealing, she clutched the other end to her chest, scrambling to hold on to it. She wasn't nearly as worried about him seeing her naked as him seeing the non-human stuff. He didn't actually try to pull the blanket out of her hands though; he just pulled the one end away, letting it drop so the entire blanket hung in a strip down her front.

And she knew he could see it all—the scales on her shoulders, elbows, hips, knees. Even the tops of her feet. And the awful, dangling tentacles that originated somewhere at the base of her spine and swayed out around her hips, the longer pair falling just past her knees. They didn't actually seem to do anything; they just hung there, not limp, but not moveable like a tail either.

Hands on his hips, Ash studied her. She pressed the blanket to her chest, the other hand holding it tight to her belly.

"You don't have tentacles," he said.

She looked down to see whether the blanket was still hiding them, but there they were, in plain sight. "Uh, are you blind?"

He stepped closer. "Do you see any suction cups? Can you wriggle them around like little arms? They aren't tentacles."

She looked down at them again. "Not tentacles?"

"No." He reached out and touched one, sliding it between his finger and thumb.

Her entire body shuddered, tingles rushing across her skin. She jerked back. "Holy *shit*, don't do that again."

His eyes widened. "Sorry."

She sucked in a deep breath. As well as the physical sensation, his touch had felt like he'd stroked the inside of her brain. Freaky as *hell*.

"Did I hurt you?"

"N-no. It just felt . . . really weird."

He let out a slow breath, and his eyes travelled down her new form and back up again. "Piper . . ."

She shrunk a little under the intensity of his gaze. "What?"

A long moment of silence. He abruptly cleared his throat and looked away from her. "We should go get your clothes."

"Huh?"

"You need to put some clothes on."

"I—I do?"

"This way." He started walking, his steps quick.

Piper blinked. Rewrapping herself in the blanket, she hurried after him—then stopped. Again she took a couple quick steps—and stopped. She looked down, sticking one leg out of the blanket to examine it. No, her legs didn't *look* any more muscular than before.

She ran three steps. Stopped. Hoooooly crap. A grin spread across her face. She hadn't moved around enough to realize it before, but she felt *strong*. Really strong. She felt strong and lithe and flexible and agile. She felt as if she could run for hours. She glanced back and wondered how long she'd been crouched on the ground without feeling the slightest twinge in her legs.

"Piper?"

"Coming!" she chirped. With a few bounding steps, she caught up to Ash. "Is it always like this?"

"Like what?"

"I feel so *strong*. Like I could pick up a car!"

"Ah, probably not."

She frowned. "Do you get weaker in glamour?"

"Yes."

"Really? By how much?"

His eyebrows rose. "A lot."

"Why would you ever use glamour then?"

"Because everyone runs away screaming when I don't."

"Oh, right." She chewed the inside of her cheek, trying to hustle her thoughts into order. Everything was bouncing around in her head, her brain still scrambled from the Void. At least the headache had let up for the time being. She turned back to him as giddiness replaced her earlier self-loathing.

"Can you believe I did it?"

"Did what?"

"The *Void*. I made it through! Can you believe it?"

His lips curved in a hint of a smile. "Yes, I can."

"Can't you pretend to be amazed at my awesomeness?"

"I knew you would be fine."

"Weren't you the one yelling for me all panicky when I didn't come out in the same spot?"

"I never panic."

She gave him a long look as they walked down the trail. He somehow kept a perfectly straight face as he looked back at her.

He pointed. "Here are your clothes. I'll wait over there."

They'd reached the same spot where they'd gone into the ley line. She could feel the line just like before, rushing magic and crackling electricity brushing against her skin. But wasn't she supposed to be able to see it now too?

As she walked over to her clothes, she squinted toward where she could feel the line. Nothing. She must be missing a step in the "seeing magic" process. Shrugging, she knelt and picked up her underclothes. After sliding on her underwear and bra, she pulled on her pants but flinched when she got them up. The waistband dug into the base of the—the non-tentacles—and made her head feel all scratchy inside from the rubbing sensation. She pushed the pants down a little but the damn things were too high-waisted, not her usual style but it was all Miysis had had available, and if she slid them lower on her hips, she couldn't fasten them.

Scowling, she picked up her shirt and struggled with it for a minute. Ash had torn half of the buttons off and then she'd tied the ends in a knot while the material was still wet. Now dried, the knot was hard as a rock. She made a half-hearted attempt to pull it over her head. Not happening. Well, shit.

She rubbed both hands over her face, then looked at the dark blanket. With a sigh, she unsheathed a dagger from her pile of belongings and cut two wide strips of material. The first she wrapped around her chest, over her bra, and knotted it at the back. The second one she wrapped around her hips twice and knotted it on one side, nicely out of the way of her non-tentacles. It would have to do. She would be back on Earth soon, where she could be human again and acquire some real clothes.

Picking up a boot, she started to shove a foot in and grimaced at the pressure on the wide scales over the tops of her feet. Then she looked at her foot. Then up the trail. She'd walked ten minutes over rocky ground with bare feet and hadn't even noticed. Sighing again, she yanked off the boot and dropped it. What was the point?

She looked down at her makeshift clothes. Her scales glittered and shimmered in the sunlight. Pressing her lips together, she touched one of the non-tentacles, lightly pinching the end between her fingers. She shivered. It was so weird feeling the physical sensation while also feeling it in her mind.

She shook her head. So strange. Mind-boggling. It really hadn't sunk in yet, that this body was *her*. She was this strange, shimmering half-daemon? Not a half-human, but half-*daemon*.

Half-ryujin.

Another shake of her head. Part ryujin. As Ash had said, it perfectly explained yesterday's encounter with the ryujin. The daemon had somehow sensed that she was one of them, and so he'd saved her. She now knew why he'd said he would be waiting: he was waiting for her to discover she was one of them. Sort of one of them.

"Piper?"

She realized she'd been standing there staring at nothing for over a minute. Patting her blanket outfit to make sure it was all in place, and wishing she looked less like some sort of Sexy Jungle Babe fantasy—now with tentacles!—she hesitantly walked over to where Ash was waiting with his back politely turned.

"Okay. Best I could do," she said, feeling a blush coming on before he'd even turned.

His eyes drifted down her body and back up. By the time they reached her face, they were distinctly darker. She blinked quickly as heat slowly rose through her. That look, that stare. She knew that look.

With two fingers, he lightly touched the scales curving over the top of her hip, above the makeshift skirt. Her heart started to pound harder. His hand curled around her hip and he pulled her slowly closer. She looked up at him, trying to play it cool.

"You promised me something, before I entered the Void," she said, the words breathless.

"Did I?"

His voice was all husky with a hint of a growl. Her stomach flip-flopped.

"Yeah," she whispered. "You definitely did."

Her arms encircled his neck and his hand slid into her hair. And then his mouth was on hers and she was pulling herself even closer. His arm was crushing her against him and she had handfuls of his hair in her grip. She kissed him harder. Deeper. Desperate for more.

He suddenly turned their bodies, and then her back was against a tree and he was pressing against her. His body was hard and warm, muscles flexing, hands running over her skin as his mouth crushed hers. She pulled him even closer and hooked a leg over his thigh, locking their bodies together. She couldn't breathe. She didn't care. Fire inside her, his hands on her, his mouth on hers.

He pulled back and she gasped for air. Then his mouth was on her neck and she couldn't breathe again. He worked his way down her throat with light kisses that made her skin tingle. She clutched his shoulders as his mouth moved lower, across her collarbone, down—

His head jerked up, a tiny surprised noise escaping him. Almost a yelp.

"What?" she demanded, breathing hard.

"You—" He slid a hand over the back of his neck and shoulder, then looked at his fingers. There were streaks of blood on his fingertips. "You clawed me."

"I—" She glanced at her hands, fingers tipped with shiny, pointed scale-nails—with blood on them. "Oh. Oops. Sorry?"

He gave her a strange look.

"Are you okay?" she asked.

"I think I'll live."

"Oh good. So—"

Her head gave a violent, sickening throb.

She swayed and pressed both hands to her forehead, swallowing to get her stomach back down as the next wave rolled over her. "Uuuugh."

The pain was back with a vengeance and ratcheting—fast. She shouldn't have wasted so much time; the rune venom had almost completely worn off. Kissing Ash should have probably waited.

"Piper, what are you supposed to do next?"

"I—I—" She struggled to think through the blinding pain.

"Ash! Piper!"

Lyre's voice echoed down the trail. A moment later, she could hear the running footsteps of the rest of the group, but she didn't open her eyes, fighting the pain as it rose and fell in burning waves.

"Piper!" Lyre exclaimed, his voice suddenly right beside her. "Holy crap, look at you!"

She squeezed her head between her hands. The world felt as though it were disconnecting, like everything was stretching away from her. Ash's arm around her waist was her only anchor in the raging ocean of pain.

Miysis arrived next, his voice ringing out in sharp disbelief. "Ryujin? She's *ryujin*?"

"Piper," Ash said firmly, squeezing her middle, "you have your daemon glamour now. What do you need to do next?"

"I—" The whole point of her new form was so she could see magic. That was it. "I need to see my magic."

"Then she should shade," Miysis said. "Magic is clearest while shaded."

"Can a haemon shade?" Lyre asked urgently.

She barely heard him as she choked back a sob. Agony. Her head was splitting, bone fracturing and brain surely boiling in its juices.

"Piper," Ash said, "can you shade?"

Shade. How the hell did she shade? She squeezed her head harder. What caused a daemon to shade? Her eyes flew open. Fear. Fear caused shading.

"Ash," she gasped, squinting through tears of pain. "Scare me."

"What?"

"Drop your glamour. Scare me!"

He looked bewildered for a second before clueing in. His body shimmered. Black wings spread wide, horns and scales, eyes like the soul of the night. She stared at him, waiting for it, waiting for the terror to hit her.

Nothing happened.

"Scare me!"

"I can't bloody do anything else," he snarled.

She shivered as his daemon voice slid across her bones, but even that didn't trigger the Nightmare Effect. It wasn't working. She wasn't afraid of him. She would have laughed at the disgusting irony had she not been in such agony.

She looked around wildly. "Seiya! Seiya, where are you?"

The draconian girl appeared in front of her, petite and harmless-looking beside her full-daemon brother. "Yes?"

"Shade. Please shade and frighten me!"

With a shrug, she dropped her glamour and spread her wings.

Terror crashed through Piper. For a moment, it overwhelmed her, mixing with the agony until she thought she might pass out.

And then something changed.

The roiling whirlwind of emotions—terror, agony, uncertainty, panic—went completely still. She hovered in the center of it all, serene and utterly composed. The agony raged just beyond her sudden calm, unable to touch her.

"Holy *shit*," Lyre breathed. "Look at her eyes. Black as pitch."

With her mind free of pain, the next step seemed clear as day. She needed to see her magic, to behold the differences in order to separate the two. And to see magic, she needed to cast magic.

She raised her hands and called on light. It was that easy. She'd seen daemons do it a dozen times. All she did was will it and it came, a melon-sized ball of rippling, heatless flame that hovered above her hands. Ash, Seiya, and Lyre stepped back at the sudden burst of light.

The fire showed her exactly what she needed to see. Dark purple flames wove through pale blue fire. Where they touched, a sickly orange glow emanated. She studied the dancing light, the two colors. Yes, she could tell them apart. The blue fire was warm and tranquil, a sun-bathed pool of water. The purple was cool, sharp, leaping and spinning. Fast, harsh. Completely different.

Narrowing her eyes, she tilted her head to one side as she concentrated. Slowly, with flashes of orange glow, the two colors began separating. They wanted to mix, to burn each other, to combust and explode until there was nothing left, but she resolutely pulled them apart. At the same time the light before her changed, she felt the same thing happening within her—two magics being pulled apart.

And then she had a ball of light hovering above each hand, one purple and one blue. And she could feel it inside her—two clear magics. The fast, sharp purple one, and the warm, soft blue one. She'd done it.

CHAPTER
-20-

WITH FLICKS of her hands, Piper cast the spheres of light away and took a deep breath. The strange state of calm dissipated but no agony followed. Just a dull ache in her head and the lingering tremble from the Nightmare Effect.

She looked up. Ash and Seiya were back in glamour. They and Lyre stared at her.

She gave them a wavering smile. Elation swept through her as it sank in: she'd done it. She'd fixed her magic—by herself. No one else had done it. No one had fixed her or saved her. She'd done it *herself*.

"I did it!" she crowed.

Grinning, bursting with excitement, she jumped forward and threw her arms around Ash—or she meant to. She'd forgotten about her daemon strength. She slammed into him and he went over backward, landing hard on his back as she came down on top of him. A blush rushed into her cheeks.

"Good job," he wheezed.

"Sorry!" She scrambled off him while Lyre laughed loudly.

They both got to their feet and she grinned at them, even feeling a certain amount of charity toward Seiya, who actually looked pleased.

Piper beamed, bouncing on the balls of her feet, freed from fear for the first time since she'd returned from boarding school, and elated by her success. She'd never felt stronger.

"Congratulations, Piper," Miysis said.

She turned toward him, surprised to see his smile—much more genuine than his usual cat-like smiles.

"I can't say how relieved I am. And your new form"—he gestured at her body—"is quite spectacular. I am extremely curious as to how you came to have ryujin blood."

She shrugged, self-consciously pulling her hair over the non-tentacles behind her ears. "We'll probably never know, though I suppose I could go ask the ryujin."

"Ah, perhaps not today. We have only just assured your continued survival. Let's not risk that so soon."

"We should pack up and get back," Ash said.

Miysis nodded and moved away to discuss something with his men. Ash turned to Seiya and led her a few steps away as he murmured something.

Fingers touched Piper's side, brushing across the shimmering scales on her hip.

"Hey there, gorgeous," Lyre purred. "You're absolutely delectable, did you know?"

She lifted her eyebrows. "Pretty sure I'm just a sparklier, freakier version of what I looked like before."

"Sparkly, yes. Freaky, no." He lifted her hand and touched the scales on her knuckles. "Our standards of beauty are much broader than the narrow, boring restrictions humans have. If every woman met human ideals of beauty, you'd all be identical. Now, this"—his eyes flicked down her and back up again—"is twice as stunning—to us, at least."

She smiled. "Thanks Lyre."

He gave her that sexy half-grin. "If you get the urge to take your new form for a test run, just say the word."

"A test run, really?" She beamed at him. "I was just thinking it would be fun to run the rest of the way up the mountain."

"Run? Up the mountain?"

"Yeah! I want to see what this body can do." She waved a hand toward the peak. "I'd love some company, so since you offered . . ."

"Um. I don't think we have time for that right now."

"Ah, I see." She smirked. "Maybe next time then."

"Yeah . . ." he grumbled.

Ash returned. Piper glanced past him and saw Seiya, Zala on her shoulder, striding toward the ley line.

"Seiya is going through. Lyre, you should go too. Koen or I will bring Piper through in a minute."

"Sure," Lyre said, then winked at Piper. "See you on the other side, beautiful."

He headed for the invisible ley line. He walked calmly like he was merely strolling in the park—and then, with a ripple of air, he vanished. She felt the blip in the ley line's power like a rock being dropped into a rushing stream. She squinted at it.

"Why can't I see it?" she asked Ash.

"I imagine you'd have to shade again." He gave his head a little shake. "I've never seen a haemon shade before."

"Have you ever seen a haemon with a daemon glamour?"

"No."

"Well." She shrugged and smiled. "Shading was weird. One minute I was terrified and the next . . . just totally calm."

"You did seem surprisingly level. I think it might be different for you than a full daemon."

"What do you mean?"

He turned to look across the valley, frowning slightly. "Shading is a calmer state, yes, but our instincts are very strong. You showed amazing instinct for working your magic, but you didn't show any signs of the overwhelming survival instinct of daemons. I expected you to attack Seiya."

"Oh. Hmm." She shrugged. "Well, it worked pretty well."

He gave her a long look. "I didn't frighten you."

She blinked. Before she could answer, Miysis joined them.

"Piper," he said, "do you feel in full control of your magic now?"

She blinked, surprised by the question. It took only a fraction of her attention to keep the two magics separated inside her body. It wasn't difficult, though perhaps it would grow tiring with time. She was a little worried about what would happen when she slept.

"Yeah," she answered. "I feel great."

"Excellent," he replied. "In that case, before we leave, I would like you to complete your side of our bargain."

"What?" she asked blankly. "*Now?*"

With everything that had happened since they'd arrived in the Underworld, she'd almost forgotten about the other half of the agreement with Miysis. In return for his help, she was supposed to use the Sahar for him.

"Now?" Ash said as well, his disapproval clear. "She should rest first. She just went through hell."

Miysis's expression hardened implacably. "It would be simpler to complete now while we are here."

"Here?" she repeated. "'Here' as in the Overworld or 'here' as in *right here*?"

Miysis took her elbow. "This way."

"But—"

"Did you agree to this or not?"

"I—well, yes, but—"

"Then come."

"Hold on—" Ash began.

Miysis shot him a cutting look. "You are not part of this bargain, Ashtaroth."

Ash bared his teeth.

Piper looked rapidly between them. Her eyes darted across Miysis's four men who were slowly shifting closer, eyes on Ash. Maybe Seiya and Lyre had been a little hasty in going through the ley line ahead of the rest of them.

She cleared her throat. "Where are we going?"

"It's not far." Miysis's aggressive bearing vanished as he dismissed Ash's presence. "I don't imagine it will take you long."

She let Miysis lead her up the trail, in the opposite direction they'd taken to Vejovis's home. His men followed her and Miysis, keeping between her and Ash. Nervousness grew in her belly.

Miysis guided her up the trail, beyond the spot where she'd come out of the ley line. The line paralleled the path, teasing her senses, a shimmer of magic she could see only out of the corner of her eye. They followed the curve of the mountain around a wide bend and her gaze swept across the view.

Though the cliff continued along the south side of the river, the mountain on the opposite side flattened out into a wide, forested plateau. If the ley line had run across the other side of the river instead, travel would have been so much easier; they could have walked straight across the plateau, a leisurely stroll through a beautiful forest instead of dangerous, cliff-side paths.

On their side of the valley, a massive, jutting piece of the mountain leaned out over the river. The trail they followed disappeared at the sheer, impassable barricade. Short of extensive mountain climbing gear or wings, there was no way to continue.

Miysis took her elbow again and pulled her with him another dozen paces down the trail, toward the dead end. She glanced back and saw three of Miysis's men casually block the path, preventing Ash from following. He stood beyond the guards, arms folded, tense.

Lifting one hand, Miysis pointed. "Do you see that crack?"

She looked again. A deep crack ran vertically through the rock blocking their path, likely caused by hundreds of years of strain on the rock. There had to be at least a hundred tons leaning over the valley.

"I see it."

"Your task is to split the rock at that crack."

Her eyes narrowed. Break away that colossal slab of rock? She could clearly see what would happen: the broken slab would tip over like a falling tree and the upper end would land on the plateau side of the valley. If it didn't shatter, it would form a natural bridge across the valley. If it did break, it would fall and damn up the river. She had no idea what that would do to the surrounding landscape, but it wouldn't be good.

No wonder Miysis wanted more firepower than any one daemon—or a dozen—could manage. It was triple the demolition job that the bridge in Asphodel had been.

She looked at the plateau again and her skin prickled. Hadn't Lyre and Ash surmised how strange it was that Miysis knew so much about the ryujin territory? That he or other Ra daemons had explored it so thoroughly that they'd found Vejovis's hidden home? If they couldn't fly safely in the territory, it had to be hard to explore the land; only small groups could move about at one time because the ley line ran along a treacherous mountain path.

But what if there were an easy route into ryujin territory? What if the Ra family could sneak unlimited numbers of their soldiers straight onto the forested plateau, easy terrain where they could spread out or even gather a large force? That plateau would give them access to a huge section of the ryujin territory.

On the other hand, if the rock broke and blocked the river, it would cut off the flow of water into a significant portion of the valley and beyond.

"Why do you need this done?" she asked neutrally.

"It doesn't matter," Miysis said. "You agreed to my terms. This is my task."

Her hands clenched. If she did as he asked, she would either be clearing the path for a Ra invasion of the ryujin territory or outright destroying the valley.

"You promised I wouldn't be hurting anyone," she said harshly.

"You won't be. There is no one on or below the rock."

Her jaw tightened. Why hadn't she learned her lesson when it came to Miysis? Why did she trust anything he said? He'd made it seem like she would be fixing a rockslide or opening up a trade route—not enabling a war on an unsuspecting people.

She turned away from the rock to face him. "You misled me."

His eyes narrowed. "I did not. I told you exactly what you would be doing."

Her gaze darted from him to Koen, standing behind the Ra heir, then to the three by Ash. Everyone was watching her.

"I won't help you start a war," she snapped.

Miysis's face went cold, and for a moment, she felt as though she were facing down Maahes, the ancient, powerful leader of the Ras. "Are you refusing to fulfill your end of our agreement?"

"I'm refusing to do *this* task. I'll do something else for you."

His eyes went black. "If you refuse, then you forfeit your life."

She took a fast step back before she could stop herself. The sheer side of the mountain blocked any possible retreat. "Are you going to kill me?"

"If you refuse, your life is mine to do with as I will."

Her mouth went dry at the icy contempt in his black eyes, the utter lack of sympathy.

"I will not ask again," he said. He slid a hand into his left breast pocket and retrieved the Sahar. He held it up between his finger and thumb. "Do you refuse to uphold our bargain?"

She stared at him. No mercy or compassion touched his eyes. Her gaze again flicked over Miysis and Koen. Two against one. She didn't fancy her odds—but she would take them over the task Miysis had given her. She wouldn't help him wage a war.

"I refuse," she whispered.

He went still, studying her with black eyes. She tensed, fingers flexing in the vain wish for a weapon.

His hand closed in a fist around the Sahar.

"Then you leave me no choice."

She had only a moment to feel fear.

Koen's hand flashed out. He grabbed Piper by the neck. She screamed as he smashed her back into the rock behind her. In the same instant, the other three Ra daemons, mere feet away from Ash, whipped toward him, blades flashing in their hands as though from thin air. Ash threw up a shield as the three attackers charged him point blank.

But that's when she had screamed.

And his eyes, in that crucial moment, flicked away from his attackers and toward her.

Again, time slowed to a crawl.

He jerked his attention back to his attackers—too late. Three simultaneous blasts of power shattered his shield. He had no time for another defense. They were already upon him, sunlight flashing on their blades.

Piper's heart stopped.

232 | ANNETTE MARIE

The first blade plunged into his chest. Then the second. Then the third.

The points erupted from his back, glistening with blood. The daemons simultaneously yanked their weapons out. Ash staggered, shock blanking his face. One of the daemons stepped forward, grabbed Ash's shirtfront, and threw him backward.

Right off the cliff's edge.

CHAPTER
-21-

PIPER'S scream of horror pierced her own ears. For a bare second, she expected to see Ash whoosh skyward with fast beats of his powerful wings, weapons drawn and magic flashing. But of course he didn't. He'd been stabbed three times in the chest. If any of those blades had hit his heart, he was already dead.

With an animal shriek, Zwi burst out of a rocky crag where she'd been hiding and shot past everyone, diving over the side of the cliff. Far, far too late to do anything.

Panic and denial closed around Piper, choking off her air. Terror and agony blinded her. It repeated over and over in her head: the blades flashing, the shining metal disappearing into his body, the spray of blood as the daemons pulled their weapons out again. Over and over she saw him vanishing over the edge, gone. Gone gone gone—

And then all the spinning terror stopped. She was suddenly floating in a state of utter calm—icy, murderous calm.

Her eyes turned onto Miysis and hatred surged even as her mind stayed cool and logical.

Koen squeezed her throat, cutting off her air. Her hands flashed up and she raked her shimmering new claws down his face. He jerked back and she struck him three times: in the face, the sternum, and the diaphragm. He staggered back, stunned, and she smashed one last blow into his face. He dropped to his knees.

She spun and launched herself at Miysis.

His hands shot up and, for the first time, she could see the magic of his shield—a glowing sheet of gold between them. Instinctively, she called on her own magic, wrapping flickering blue and purple flames around her fist as she let it fly straight at his shield. Her scaled knuckles hit the barrier, and with a burst of orange light, the shield vanished.

Shock flashed across his face, and then she was on him.

She loosed a swift kick at his knee but he sprang back, lighter on his feet than she'd expected. She reached out in a fast strike, claws hooked as she went for his throat. He blocked her attack and suddenly reversed direction, slamming her with his greater weight. She staggered then ducked fast as he unleashed a glowing ball of gold light that exploded in a shower of stones when it hit the rock behind her.

Baring her teeth, she sprang for him again. The calmness of shading kept her levelheaded as rage pulsated through her. She feigned a strike to his torso, then dropped and swept out her leg. It hit his ankles and he stumbled. She coiled her body and launched herself into his legs. He fell.

She jumped on top of him, claws going for his face. He grabbed her wrists, teeth bared, eyes black. For a brief second, she strained against him, forcing her hands down, her half-daemon strength overpowering him.

Then his body shimmered as he released his glamour.

He flipped her off him and came down on top of her in one smooth move. Wings rose off his back, golden-brown feathers sweeping outward. With twice the physical power of his glamoured form, he crushed her into the rock and pressed his forearm into her throat. She fought to keep the pressure off her windpipe and called on her magic. As soon as she did, he slammed some kind of spell down on her and her magic fizzled out like a snuffed flame.

His other hand grabbed her chin and she knew exactly what he was planning to do—knock her out with a sleep spell.

As tingles rushed over her skin from his magic, she grabbed the fist of his other hand and dragged her claws across the heel of his hand and into the palm, forcing his fingers open. With her other hand, she snatched the Sahar from his grip.

Raging magic rushed into her, eclipsing her own reserves. It exploded out of her in an uncontrolled blast, hurling Miysis off her. He crashed down on his back and nearly slid off the edge of the cliff. She rolled to her feet—and felt a ripple of magic from the ley line.

Six daemons flashed into being out of the line, hurtling straight for her.

She spread her arms wide and called on the Stone. Violence erupted in her head but her calm, shaded state held. As the daemons charged, she spun in a fast circle, arms cutting through the air. Two blades of white magic spun out from her hands and whipped outward at chest-height. Blood sprayed. All six daemons collapsed.

She turned toward Miysis. He had been far enough away to successfully shield against her last attack. He stood rigidly, wings half-furled, waist-length braid of golden hair hanging over one shoulder. Another time, she would have been in awe of the beauty of his daemon form, nearly as stunning as Lyre's. Instead, she just wanted to kill him.

Rage and hatred built inside her, pumping into her from the Sahar and mixing with her own burning fury. Her barrier of tranquil logic started to crumble and she bared her teeth, overcome with the need to see him bleed. To rip out his heart and watch life fade from his deceitful green eyes. To make him pay for what he'd done to them.

The ley line stuttered again, the magic shuddering as another dozen daemons appeared.

Shocked out of her haze of savagery, she spun away from the line. Hatred still seethed in her, demanding she destroy them, rip them apart, feed their blood to the earth. But they weren't important. It had been less than a minute since Ash had disappeared over the cliff. He hadn't given up on her when she'd fallen into the river. She wouldn't give up on him.

Sahar clenched in one hand, she took two running steps and leaped off the cliff.

She plummeted, the wind screaming in her ears. The water rushed toward her while also seeming to approach her in slow motion, gradually filling her vision. Rocky cliff walls whipped by on either side, faster than she'd ever experienced, but the fall was strangely calming, almost serene, her fear of heights forgotten. Pointing her feet downward, she plunged into the river.

Pain ricocheted through her legs on impact. Water engulfed her. The moment she was submerged, she knew why her non-tentacles felt so weird when touched. They were made for the water.

Sensations flooded her mind—every shift of the current, every dart of a nearby fish, every rock, tree branch, and obstacle. The river welcomed her like a long-lost but deeply beloved child, a warmth she could feel inside her head, the touch of a deep and ancient power.

She shot for the surface, her head bursting into the cool air. She didn't have to swim. The water held her up as she was swept downstream.

Ahead. Far ahead. She could see flashes of black—small wings beating frantically in the air. Zwi had grabbed on to Ash and was desperately trying to keep his head above water. Piper could feel his presence in the river ahead of her. She could even feel his blood, foreign Underworlder blood, tainting the pure waters.

And beyond him she could sense the sharp, crashing violence of rapids.

She had to reach him before he hit the rapids. No sooner had the thought come to her than the current of the river gave a strange shudder. With a reassuring caress inside her mind, the river surged— and then she was nearly flying, the current carrying her at an impossible speed downstream, shooting her toward the flashing black flag that was Zwi. She stretched out her arms, reaching for Ash.

The moment her arms closed around him, another shudder ran through the river and the current abruptly gentled. She clutched Ash to her, his back against her front as she leaned back to keep his head up. Zwi flew above them, crying out in fear with each flap.

The river carried them into the tamed rapids. She could feel the current and the rocks, and she knew nothing would harm them. The alien power in the river helped her, whisking her this way and that along the gentlest path. She spotted a stretch of gravel along the bank, an easy place to go ashore.

The current swirled, pushing them toward the spot. Her feet touched the slick bottom. She pulled Ash through the water and dragged him halfway onto the rocky slope.

"Ash!" She knelt beside him, her feet still in the water. Panic threatened to blank her mind.

Three stab wounds to the chest. They'd missed his heart, but both lungs had to be punctured. Blood seeped from the wounds. She touched his face. His skin was clammy and his lips were tinged blue either from the cold river or from shock. She put a hand over his mouth and felt his warm breath on her wet skin. He was still breathing—barely.

Zwi landed beside her master, pawing at his shoulder as she mewled.

"No," Piper moaned. "I don't know how to heal you. Ash, I don't know how!"

His eyelids flickered but his eyes didn't quite open. He couldn't have much time left. What did she do? What should she do?

"Help," she whispered. "Help!" This time she screamed it, head whipping around to scour the barren, rocky bottom of the gorge. "Please help me!"

And she felt it, whispering through the river. An answer. An affirmative.

Help was coming.

Zwi let out a sharp chirp—a warning. Piper looked up.

High up on the cliff's edge, almost out of sight around the bend, she saw the dark silhouettes of a dozen people. And then their wings spread. They jumped off the cliff, soaring out over the canyon. Piper's heart stuttered.

Ra daemons were griffins—and just like Miysis, they had wings.

They were coming for her and for the Sahar. She bared her teeth. "Over my dead body," she growled.

Reluctantly letting go of Ash, she stepped into the water until she was submerged up to her waist. The river swirled around her, waiting for her command. It knew what to do, as it had done it a hundred times before at the call of other ryujin. Piper could see it in her mind, a vision of how to form her attack. The river was willing. All she had to do was provide the magic.

A dozen griffins soared toward her. She could just make out the golden brown feathers of their wings and the long-handled halberds in their hands, the perfect weapons for diving at your enemy without ever making yourself a target.

She had no intention of letting them get that close.

She tapped the Sahar again. Roaring power surged into her, filling her body near bursting. Every nerve burned with agony, but locked in the shaded state of a daemon, she barely registered it. The griffins were descending, blades flashing in the sunlight. Their long golden braids trailed behind them.

She extended her hands over the water. The river shivered as she flooded it with power. Hatred pounded through her. No one would take the Sahar from her. No one would hurt Ash again.

She flung her hands skyward.

Massive jets of spinning water whipped into the air like a dozen immense waterspouts. The flailing spirals writhed fifty feet above the river, waving and undulating with wild force. The griffins scattered as the spirals crashed into their midst. One, two, three griffins got caught in the spirals.

She dropped her hands and the water jets lost their form, crashing back into the river. The remaining griffins had lost elevation, though already they were beating their wings to regain altitude. Too slow. Her lips stretched into a merciless smile.

She extended her hands and felt the river's will join her own for a second time. Power poured from the Sahar, through her body, and into the water. Another half dozen spirals of water launched into the air. Five griffins couldn't get away fast enough and the enormous spouts smashed into them.

Five left. She pulled on the Sahar again—and agony shredded her concentration.

She doubled over, clutching her middle, unable to breathe. Burning, searing pain coursed along every nerve. She'd been so focused, so shaded and immune to pain, she hadn't really felt it—the Sahar's power tearing through her body. With effort, she let go of her connection to the Sahar. The consuming hatred from the Stone vanished, clearing her mind.

Gasping, she looked up as the first griffin dove at her. She threw up her arms, barely able to think through the pain, let alone defend herself. The blade of his weapon sped toward her.

Zwi leaped in the griffin's face, clawing at his eyes. He overshot Piper, his halberd swinging by mere inches above her head. Zwi darted away.

Piper spun as the griffin landed and pivoted to face her. Blood ran down his face. Teeth bared, flared wings making him look huge, he charged with his halberd a spinning blur. She flung a hand out and a five-foot wave of water leaped over Ash and smashed into the griffin, knocking him off his feet.

She dove toward Ash and a blade whooshed past, slicing the air where her head had just been. The second griffin—she hadn't even seen him coming—swept past, circling around for another strike.

Dropping to one knee, she pulled both of Ash's short swords from the sheaths along his thighs. Holding both in one hand, she jammed the Sahar into her bra. Breathing hard from the pain of her magic overdose, she ran at the griffin on the ground.

Her left sword hit the blade of his halberd. He nearly ripped it out of her hand when he twisted the handle of his weapon. She slashed with the other but he stepped sideways. Freeing her blade, she darted in, faster as a half-daemon than she'd ever been as a haemon, but he was a hardened, experienced soldier.

A flick of his hand and a magic blast shot at her. Unlike past fights, she could see it coming—golden light rushing toward her chest. She threw up both swords and pulled on her magic instead of the Sahar. Her shield formed: a shimmering sheet of blue magic with streaks of purple.

As his blast was deflected, the griffin lunged in, his halberd sweeping low. She leaped over it, but he reversed the direction and the blade whipped toward her face. She blocked, his halberd crashing into her two blades. If her daemon form hadn't been so much stronger than her haemon one, she would have been knocked off her feet. She slashed three times in quick succession, trying to hold him off as she desperately searched for a hole in his guard.

Zwi appeared out of nowhere, landed on his head, and wrapped her wings around his face.

He shouted furiously, reaching for the dragonet, but Piper was already lunging forward. Her first strike cut his arm down to the bone and tore the halberd from his hand. Her second pierced his chest between two ribs and went straight into his heart.

He fell backward, the sword stuck in his chest. Piper whirled and ducked with a shriek as two more griffins dove at her. The first blade missed her but the second cut a shallow line across her back as she dove for the ground. She rolled to her feet and whirled around to face them. For a moment, the three of them paused, sizing one another up.

Piper called up a sphere of blue and purple flame and threw it at the two griffins. They both cast shimmering gold shields, but she was charging in right behind as the fire burst harmlessly against their defenses. She slashed at one and ducked as the other tried to stab her in the back. Their damn halberds had so much more reach than her short sword.

Zwi swooped in again. She grabbed a mouthful of feathers from one griffin's wing and ripped them out. The griffin yelped and flailed at the dragonet.

Piper focused on the other one. His halberd spun in his hands, too fast to follow. He moved toward her, his steps slow but implacable. She retreated, holding her guard position as she watched his black eyes. A flicker of a glance. She sprang back and lifted her sword in a block as the halberd flashed out. It struck the sword so hard that it was knocked out of her hands.

She didn't waste time being scared shitless that she was now unarmed. His halberd had swung wide in his last attack, leaving a clear opening—so she jumped on him.

Her attack took him completely by surprise. She landed with one foot on his halberd's handle and used it to spring even higher. She grabbed his shoulder and swung her body around to hook her leg around his jaw. With his head squeezed in the crook of her knee, she flung herself upside-down over his back.

His neck made an awful crunching sound when it broke.

She landed hard, the griffin falling half on top of her. In the sky above, the last two griffins circled. Beyond them, flying hard, was another dozen, newly arrived from the ley line. Holy shit, was there no end to them?

Breathing hard, she started to shove the body off her when a shadow fell across her. She looked up and her heart skipped a beat. The other griffin, chunks of broken feathers sticking off his wings, stalked toward her. She didn't see any sign of Zwi.

She wrenched at the weight of the fallen griffin, his torso still pinning her leg, her muscles shaking from adrenaline and the residual burn from her magic overdose. He rotated his halberd, aiming the point at her chest. His arm drew back, readying the strike.

She threw up her hands, casting a shield at the last second. The blade hit it. Her shield shattered but deflected the trajectory of the blade. It hit the top of her shoulder and scraped across the shimmering scales. Piper grabbed the handle of the halberd as the griffin yanked it back. The force pulled her free from the dead griffin, but her legs buckled before she could get them under her. The griffin wrenched his weapon free and she fell forward, barely catching herself on hands and knees.

The other two griffins swooped in and landed on her other side, blocking any escape.

The first griffin drew his halberd back a second time, taking aim. Magic sparked down the length of the weapon, a spell to break any shield she might cast. She recoiled, calling on the Sahar to create a shield anyway, the only thing she could do.

With a huge splash, a shimmering white beast surged out of the river and crashed headlong into the first griffin. The water dragon's massive jaws closed around the griffin's head, crushing it. Flinging the griffin aside, it whipped its tail over Piper, smashing it into the other two griffins. They both slammed into the wall of the canyon and crumpled.

The griffins in the sky roared battle cries and dove.

Piper scrambled to her feet, looking around wildly for a sword. Before she had the chance to find one, another dragon surged out of the river, spraying water everywhere. And then a third a little ways down the bank. And another. And another.

Suddenly, silvery blue water dragons lined the bank, half a dozen on either side of her, the scales on their foreheads glowing and their jaws opened wide in threat as they gazed upward. The griffins had aborted their dives and were hovering awkwardly out of reach of the creatures.

A strange ripple ran across the river—and a dark head broke the surface.

The ryujin floated in the middle of the river, untouched by the current, head and shoulders visible as he looked up at the griffins. One of the flying daemons hurled his halberd. The ryujin vanished beneath the surface a moment before the weapon splashed into the water.

The river rippled again. The current churned. The griffins started flapping frantically, retreating toward the high cliffs. Too slow.

Pillars of water exploded out of the river—and Piper saw what Miysis had meant about the ryujin's good aim. Twelve pillars. Twelve helpless griffins. Each waterspout slammed into a fleeing griffin. The water folded over them like breaking waves and yanked them down. Twelve griffins disappeared beneath the surface.

And then there was no sound but the mundane rush of the river. No more wings in the sky. No more blades flashing in the sun.

Piper launched to her feet and ran down the bank, her heart squeezing in her chest.

Ash lay exactly where she'd left him. He'd lost his glamour, dark wings splayed awkwardly against the rocks. She dropped to her knees beside him. His chest rose and fell, breath fast and weak. His face was white as snow and his skin icy to the touch.

"Ash!" she gasped. "Help!" she yelled over her shoulder. "Help him!"

She clutched his hand and pressed her fingers to his wrist. His pulse was fast and erratic. He had no time left.

"It's okay, Ash," she said, her voice shaking. "The griffins are gone now. And there's a ryujin. He's going to help you. He can heal you."

She clutched his hand. His chest rose and fell, faster and faster as he fought for air, slowly drowning in his own blood.

"You'll be okay," she whispered. "Just hold on. Don't give up. Help!" she screamed toward the water.

Ash's breath came in gasps. She squeezed his hand, her heart in her throat as she watched his chest rise and fall, counting each desperate breath he took. The ryujin—she had no idea if it was the same one as before—ran through the shallow water and knelt beside her. He reached for Ash.

Ash let out a gurgling breath—then silence.

His chest didn't rise again.

CHAPTER
-22-

PIPER paced. Back and forth. Ten steps, then ten more. She couldn't stop moving even though her muscles trembled with each step. Even though her head and chest were burning from using too much of the Sahar's magic. Even though the scabbed wound on her back kept reopening from the constant movement.

She couldn't stop until she knew Ash would live.

Seconds after Ash had stopped breathing, two more ryujin had burst out of the water, and she'd recognized the one who'd healed her. They'd circled Ash, kneeling around him, magic sizzling in the air. A long minute had passed as they worked on him—and then Ash had taken another breath. And another. But each one was so weak it sounded like it would surely be his last.

Once it was clear Ash wouldn't immediately expire, she'd left for a minute to find Zwi. The poor dragonet had been lying in a crumpled lump behind a cluster of rocks, probably knocked out of the air by the griffin. When Piper had picked her up, Zwi had opened her eyes and mewled softly. She'd seemed to be only bruised, for which Piper couldn't be more grateful.

The dragonet's master, though, was in far worse shape.

With Zwi in her arms, Piper had turned to rejoin the ryujin and Ash, when movement had caught her eye. Far above on the cliff's edge, a line of figures had stood watching her. She couldn't say how she knew, but she had been certain that one of them was Miysis. She'd stared up at him, hatred scorching her soul.

"Child."

The ryujin who'd healed her before had stood, and he too was looking up at the cliffs.

"This place is not safe. We must move."

The other ryujin had carefully lifted Ash between them, their hands gentle as they laid him across the back of the nearest water dragon. She'd wanted to ask them why they were helping her, why they were helping Ash—but clearly they were, and she would worry about their motivations later.

"Will he be okay?" Piper had asked, her voice shaking.

"He is stable . . . for now."

That had been two hours ago. The ryujin had taken her down the river, back to the cave where she'd nearly died. Deep inside the snaking underground cavern system that no one but a ryujin could enter was their home.

Piper had only seen two daemon dwellings. Asphodel in the Underworld had been old world elegance mixed with modern design, striking with a cold, stark beauty. But the ryujin city was something else entirely.

The main cave was long and winding, with a small branch of the river flowing casually through the middle. Much of it was natural stone, carved long ago by flowing currents and dripping water. Stalagmites hung high above. Veins of quartz or some other colored stone glittered in the ceiling of the cavern, ice blue and amethyst and champagne pink.

The rest had been carved by the ryujin—smooth, swirling lines and curves that mimicked flowing water. From the wide doorways to the footbridges to the walkways leading up to the higher levels, there were no straight lines to be seen. Uncut gemstones the size of melons had been set in the walls and imbued with spells that made them glow, lighting the darkness with soft colors.

It was more beautiful than a dream. Once she knew Ash would be okay, she would appreciate it properly. But for now she continued to pace, occasionally glancing toward the shadowy crevice of rock where Zwi was hiding, as there were too many strangers for the shy dragonet to show herself.

The city didn't have houses. Instead, doorways led to the interior of the mountain, covered by curtains woven from leaves and vines, and decorated with glittering gems. Wide avenues led to entirely different branches of the city where more ryujin lived. She couldn't even begin to guess how many called this place home. It could have been anywhere from few hundred to a few thousand.

And this was just one small city. Similar cavern systems existed throughout the mountain range. How many cities had they built beneath the mountains?

She kept her line of pacing contained to the stretch of smooth stone in front of what she assumed were guest rooms of some kind. Inside the guest room, on the other side of the woven curtain, a group of ryujin was working to heal Ash. They had stopped him from dying on the rocky shore of the river, but he wasn't anywhere near out of danger. He could still die. If his heart stopped again, that would be it.

She'd been kicked out of the room before they'd even laid him out on the bed—a mattress of soft sheets and a plush rug that the ryujin probably hadn't crafted themselves. More of the strange daemons had been waiting outside the room to greet her. They'd tried to get her to come with them, to have her injuries treated, to get food and some real clothes, but she'd refused. They'd tried to get her to at least sit down, but she'd refused that as well. Some of them lingered, watching her as though she was some shy, exotic creature they didn't want to frighten.

She had to make a conscious effort not to stare at them as she paced. The ryujin were a beautiful people despite their alien looks. Their scaled bodies shimmered in the faint light of the glowing stones. Men and women both wore their dark hair long, some loose, some braided with beads and gemstones. The men wore garments similar to shorts, fitted to minimize drag in the water. The women wore similar bottoms, as well as halter tops. The garments shimmered too, by all appearances waterproof, and were decorated with intricate stitching and more gemstones.

The presence of the nearby ryujin was like a comforting spot of warmth in her mind. She didn't understand their telepathy, but somehow she could *feel* them around her. Every individual was a presence in her mind. Maybe her new form was more receptive than her human body, or maybe she just hadn't been near enough of them before. If she had felt this before, she never would have been afraid of the first ryujin. She could literally sense their welcome and acceptance.

She would never again judge a daemon based on reputation alone. So many feared the ryujin. Even Underworlders knew their reputation as vicious killers. But they were clearly not a violent people at heart. She still didn't understand why they were helping her and Ash, why they were so welcoming and concerned, but she couldn't doubt their sincerity.

As much as they were generally placid, she'd seen their other side too. The one who had arrived first to help her had destroyed the attacking griffins with cold precision. Her water attacks had been clumsy and childish in comparison. He had been utterly lethal, more than living up to his people's reputation. But then, immediately after when she'd asked for his help to save someone who, to him, was an enemy, he hadn't even hesitated.

No one had questioned her. No one had asked her to justify why they should heal an enemy at her request—her, a half-breed they'd never met. It was a level of generosity and acceptance that she'd never encountered before.

She rubbed a hand over her chest. Her head and lungs still burned from the Sahar's magic. Although brief attacks with the Stone didn't cause her pain, she'd known it was possible to use too much. When she'd used it to break the gold collar off her neck, the pain had been intense. As Ash had told her months ago, her body could only hold so much at once, and she'd clearly pushed her limits too far today.

Aside from the physical pain, she was confused by the Sahar's emotional effect on her. When she'd used it two months ago, it had overwhelmed her with bloodthirsty rage until she could barely think, until all she'd wanted to do was kill. But this time, that side effect of the power had seemed almost muted. She wasn't sure if the difference had to do with her being shaded or something else.

A rustling sound to her left stopped her mid-step. She turned quickly as four ryujin filed wearily out of Ash's room. Their tired faces told her nothing as they swept past her, likely in search of their beds. The last one to exit was the ryujin who'd healed her. His name was Hinote—as in "he-no-tay." She'd had to practice it out loud so she wouldn't garble it later.

His dark eyes rose to her face. "Come, child."

She couldn't read the emotion behind his words. She ran for the doorway.

Ash lay across the bed on his back, his wings cradled by the mattress, half-furled. His weapons had been removed and laid near the far wall. Eyes closed. Wounds gone. Chest rising and falling with smooth, quiet breaths.

Gasping for air from her relief, she rushed to his side and knelt on the edge of the mattress. She gently touched his chest, delighted to feel warm skin under her touch. She looked up at Hinote. He crossed the room, movements slow and flowing like water, and knelt beside her. His eyes slid across Ash's sleeping form.

"His injuries are healed," the daemon said in his deep, measured voice, "but he is not yet out of danger."

"What do you mean?"

"His body is weak. His lungs and viscera were contaminated with water. It will be many days before the danger has passed, and many more until he regains his strength."

Her hand blindly found Ash's and closed around it, warm skin and cooler scales.

"He's tough," she said, her voice wavering. "He'll pull through."

Hinote nodded.

"I—" She cleared her throat. "I don't know how to thank you. You saved us both."

"There are no debts among family, child."

Her heart caught in her throat. "But—I—I'm not . . ."

"The river knew you as kin even as a human. So did I."

She licked her lips, struggling to discern any emotion from him. She could sense the warmth of his mind in her own, but the telepathy told her nothing of what he was thinking.

"How is it possible?" she asked quietly. "I thought your people never left the Overworld."

Hinote's dark eyes were unreadable but his voice became even more neutral. "Only one among us has ever left our homeland."

"Only one?"

"We knew him as Yuushi, but he took a new name long ago."

"What is it?" she whispered.

"His chosen name is Vejovis."

Without further comment, he rose and left the room, giving her privacy.

She stared at nothing, her mind spinning. Hinote's voice echoed in her head. Vejovis. The mysterious Overworld healer, caste unknown, past unknown, his healing skills elevated to legend.

Of course. Of course he would be a ryujin. She'd experienced firsthand the unrivaled healing skills of the caste. It was now clear where Vejovis had inherited his talents, and how he'd lived within the ryujin's territory with impunity.

And he was her grandfather.

She slowly shook her head back and forth, barely able to comprehend it. So that's why he'd sealed her magic as a child. Why he'd followed her from the medical center. Why he'd spared her life in Asphodel, then helped her escape. Her throat closed. He was her grandfather, and he'd died because he'd helped her.

Opening her eyes, she put Vejovis out of mind and turned to Ash. She held his hand in silence, watching his chest rise and fall, face peaceful. Slowly, she ran her fingers over the smooth ridged texture of one of his glossy horns. She touched the scales across his cheekbones and traced the faint, dark design in the hollow of his cheek. Then she brushed a fingertip over the blue material braided into his hair, her gift to remind him of his promise to protect her.

Could she have been any more selfish?

Her eyes squeezed shut. She saw it again in her head. The Ra daemons drawing their weapons to attack. Ash, ready to defend, shielding, focused. And then she had screamed. *Why* had she screamed? Why couldn't she have kept her stupid mouth shut? Again, she saw Ash's fatal glance in her direction, that involuntary break in concentration that had almost cost him his life.

It was all her fault. Seiya had been right all along.

Her entire body trembled as the inner anguish built up. The quiet stillness of the ryujin city pressed in on her, suffocating. Biting the insides of her cheeks, she lay down beside Ash, careful of his wing, and pressed her face against his neck. She now fully understood Seiya's commitment to Ash that he would never have to bleed for her again.

She lost track of time as she lay beside him, holding him close. Minutes slowly passed as she listened to his heartbeat. Thoughts whispered through her mind, taunting her. When Ash had been stabbed, she'd felt as though the knives had pierced her own chest. When he'd stopped breathing, she'd felt her own heart stutter and struggle. The thought of losing him had scared her more than her own impending death from her magic had.

Perhaps it was time to admit that her feelings for him ran deeper than mere attraction.

Slowly, as if in a dream, she rose up on one elbow to look down at him. Her eyes traced his face, alien but so familiar. She lightly touched his jaw, emotion rising up inside her until she couldn't breathe. What kind of fool was she? She could deny it all she wanted, but deep down, she knew the truth. He wasn't just a friend. He wasn't just an infatuation.

Trepidation bordering on panic slid through her. If she acknowledged it, his ability to hurt her would increase tenfold. She knew what rejection could do to her. She knew that pain, and her feelings for Micah had been the blind, foolish obsession of a teenager. She couldn't imagine ever risking her life for the incubus, even when she'd thought he was the only thing that mattered in the world.

Ash had done so much more than capture her heart. He'd changed the very landscape of her soul.

Heart beating hard, she pressed her hand against the side of his face. She didn't know if his feelings matched hers. She wasn't sure if it even mattered. All she knew was that she would do anything to keep him alive—even if that meant doing the very thing Seiya had been demanding all along.

Even if that meant letting him go.

Her hand trembled against his cheek. Slowly, she leaned down until her lips hovered just over his. His warm, slow breath brushed across her skin. She closed her eyes, fighting to contain the rush of emotion within her. She couldn't tell him. He couldn't know. It would make everything more difficult. Seiya had said it, hadn't she? What future could she and Ash have together? But she couldn't hold it in.

Her lips brushed across his as she whispered the forbidden words.

"I love you."

Tenderness laced with pain twisted inside her. She pushed away, climbing to her feet and clenching her hands against the tremble in her fingers. The first and last time she would say those words to him. Her feelings were her own problem. He'd almost died protecting her too many times already. She wouldn't ask that of him again. She wouldn't allow it again.

She paused in the midst of taking a step toward the door and glanced back. Her heart squeezed. She knelt again and reached for the braid alongside his head. With fumbling fingers, she loosened the plait and slid the strip of blue material from his hair. Clutching it in one hand, she rose and strode for the door. As she pushed the curtain aside, she couldn't stop herself from looking back one last time.

Hazy grey eyes stared at her.

She blinked hard—and saw he was still deep in the healing sleep. Taking a deep breath against the rush of alarm that he'd somehow woken up, she dismissed her overactive imagination—fueled by longing—and slipped silently out of the room, leaving him to his recovery.

As she walked away, she vowed that she, too, would never let him bleed for her again.

CHAPTER
-23-

PIPER crouched on the edge of the path, a hundred foot plummet a few inches from her toes. The Kyo Kawa Valley stretched before her in the dim light of dusk. Glowing blue orbs dotted the landscape like scattered stars.

She closed her eyes, letting the breeze caress her face as she inhaled the quiet scent of this world. The ryujin territory was dangerous, beautiful, mysterious. In a way that the Underworld hadn't touched her, something about this world drew her. Maybe it was all in her head. Maybe it went down to her bones.

Behind her, the ley line flowed past, shivering across her senses. Somewhere farther down the path, Ash's blood smeared the stones.

She let out a long breath. It had been over five days since Miysis's betrayal. For five days, she'd stayed in the ryujin city to make sure Ash's healing continued. Two days ago, he'd developed a lung infection, which he was still fighting. He hadn't woken up properly since he'd fallen off the cliff and out of her sight.

Hinote had assured her that Ash would fully recover with a bit more time. She had to believe him.

She'd waited as long as she could. With nothing but Hinote's assertion that Ash would be okay, she'd thanked the ryujin for their kindness. Hinote had promised to care for Ash like his own family until he was well again. It was the best she could hope for.

The time for waiting was over.

She rose to her feet. Lyre and Seiya hadn't returned since going through the ley line five days ago. Considering the speed with which Miysis's backup force had arrived, it was entirely possible he'd had an ambush waiting for them on Earth. Piper had no idea if Lyre and Seiya were alive, but if they were, she wouldn't abandon them.

She stretched her arms out in front of her. Each forearm was wrapped in pale leather that shimmered in the soft dusk light— dragon scale. The armguards were magic resistant and nearly impenetrable, a gift from Hinote. Beneath the left one, the Sahar lay against the skin of her inner wrist. Her torso was clad in a halter top of dragon scale like the other ryujin women wore, and she'd already recovered her boots and pants from the trail. She wore both despite the discomfort. It wouldn't be a problem for long.

The tentacle-like appendages drifted around her thighs. She'd finally learned what they were called: dairokkan. As Ash had surmised, they weren't tentacles at all, but sensory organs that allowed her to sense water currents as well as the strange, sentient elemental power within the river. Hinote hadn't been able to explain very well what that power was, and she knew almost nothing about elemental magic.

She let out a long breath and slipped a hand into her pocket. She pulled out the strip of blue material she'd taken from Ash's hair. Sliding it through her fingers, she hardened her resolve.

As much as it burned her to admit it, Seiya was right. Piper hadn't been strong enough, and her weakness had nearly gotten him killed. She hadn't learned when he'd almost died after the fight at the medical center so many months ago. She hadn't learned when he'd been tortured in front of her. She hadn't learned when Samael had used her to poison him.

He'd almost died for her selfishness. She hadn't *needed* him to accompany her to the Overworld, but despite the obvious danger, she'd let him come for her own comfort. She'd even let him come knowing Miysis couldn't be trusted—and she'd been right. The Ra heir had obviously planned to eliminate Ash the moment Piper completed, or broke, her side of their agreement.

She couldn't count on Ash anymore. She couldn't ask for his help anymore. Next time there wouldn't be a team of the best healers in any of the worlds standing by to save him. Next time they wouldn't be so lucky. Next time he would die. She couldn't let that happen.

If she really loved him, she wouldn't put him at risk again. How could she justify that? Until she was as strong as Seiya, until she was so strong that she didn't need Ash's protection, she had no business being near him. No matter what she said, he *would* try to protect her if they were together.

She was done letting other people risk their lives for her. She was done letting Ash bleed for her. She would fight her own battles from now on.

Jaw tight, she pulled the second item from her pocket: the narrow leather band Ash had given her, imbued with a tracking spell. Selecting a blue-tinted rock from the path, she tied the material around it, then wrapped the belt over top that. Weighing it in her hand, she drew her arm back and hurled it as hard as she could into the gorge. The rock plummeted out of sight.

Turning her back on the valley, she took a moment to just breathe. It was time to go.

She stepped closer to the ley line. Although it had been days since the Ra ambush, she didn't dare go back to the same spot where Miysis had taken them through the ley line on Earth. Lyre and Seiya had gone that way and hadn't been seen since. It could easily be a trap; Miysis would surely be watching for her.

She needed to come out of a different Earth ley line, but there was only one other she knew of. Two months ago, she, Ash, and Seiya had used it to return to Earth from the Underworld. It would work equally well from the Overworld to Earth, so that's the line she would use.

Her only experience with the Void had been a single step out of it; she hadn't tried to travel anywhere. But she couldn't wait for Ash to wake up and coach her, and the ryujin had no advice to offer her on interworld travel. She would have to wing it.

She inhaled one more breath of Overworld air, trying to slow her speeding heart rate. Then she wrapped her mind in a barrier of magic as she had last time, visualized where she wanted to go, and stepped into the ley line. Magic rushed over her, sliding across her skin like an unseen river.

She could sense the Void, out of sight but not out of reach.

Squeezing her eyes shut, she stepped into the shrieking, shattering darkness.

o   o   o

She hadn't properly appreciated the strength of her daemon body until it was gone.

Her muscles felt limp and feeble with each trudging step. She walked listlessly through the balmy evening shadows, following a long-abandoned road. Plant life had destroyed the pavement, leaving nothing but treacherous chunks of concrete hidden in the grass. She vaguely recalled this road from last time, when she'd followed the dark silhouette of Ash's back through the night. It could have been a completely different road, she supposed, but based on the setting sun, she was at least going in the right direction.

She lifted her hands as she walked, studying her familiar, human fingernails. When she'd come out of the ley line, she'd been human again, forced back into her usual form by Earth's magic. She had no idea if she could switch to her daemon glamour the way a daemon could drop his human glamour. She missed her shimmering scales and extra strength, but she was also relieved to be herself again.

The only thing left of her trip to the Overworld was her magic. She could still sense the difference between her two magics even though she was once again blind to the supernatural forces. Even if she never shifted back into her daemon form, she could keep her magic under control. There were many things that might still kill her, but her magic wasn't one of them.

As she plodded steadily toward the distant city, loneliness closed around her like a suffocating cloak. The last time she'd made this journey, she'd been with Ash. She'd just helped him escape a living hell, having just escaped it herself. She'd been closer to him than ever before. Now he felt a million miles away—a world away. Unreachable and untouchable.

With effort, she put him out of her mind and focused on the problems at hand. To start, she would find out what had happened to Lyre and Seiya. They would be with Ash and safe if it hadn't been for her. She had to believe they were alive. Maybe they were on the run and hadn't been able to make it back to the Overworld? Maybe they'd returned and had left again when they couldn't find Piper and Ash? Either way, she would find out for sure.

She hadn't forgotten about Miysis either. Hatred boiled inside her at the thought of him. Although she relished the idea of revenge, she didn't plan to go looking for him; that would probably be suicide. But if he crossed her path again, she wouldn't hold back.

As she walked, the condition of the highway gradually improved until it was mostly level. The sun crept lower, edging toward the horizon. She marched methodically around a wide bend in the road. As she came around the corner, her steps slowed then stopped.

Devastation spread out before her.

To her right was a piece of a highway ramp, jutting fifteen feet into the air. Memories engulfed her: the gritty air in her mouth, the deafening sounds of explosions, the drifting clouds of dust. She remembered climbing on top of that ramp to peer, horrified, at the battle before her, trying to identify where her father was amidst the Hades forces.

It took her a long moment to make her body move again. She walked numbly, eyes travelling across the rubble and debris, the scorched concrete, the craters from magical explosions. Here and there, dark stains formed haphazard patterns across the ground. Another flashback hit her: her astride the Underworld horse, slamming her dagger into a daemon's throat.

Clenching her shaking hands, she forced herself to keep going. Slowly, she walked through the battlefield, memories assaulting her senses. She should have realized she would encounter this place; she'd come out the same ley line as Samael's small army and was following the same path toward the Consulate they would have travelled two months ago.

Her steps carried her to the crest of a hill. Spreading out beyond it was nothing but a hundred yards of flattened ground covered by a layer of fist-sized concrete chunks and charred bits of tree. In her mind, the explosion of ebony power eclipsed the world again—Ash's attack with the Sahar. Over a hundred daemons had died there.

She squeezed her eyes shut. Again, she could see him. Black eyes, empty of everything but rage, lost in the Sahar's power. Then the black had shrunk and vanished, and wide grey eyes had stared at her.

Then he'd crushed her in his arms and kissed her as though the only thing in the world that mattered to him was holding her close.

She opened her eyes, angrily brushing away an escaped tear. Turning her back on the destruction, she crossed the last of the area at a fast walk and found the overgrown highway on the other side. Putting the ghosts of the battleground out of her mind, she focused on walking.

Soon, the light was disappearing as night approached. Shouldn't she be there by now? It felt like she'd been walking forever.

To her right, the dark silhouette of a large, rocky hill rose above the trees. She pushed her way into the forest, ignoring the slap of branches against her bare upper arms and midriff. The dragon-scale halter top she still wore didn't offer a ton of coverage, but the summer evening was warm. Her legs ached as she started the climb. She trudged upward until she reached the crest. Breathing hard, she looked across the landscape ahead of her.

She could see the city—and it was on fire.

A red glow lit the sky. The metropolis—scattered lights and silhouettes of downtown skyscrapers—stretched across the horizon. Even from that distance, discernible flames leaped skyward from a huge fire that was at least a city block long. Orange-tinted smoke billowed into the darkening sky. Half a dozen smaller fires, scattered among the lights, marred the view.

Staring, she pressed a hand to her mouth. The city was burning. Why? Why was it on fire? She slowly lowered her hand. Who did she know who liked burning buildings to the ground? Who had violent plans to enact their vision of the future?

Had the Gaians started some kind of battle with the daemons in the city? She'd seen what magic in a battle could do. Haemons might not have the firepower that daemons did, but if they'd brought technology and modern weapons to the fight, the results could be catastrophic.

They had to be stopped. The city was going to burn to the ground if they kept this up. The Gaians didn't understand what they were getting into. Their experiences with daemons were limited to small skirmishes with the thugs and mercenaries that inhabited the city's darker quarters. They'd never seen what a daemon trained for battle could do.

Gritting her teeth, she half-ran back down the hill to the road. Picking up the pace into the fastest walk that she could maintain, she strode through the shadows. Her lungs and legs burned. Darkness gradually fell, the sky growing darker and darker until the horizon glowed the faintest blue of twilight. She lit an orb of flickering blue light but couldn't figure out how to make it hover in the air like daemons did, so she carried it on her palm. She was so focused on the treacherous road that she almost missed it.

She stopped and backed up a couple of steps, staring down the dark gravel drive, almost invisible amidst the trees. Exhaling, she started down the road. She'd walked it countless times before, every day to and from school. The path was so familiar she could have walked it without any light at all.

Her heart rate picked up as the trees thinned, and then she was standing on the curving driveway staring at the remains of her home.

Only one corner of the building still stood. The sight of the destroyed Consulate made it feel as though the entire system had died with the building. The Gaians' claims that the Consuls were powerless, that she'd dedicated herself to a critically flawed system, whispered through her, beating at her, wearing her down.

The manor looked like her future: burnt, crumbling, a few charred pieces stubbornly standing despite the surrounding devastation. The Consulates had rejected her. She'd rejected the Gaians. What did that leave her? What was she supposed to do with herself?

She closed her eyes. Ash had been asking himself those same questions since escaping Asphodel. His future was just as uncertain as hers.

Her eyes opened again. She would worry about the future later. Tonight, she would start looking for Lyre and Seiya in the city. But first she needed weaponry to supplement her burgeoning magic skills and the Sahar—and she hoped to find some here.

Burying her roiling emotions, she circled the remains of the Consulate until she was standing in front of the last vertical section, the southwest corner. The rain on the night of the attack must have put out the fire before it could devour everything. Climbing over the charred wood in the kitchen, she slipped into the cracked, sagging hallway. She glanced warily at the ceiling, remembering how the other hall had caved in just after she'd escaped it. Passing the infirmary, she tried to open the door to the sparring room. It was stuck. Tossing her light orb aside, she shoved the door with her hands, then slammed it with a shoulder. The wood cracked and the door swung open on one hinge.

She glanced back. Her light orb was hanging in the air, flickering sedately. Huh. So that's how she was supposed to do it. Calling up another one—purple this time, because why not—she tossed it into the sparring room.

The far side had collapsed when most of the upper floor had come down. She remembered that quite vividly, having been up there when it had happened. But the nearer side of the room was untouched. The wall was lined with weapons of all kinds, from swords to crossbows to bokken.

It took several minutes to load up. A belt around her waist held a long and short sword, one on each side. Long daggers were strapped to her thighs, throwing knives bound to her upper arms. She'd even smashed the cabinet in the corner and had helped herself to two handguns and extra ammo, attaching those to the back of her belt.

Yes, she could use magic now, but she'd learned how to survive without it her entire life, so she wouldn't be tossing her training out the window just yet. Magic was great and all, but punching someone was just so satisfying.

Armed and pleased about it, she climbed over the broken door and headed back down the hall. As she stepped into the scorched kitchen, she froze at the loud crunch of breaking wood from the east side of the building. Tensing, she pulled a gun from her belt and held it in both hands. Creeping to the edge of a broken wall, she peeked around the corner at the crumbled debris of the east end of the building.

For a second, she couldn't see anything. Then a shadow moved — someone digging through the debris. Another crunch as the figure, a solidly built man, heaved a two-by-four out of the way. Fury seared her. Who was this vagrant looting the Consulate's remains? Jaw clenched, she stepped out from behind the wall and leveled her gun at the man twenty paces away.

"Stop right there or I'll shoot!" she yelled.

The man stilled.

"Stand up," she ordered.

He clambered to his feet and turned to face her, hands held up in the air, no more than a silhouette in the darkness. Her eyes narrowed. Keeping the gun steady in one hand, she lifted the other and called up a blue orb of light. She threw it into the empty space between them.

Light fell across his face, illuminating a bald head and one eye wide with shock. He stared at her as though he were seeing a ghost.

Her fingers went numb and she nearly dropped the gun. Swallowing hard, she struggled to find her voice.

He spoke first in a dazed croak. "Piper?"

She drew in a shuddering breath. "F-father? What—what are you—"

Quinn surged into motion, striding across the debris as if it wasn't even there. She tensed at his fast approach, but he reached out and grabbed her before she could react. He pulled her into a suffocating embrace.

"I thought you were dead," he said roughly. "How are you not dead?"

"I—" She hesitantly wrapped her arms around him, the gun still in one hand. "I made it out after the attack. I wasn't hurt."

He stepped back, holding her shoulders as he stared at her. "Where have you been?"

"Um, it's a long story."

His mouth opened, disbelief still etched across his face, but she jumped in before he could ask for a real explanation.

"Did you see the city? It's on fire. What happened?"

He visibly pulled himself together, sealing away his shock at finding her alive. "Multiple attacks on daemon establishments. The same group that's been taking out Consulates. Daemons quickly started grouping together to defend themselves, and the fires are the result."

"That group," she said quickly. "Do you know they're—"

"The Gaians, yes. We discovered that shortly after the attack here. We've yet to learn what their plans are, but—"

"I can tell you that," she interrupted grimly. "I know part of their strategies, what their goals are, and how they plan to make it happen. We're in big trouble." She looked toward the unseen city, then back to him, frowning. "Why are you here? The Consuls need to stop the fighting, Gaians or not. That's our—your—job."

His face hardened. "Not anymore."

"What do you mean?"

He dropped his hands from her shoulders. "I was relieved of my position four days ago."

"*What?* You—you're not Head Consul anymore?" Impossible. Her father was the Head Consul. It was a fact as solid and unchanging to her as the sun rising in the east.

"I was deemed incapable of leadership," he said flatly.

"Why?" she demanded, hand tightening on the gun before she realized what she was doing. She quickly stuck it back in the holster.

"It was an excuse to remove me." His voice took on a mocking note. "In light of the destruction of my Consulate, the tragic death of my daughter, and my ex-wife's role in the attacks, my unwillingness to use lethal force against the Gaians was construed as a sign of my inability to effectively lead in this difficult time."

Her head spun. The bedrock her entire life had been built on was crumbling beneath her feet. She hadn't realized how much her father's position had been tied to her own identity until it was gone.

"But . . ." She didn't even know what to ask next. "What now?"

He took her elbow, his calloused fingers tight. "We try to salvage whatever we can before it's too late."

She nodded. The rest of her questions could wait. He pulled her into motion, leading her out of the ruins of their home. She may have lost her apprenticeship months ago, but like her father, her commitment to the core principles of a Consul hadn't wavered. It was their job to keep the peace, and they would do whatever it took to make that happen.

To be continued in
Book 4 of the Steel & Stone series:
REAP THE SHADOWS

Visit **www.authorannettemarie.com** for more information about the Steel & Stone series, to sign up for Annette Marie's newsletter for alerts about new releases, and for an opportunity to read the next book before it comes out!

ACKNOWLEDGEMENTS

Thank you for reading *Yield the Night*! I hope you enjoyed it!

Thank you to Breanna, for your ceaseless support, encouragement, and sympathy. I can always count on you to cheer me up when I feel like the book is getting the better of me.

Thank you to Elizabeth, for being the perfect editor for me. We're so much on the same vibe now that we might as well share a brain. Okay, maybe not, but close.

Thank you to Valerie and Karen, for dropping everything (or close to it) to rescue me in the final hours of publication. Your feedback was invaluable.

Lastly, thank you to my fiancé. I'm so lucky, and grateful, that we get to undertake this journey together. I may have already mentioned it, but did you know you're the best?

ABOUT THE AUTHOR

Annette Marie lives in Western Canada with her fiancé. Someday she'd like to get a cat. Maybe two.

Printed in Great Britain
by Amazon.co.uk, Ltd.,
Marston Gate.